Praise for Paul Burke

'Funny, thoughtful and original' STEPHEN FRY

'A warm, funny, blisteringly good read' TONY PARSONS

'Warm, tender, funny and engaging from start to finish. It's full of sharply written dialogue, filled with characters you can take to your heart, and driven by a classic will-they/won't-they narrative' *Scotsman*

'Fast-moving, witty and highly digestible' TIM LOTT

'A thoughtful read . . . Burke's characters and their unfolding story have depth and charm' *Hello!*

Also By Paul Burke

Father Frank

About the author

Paul Burke has worked in advertising since he left school and his work has included campaigns for Barclaycard, VW, PG Tips, British Gas and Budweiser. He has also worked as a DJ on both radio and in clubs, and has written for various newspapers and magazines. He is the author of one previous novel, the highly acclaimed *Father Frank*.

PAUL BURKE

Untorn Tickets

FLAME
Hodder & Stoughton

Copyright © 2002 by Paul Burke

First published in Great Britain in 2002 by Hodder and Stoughton
A division of Hodder Headline

The right of Paul Burke to be identified as the Author of the
Work has been asserted by him in accordance with the Copyright,
Designs and Patents Act 1988.

A Flame paperback

2 4 6 8 10 9 7 5 3 1

A CIP catalogue record for this title is available from the
British Library

ISBN 0 340 79348 1

Typeset in Sabon by Palimpsest Book Production Limited,
Polmont, Stirlingshire

Printed and bound in Great Britain by
Mackays of Chatham plc, Chatham, Kent

Hodder and Stoughton
A division of Hodder Headline
338 Euston Road
London NW1 3BH

To my two wonderful children, Jack and Eleanor,
for not disturbing me (much).

Acknowledgements

Even more eternal gratitude this time to Philippa Pride and Georgina Capel whom I now know to be the best editor and agent in the world respectively. Huge thanks, of course, to my wife Saskia for doing so much while I did so little and to Frank Waites, Renee Kaufman, David Redmond, Helen Style, Claude Agius, Mark Kermode, Rachel Music, Philippa Roberts, Jesse Birdsall, Sue Ross, Phil Style, Anni Cullen, Sheila Crowley, Rob Williams, Lucy Dixon, Sheena Craig and especially Andy Daruk without whom you would not be reading this. So blame them.

1

Let's start with the last word: Zymanczyk. The last word in Polishness. Just look at it. Isn't it the most Polish word you've ever seen? That old joke about Polish names being formed by hurling Scrabble letters into the air and just letting them land would appear to be true in this case.

Zymanczyk was also the last word – the last name – in the London phone book. Zymanczyk, J., 67 Askew Crescent, London W12. Almost from the day he was able to read and recognise that peculiar selection of consonants as his own family name, Andy Zymanczyk (pronounced Zer-man-chick) would gaze proudly at its inverted 'pole position' right at the end of the book. The final attraction. Top of the bill. Until, unfortunately, the Zysblat family moved in down the road and usurped that position for ever.

Andy was the only child of Jerzy and Ewa Zymanczyk, parents who were old enough to be his grandparents, parents with three distinguishing characteristics: they were very old, very strict and very, very Polish.

The force of Catholicism to which Andy was domestically subject was the most potent known to man. In his class at St Bede's, those with English parents got off fairly lightly. As long as mass was attended on Sundays and on Holy Days of Obligation, not much more was expected. Those with Irish parents usually had it a bit harder: a tendency towards Republican sentiments, a holy-water font by the front door and Dave Allen banned from the TV screen. Those with Polish parents had many more crosses to bear. Dave Allen, for instance, was not banned from the Zymanczyks' TV screen because there was no TV screen from which to ban him. Andy's father refused to let the insidious cathode-ray tube bring 'the ideas of the devil' across his threshold. Andy's only glimpses of Slade and Gary Glitter on *Top of the Pops* had been stolen by standing on tiptoe on the lavatory seat and gazing excitedly down through next door's sitting-room window.

The Zymanczyks, like countless other Poles, were strong adherents to the Marian creed, which meant that they worshipped both God and Our Lady with equal zeal, so double quantities of religious belief were required. Pictures and statues of the Madonna adorned almost every room in the house and the sitting room boasted a particularly fine example – a huge gilt-framed portrait of Our Lady of Czestochowa, which hung above the fireplace and was the focal point of the room. This was the Zymanczyks' equivalent of a television set starring Our Lady as a sort of Immaculate Test Card that was never switched off.

Andy's father was intensely patriotic and chest-puffingly proud of being Polish, which always struck his son as rather odd. You can be pleased to be Polish, of course, but your nationality was something for which, Andy always felt, you could take neither credit nor blame. A mere accident of birth. Surely saying 'I'm Polish and proud of it,' was a bit like declaring 'It's Thursday and I'm proud of it.' But proud of his roots Jerzy most certainly was, and since this was combined with a stern pride in his Catholicism, life in the Zymanczyk household was never going to be a barrel of laughs.

Andy longed to spend his Saturday mornings with the other Shepherds Bush boys, at Saturday-morning pictures or playing football in Wendell Park. Instead, he was packed off to the Polish Social and Cultural Institute in Hammersmith for Polish School where he was taught, among other things, to say, '*Chzqszcz brzmi w trzcinie*', which means, 'A bug is buzzing in the reeds,' and occupies a place in the *Guinness Book of Records* as the most difficult phrase in the world for a native English speaker to pronounce. With that sort of grounding, it was little wonder that Andy could repeat, 'Red lorry, yellow lorry,' *ad infinitum* with no difficulty at all.

Polish School had many other delights. Andy soon became a dab hand at making *pisanki* – ornate table decorations, intricately fashioned from eggshells and brightly coloured wax. This compensated for his never having seen what Valerie Singleton could do with two loo-roll holders, an empty cornflakes box and a yard of sticky-backed plastic. At the age of fourteen, although forbidden to watch *Blue Peter*, Andy had nonetheless appeared on it in full national costume as part of a Polish folk-dancing troupe, cavorting with a pig-ugly partner. When he got home, he prayed that no one in his class had seen it, and if they had that they had failed to recognise him. Mercifully, on this occasion, his prayers were answered.

Andy's birthday was 5 January but he received his presents on 21 May, his 'name day', the feast of St Andrew Bobola, the seventeenth-century Polish martyr after whom he'd been christened. This tragic figure, murdered by the Russians for refusing to renounce his Catholicism, had also lent his name to the old Victorian church round the corner. It had been taken over by the local Polish community in 1962 – and guess who was the first baby baptised there?

The church of St Andrew Bobola was the centre of the Zymanczyks' lives and the lives of other strong, devout people with unpronounceable names. Every mass was conducted in Polish and there, at least, Andy could draw comfort from the fact that he was not the only child in West London to be living under a benign Polish dictatorship. He was, however, the only child in his house, with just his ageing parents for company. Never was this more painfully apparent than on Christmas Eve when the window of Czyrko's, the fishmonger, on Askew Road was crammed with pike, the Polish alternative to turkey, all awaiting collection. Names would be pinned to each one, Drzewuki, Scislowicz, Mruk, Pyrtek, Niziolek, Karpinski, Szczudlo, but Zymanczyk was always attached to the smallest, the one that only needed to be big enough to feed three.

That night, after beer soup with eggs, the little poached pike would be served up with baby carrots and hot Polish chicory as part of the traditional Christmas feast, which the Zymanczyks would solemnly consume before walking round the corner to midnight mass. As was customary, an extra place at the table was always laid for the unexpected visitor. 'A guest in the house,' said the old Polish proverb, 'God in the home.' Over the years, Andy hoped that God would turn up in the form of Lesley-Anne Down, Lynsey de Paul or even his beautiful blonde cousin Alison Gomoulka. But, every year, he was disappointed.

As he grew older, he would reflect on the irony of his situation, with a mixture of amusement and dismay. His parents, and thousands like them, had fled from Poland to Shepherds Bush and Ealing, Willesden and Balham to escape the brutal repression of a Communist dictatorship. Yet here they were imposing a benevolent but nonetheless unyielding form of tyranny on their own families.

Still, things were looking up. It was Thursday 15 June 1978, Andy was sixteen and his parents were pleased with him. He'd completed nine O levels. His grade A in Polish meant that Polish school on Saturdays could now be a thing of the past. For the first time in his life, he was to be allowed a part-time job to earn a little extra cash. Very gradually, the reins were being loosened and with them the constraints of Catholicism.

Was it Andy's imagination or was his father's fanatical fervour on the wane? Well, it might have been, except for one thing: the sudden death of Pope John Paul I after just thirty-three days in office. He was succeeded by Pope John Paul II, formerly known as Cardinal Karol Wojtyla.

'Oh, God,' groaned Andy, when he first heard the news on the Grundig Yacht Boy, which, unlike the TV, was not seen as a corrupting, Satanic influence. 'I don't believe it. He's the new head of the Roman Catholic Church. He's the most prominent religious leader on earth. And he's bloody Polish.'

Andy got on to his bike, pedalled out on to Goldhawk Road, round Shepherds Bush Green, up Holland Park Avenue and left into Ladbroke Grove. Little did he know that, approaching Ladbroke Grove from the other direction, heading for exactly the same place for exactly the same reason, was his schoolmate Dave Kelly. Dave would get there first. Dave usually did.

2

Dave Kelly had been born into the wrong family. In fact, his whole family had been born into the wrong family. His sister Kathy would have preferred to have been the daughter of an eminent country doctor and his ample-bosomed wife. Heaven for Kathy would have been her own bedroom overlooking green fields in a cosy, book-lined cottage where, every Sunday around four o'clock, the old oak refectory table would be creaking under the weight of freshly made cakes. His sister Nuala would have favoured something more modern: dark brown carpets, soft, cream sofas and a twenty-six-inch colour TV. She would have loved a handsome, generous father who drove a Mercedes and a mother who could still wear hot pants.

As for Dave, he yearned, despite his Irish-Catholic provenance, to be part of a warm, all-embracing Jewish family in a rambling Manhattan apartment on the west side of Central Park. A place where music, films and personal neuroses could be discussed every Friday night over chicken soup and latkes.

Instead, the Kellys had to be content with 76 Kilravock Street, one of a thousand tiny council houses crammed inbetween Kilburn and the Grand Union Canal.

Nowadays, their house would be described as 'bijou', and the owners would knock through walls, insert a chic spiral staircase and augment the kitchen-diner with a Scandinavian-glass conservatory. But in 1978, its owners were Westminster Council and such details were not high on their list of priorities. Bijou? The house was just plain poky. Two short strides from the front door and you were half-way up the stairs. Two more would take you into any of the three bijou bedrooms, which led off a landing the size of a beer mat. The tiny front room could barely accommodate the green Dralon three-piece suite, which was still being paid off at four pounds a week, the sideboard (two pounds a week) and the rented Rediffusion TV. However, many front rooms on the Queens Park estate had even less space than the Kellys' since they also contained a large Alsatian, usually called Prince, growling malevolently under the sideboard. The bathroom was downstairs but with three outside walls, a flat roof and no central heating, it was generally out of bounds from September until March. The walls of each room were woodchipped and magnolia'd every five years by the council and were so thin that, on the rare occasions when the TV wasn't switched on, you could hear next-door's budgie pecking its seed.

You could hear most things in Kilravock Street and be privy to your neighbours' innermost secrets whether you wanted to or not. Only the other night Dave had heard a startling revelation from number sixty-eight –

something along the lines of 'She ain't your bleedin' kid anyway, Ken.'

However, as council estates go, this one was almost picturesque, with its neat rows of terraced cottages set along wide tree-lined avenues. The previous year, Kilravock Street had even won a prize for the best decorations during the Queen's Silver Jubilee celebrations. Without those adornments, it was drab but not forbidding, rough but not dangerous – and more difficult to escape from than almost anywhere else on earth.

If your home is a squalid tower block on a desolate, crime-ridden estate, escape can be far more simple. With surroundings so horrific, you are impelled to get yourself out or risk being found dead on a concrete stairwell with a hypodermic needle in your arm. Similarly, if your parents are prosperous, middle-class and understand the importance of education, they or their friends from the golf club, the Rotary Club or the lodge can often provide you with the leg up you need to hop effortlessly into the career of your choice. Dave, though, was stuck somewhere between the two and had little chance of altering his circumstances. But then, why would he want to? His family was not dysfunctional. His life had never been blighted by violence, alcoholism or drug abuse. It might have been better if it had – at least that would have given him the impetus to escape, though any desire to flee from Kilravock Street was not evident this morning.

It was Thursday 15 June 1978. Dave was sixteen years old and had finished the last of his eight O levels. An eleven-week summer holiday stretched out ahead of him and it was warm enough for him to stretch out in a tub full of suds in that downstairs bathroom. One person occupied centre stage in his mind. All right, so she was twice his age but she had pushed Debbie Harry and Kate Bush down to numbers two and three respectively. The object of his desire was Olivia Newton-John, and what had made her so sexy was the fact that it was all so unexpected. She was like the pretty but innocent girl next door whom you had always known but never noticed. Now thanks to that tantalising clip from *Grease* on *Top of the Pops* last week in which she had performed 'You're The One That I Want' in a black leather jacket, skin-tight satin pants and an unseemly amount of makeup, the record had gone to number one, so the clip would be shown again that night. Lying in the bath, Dave thought of a way to ensure that he saw it again and again and again.

Like Archimedes, he cried 'Eureka' and leaped out of the bath. At least he would have done if he'd ever heard of Archimedes or had the faintest idea what Eureka meant.

3

It was the animal blood that had done it.

The blood of a dead cow had finally convinced Dave that it was time to look for another part-time job. He'd had a Saturday job at the Irish Meat Market in Kensal Rise for the past year but it had proved less than rewarding employment. Although bright, cheery and numerically nimble, he was seldom allowed to serve customers. Instead, he was consigned to the back of the shop, where Tom Riordan had taught him how to chop and chine. This wasn't something for which Dave had shown any aptitude. He was not a natural butcher. Those big knives had to be sharp enough to cleave their way through great sides of beef and Dave, terminally clumsy, was always cutting himself.

Getting salt in a fresh wound is bad enough, but animal blood is pure unmitigated agony. Some sort of chemical reaction occurs when the blood of an animal meets that of a human and it's enough to send even the bravest butcher screaming to the nearest cold tap. As Dave ran his hand yet again under cold water, he decided to quit while he still had the full complement of fingers.

The magnificent Gaumont cinema in Westbourne

Grove would be a far more palatable place to work. Maureen Breslin, devout Catholic and Irish, was the assistant manageress. Now almost fifty, Maureen lived alone at the other end of Kilravock Street and was a friend of Dave's mother. Maureen had been married for twenty-five years but hadn't seen her husband for twenty-three of them. Jim Breslin had run off with a younger woman but Maureen, whose strength of faith absolutely forbade divorce, was still legally married to him. Dave's mother maintained that Maureen still 'held a candle' for the old rogue and sincerely believed that one day he would return to her. However, since Maureen also believed in a bearded man's ability to walk on water and rise from the dead, this was no surprise.

For the moment Maureen's blind faith in these two men didn't concern Dave. In the bath, he had remembered his mother mentioning that the cinema might need part-time staff over the summer holidays, which was why he was now pedalling along Ladbroke Grove.

The Gaumont had always occupied a special place in his heart. Along with practically every other child on the Queens Park estate, he had gone to Saturday-morning pictures there. It was where the furtive fumblings of his first date had taken place when Christine O'Connor had clung to him in the back row during the scary bits in *Jaws*. The cinema had seen better days and was under constant threat of closure. In an effort to make it a little more profitable, it had recently been 'tripled' – instead of one huge thousand seat cinema, it now comprised three smaller ones. Screen One was upstairs in what had been the circle; with 600 seats, it was the biggest and always showed the latest release. Screens Two and Three were downstairs, each containing 200 seats. Screen Two usually showed the big release from the previous week and Screen Three the more 'esoteric' films. Soft-porn offerings, with titles like *Erotic Inferno* and *Keeping It Up Downstairs*, ensured that every potential patron in London W11 was catered for, and that the beautiful art-deco cinema remained an important part of their lives too. It stood on the corner of Chepstow Road, which meant that, geographically, it was Over There.

Over There was a place nervously pointed at from Kilravock Street with a trembling finger and a look of dread in the eye. Over There was where the kerbsides were littered with discarded mattresses, gearboxes and, quite often, people. Inhabitants from Over There, when not menacingly roaming the streets, were imprisoned in crumbling tenements or nineteenth-floor concrete cells, the lifts to which were almost permanently out of order.

Over There was Notting Hill, and the Gaumont was slap-bang (very appropriate words) in the middle of it. Even the cats seemed to behave differently Over There. Whereas the Kilravock Street cat was relaxed and happy, his Notting Hill counterpart was nervous, edgy and constantly on the run from the screaming sirens of the SPG vans or from horrible little oiks wanting to tie a rocket to his tail.

The most frightening embodiment of Over There was Trellick Tower. Its thirty-one floors cast a grim, forbidding shadow over vast tracts of West London. Its terrifying presence seemed to punch out a dire warning to any people within a ten-mile radius who might be disaffected with their lot. 'You think you're badly off,' it would say, 'well, how would you like to live here? You'll never escape. The only way out will be in a wooden box. And guess what? They made the lifts too small so you'll suffer the final indignity of having your coffin shoved in upright for your final journey down to the street.'

The fear of ending up in Trellick Tower was not unlike the Victorian fear of ending up in the workhouse. Though completed only six or seven years earlier, this monolithic social experiment had already fallen into dangerous disrepair. Residents had been herded in, usually against their will – their homes and communities had been destroyed to make way for the Westway. Now they were hundreds of feet in the air, squashed together yet strangely lonely and isolated. The long, sinister, poorly lit concrete walkways were like little streets in the sky. Streets the police could not patrol where W10's hoodlums and drug-dealers were free to go about their business with total impunity.

Yet if you headed south towards Notting Hill Gate and Kensington, the area became more prosperous and genteel. Elsewhere in the vicinity, there were concentrations of Irish, West Indian, Spanish and Portuguese immigrants. Add to this the Arabs further east around

Bayswater and the more Bohemian characters to be found along Portobello Road plus, of course, the ordinary indigenous families, who filled the red-brick terraces around Oxford Gardens, and you had one of the most culturally diverse neighbourhoods in Britain. All human life was within walking distance of where Dave Kelly was now parking his bike.

'David.' Maureen Breslin's warm Wexford lilt and outstretched hand emerged from the manager's office to greet him. 'As it happens, we're very short-staffed now and Screen One is full of kids. Can you start right away?'

'Er . . . well . . . yeah,' said Dave, taken aback by the brevity of his 'interview' and mentally sticking up two bandaged fingers at Tom Riordan and the Irish Meat Market.

'Ah, that's grand. C'mon. Let's get you into a uniform.'

Dave glanced over at the other usherette, whose name turned out to be Doris, and hoped that he wouldn't be expected to wear a red nylon pinafore dress and American Tan tights. His uniform was only marginally better: red Crimplene jacket with a narrow shawl lapel, white shirt, bow-tie and black trousers.

He was introduced to the rest of the day shift and noticed that he was the only one not entitled to a bus pass. George the doorman – or 'commissionaire', as he preferred to be known – was tearing the tickets. He could remember the Gaumont's opening-night ceremony being performed by Jessie Matthews and Sonnie

Hale. Unfortunately, he couldn't remember that he'd told you the same story about half an hour earlier. And about half an hour before that.

Lily was the senior usherette and outranked George because she had worked in the drapery department of Arthur's Stores, which had been knocked down and replaced by the cinema. That was in 1936. Then there was Doris, the more junior usherette, sixty if she was a day, who would only stand on the 'smoking' side of the auditorium so she could show patrons to their seats with a torch in one hand and a lipstick-smeared filter tip in the other. Behind the sweet kiosk stood a fearsome septuagenarian named Ida, who ran it as though her life depended on it and was not afraid to administer a clip round the ear to any light-fingered child attempting to purloin a family-size bag of Maltesers.

Maureen was manning the box office. She thrust a torch into Dave's hand and directed him up the grand baronial staircase to Screen One where Disney's latest, *The Cat From Outer Space*, was being shown to a couple of hundred noisy children. One child, whose five-year-old stomach had been overfilled with a lethal mix of popcorn, Pepsi and Payne's Poppets, suddenly emptied it all over the maroon, monogrammed carpet.

Dave's first task was to get down on his hands and knees with a large cloth and a bucket of disinfectant to remove all traces of vomit. As nausea gripped him, he began to think that perhaps animal blood wasn't so bad, after all.

4

Once Dave had finished scrubbing the carpet and had returned to his position on the usher's seat, he remembered another thing that made him feel ill. They say you can become allergic to anything at any time, and for as long as Dave could remember he had been allergic to Ireland. In an age when the Irish are rightly regarded as eloquent, romantic, fashionable and funny, it is hard to remember a time when they weren't. Yet Dave and many others of Irish extraction were embarrassed by rather than proud of their provenance. His parents, though they waxed lyrical about 'home', had little desire to return there. They had been glad to escape from a place they found cold, harsh, bigoted and backward. Yet every year, they headed down to Pat Carroll's travel agent on Kilburn High Road to book the two-week pilgrimage to Granny Kelly's farm just outside Ballina, and every year Dave dreaded the trip. He broke out in a psychosomatic rash at the thought of the wet misery and mind-numbing boredom of the fortnight that lay ahead.

It started with the tempestuous crossing from Holyhead to Dublin, sloshing up on to the open deck ankle deep in salt water and vomit, then the coach journey across 'roads' so rough and rutted that his fillings were almost shaken out of his mouth. On arrival at Granny's, they were welcomed with a steaming plate of fatty bacon and watery cabbage, nostrils further assailed by the vile stench of stewed tea from the big brown pot on the stove. In later years, whenever he thought of tea, he remembered how far his grandad has been from becoming a 'new man'. His sister Kathy had once been making the old man a cup of tea. 'Grandad?' she called out. 'Do you take sugar?'

There was a pause. 'I don't know,' he replied. 'Ask your granny.'

If they arrived on a Sunday, they would be hurried straight out to mass, to a style of service and atmosphere that bore little resemblance to mass in London. In the sunny, stained-glass church in Kensal Rise there was a warmth and a familiarity that was not evident in Ballina. This was not a social occasion; the congregation seemed terrified. They hadn't come along out of love for God, but through fear of Him. Dave never knew any of the ancient hymns but he remembered the old maxim that if you mimed the words 'forty-three, forty-four' over and over again, you could look like you knew what you were singing. Thus he managed not to incur the wrath of Father Mallon. The candlelight reflected in the priest's glasses made it seem to every member of the flock that his harsh, reproving glare was directed solely at them. Bored, cold and unhappy, Dave had worked out that a mere 336 hours of Ireland was all he had to endure before he vomited cheerfully back to Holyhead.

He counted those hours religiously. Sometimes they passed so slowly that he'd find himself squinting at the second hand of his Timex to check that it was still going round. Occasionally he'd bring it up to his ear in the vain hope that it had stopped ticking. It never had. It really was only five minutes, or one-twelfth of just one of those 336 hours, since he'd last checked the time.

He was happiest during the night when eight or nine whole hours might pass unnoticed. However, it was usually only a matter of minutes before he was awoken by one of three things: the severe discomfort of the old iron bed with its thin and crispy mattress; his grandfather's whiskey-fuelled snoring; the rain, which poured down hard and unrelenting to make an already miserable fortnight about a hundred times worse.

The views from the farm were said to be spectacular: the magnificent untamed majesty of the mountains, the verdant meadows rolling down to glorious unspoilt beaches set against huge open skies. Yet Dave could scarcely remember ever witnessing this splendour. It was invariably sheathed in cloud or obscured by a grey veil of driving rain. Dave's abiding memories were of sopping wet and mud-spattered cattle being herded into barns to shield them from yet another spiteful meteorological onslaught.

As a child, he began to think that the whole of the planet's rain supply must fall on County Mayo. Surely there would be none left for the rest of the world.

Would they return to find London a desert and camels wandering along what was once Kilravock Street?

Ah, Kilravock Street – at least when heavy rain fell on the Queens Park estate there was still plenty to do. There were TV programmes to watch, records to play, comics to read, friends to hang out with. A wet Sunday afternoon in Ballina made a Sunday in England seem like Rio at carnival time.

Contrary to romantic belief, children from London do not enjoy cutting peat or gathering hay. Neither have they a burning desire to get up at the crack of dawn and sit fiddling with cows' udders in a hopeless attempt to elicit a tiny squirt of liquid into a pail. They find it boring, smelly and actually quite repulsive. One year, having read *Cider With Rosie* at school, Dave fancied emulating Laurie Lee and experiencing a seminal sexual encounter in a lush meadow with a creamy-shouldered wench. A sort of *Guinness With Bridey*. Needless to say, no luscious farmer's daughter was willing to frolic in a field that was gurgling under six inches of water.

So for Dave, that was the best thing about working at the Gaumont. It wasn't the films; it wasn't the money. It was simply the first summer in his life when he wouldn't have to spend those two weeks 'at home'. He was his own man now. He'd never have to go there again.

5

Dave had no idea what his dad did for a living. It wasn't as though Joe Kelly disappeared on top-secret assignments for MI6: he worked at the gasworks between the railway and Ladbroke Grove. Whatever the nature of his work, it was of no interest to Dave – in fact, it was of very little interest to Joe. It was a means to an end, not a career. Residents of the Queens Park estate did not have careers; most were satisfied just to have jobs.

Joe might have been a very bright man but he'd never had the chance to find out, hamstrung by absence of opportunity and that quintessentially Catholic lack of ambition. Somehow pushiness was sinful: professional progress was almost always at someone else's expense and the humility of Catholicism frowned upon this. Joe was a man who lived by his faith, a paragon of unhypocritical goodness, wedded to the Catholic Church. Mass every Sunday morning, benediction every Sunday night, charity work with the St Vincent de Paul Society and the Knights of St Columba. Yet quiet, unassuming Joe was actually the fast-living member of the family. After all, he had left Ireland and journeyed to the throbbing metropolis. His brother Michael was a Trappist monk.

His father's unimpeachable virtues had always made Dave feel rather sorry for his mother, who had to endure the strain of being married to a 'good man'. It was almost as though the Church was another woman, Joe's 'bit on the side', with whom his wife could never compete.

Even for a Catholic, Joe had a remarkable indifference to material wealth. His wife allowed him strictly rationed 'pocket money' to prevent him putting all his spare coins into the poor box. Dave remembered his mother exploding at him one night for doing just that: 'What the hell do you think you're doing?' she'd yelled. 'Look at us! We are the bloody poor.'

Joe was content with his lot. He was far happier in London than he would have been in the bleak, rural wilds of Mayo. Even though he and his family were falling over each other in that tiny house. Even though he had no car and his weekly wage packet contained far less than was necessary to bring up three children in any sort of style.

Andy Zymanczyk, on the other hand, was only too aware of what *his* father did for a living. Every morning at nine, Jerzy Zymanczyk's first patient would press the buzzer at the side of the house before settling into the chair and being told to '*Otwuz usta, szeroko*' or 'Open wide, please.' Jerzy had served as a dentist in the RAF before settling in London immediately after the war like thousands of other Polish ex-servicemen. He was not generally known as 'Jerzy' or even 'Mr Zymanczyk' but as *Pan Dentysta* – 'Mr Dentist'. The reason he wasn't known as *Pan Doktor* was that he'd always preferred the certainty of dentistry to the uncertainty of medicine.

When a doctor sees a patient who doesn't know what's wrong with him, chances are the doctor won't know either and will be forced to opine that 'It's probably a virus,' or 'There's a lot of it about.' Such woolly diagnoses are rare in dentistry, but as Andy got older and understood more and more (or, rather, less and less) about the Catholic faith, he found this paradoxical. How could his father, a man so rooted in certainty, be such a keen adherent to a faith where nothing could be regarded as fact? Perhaps it was his only streak of recklessness. Maybe he was indulging a deeply suppressed urge to gamble – the equivalent of backing a horse called Catholicism in the three-thirty at Doncaster, with his whole life as the stake.

Almost all *Pan Dentysta*'s patients were Polish, as was his loyal assistant, Mrs Wizbek, so it was small wonder that, even though he was an intelligent man who had lived in London for thirty-three years, his command of English was no more than rudimentary.

The Zymanczyk household on a weekday was not a place where Andy felt relaxed or comfortable. It was deathly quiet, for a start, enlivened only by polite Polish chatter followed by the fearsome whine of the dentist's drill, the occasional scream, and the 'dang' of a tooth falling into a kidney-shaped metal dish.

Andy never invited his friends home. There was no

TV and no drinks, unless you had a penchant for pink dental mouthwash. An eleven-week summer holiday spent there would be unbearable. His parents were always around. Unlike Dave's, they didn't even go 'home'. They harboured a great desire to return one day to Poland but while it remained under the iron heel of General Jarulselski even a brief visit was out of the question. In fact, since they first arrived in Britain, Jerzy and Ewa had never left. They feared that something might happen while they were away and they wouldn't be allowed back in, so they'd never even taken a holiday. Perhaps they regarded their life in Shepherds Bush as a permanent holiday – which, compared with life in Communist Poland, it probably was.

So, for the summer at least, Andy would have to spend as much time as possible away from his house. He'd drawn up a shortlist of places he'd like to work over the break. It was a shortlist of one. He couldn't believe his luck when he found himself being measured up for a red Crimplene jacket.

As he and his torch began to show patrons to their seats in Screen Two, Andy was thanking God and Our Lady of Czestochowa for his good fortune. This place was more special to him than to possibly anyone else in the area for one simple reason: having no TV at home, he was besotted, to the point of obsession, with films.

He had occasionally been brought to the Gaumont as a child to see films like *Mary Poppins*, *Peter Pan* and *The Railway Children*, but as he got older, his visits became more frequent. On Saturday afternoons, his father – a good man, wholly committed to the NHS – would often be carrying out emergency dental work at Charing Cross hospital and his mother was usually visiting her sister in Ealing, so Andy would race out to see his friends. Over the years, those friends had included Sylvester Stallone, Jack Nicholson, Robert de Niro and Harrison Ford. Each had been there to greet him at the Gaumont as he had lapped up the delights of *Rocky*, *Chinatown*, *Taxi Driver* and *Star Wars*. He had seen the middle two and many other X-certificate features by buying a ticket to the U or A-certificate programme showing on one of the other screens and sneaking in when the usherette (probably Doris) was having a fag break. He would watch the film slouched down in his seat so that his under-age head was hidden from view.

Not surprisingly, Andy was shy and awkward in social situations. For him, going to the cinema was a way of socialising *without* socialising. It was a purely solipsistic activity, like reading a book, and he couldn't understand why anyone would want to go to the cinema *with* someone. He liked to sit in the same seat each time so that he could always view the film from the same angle – two-thirds of the way down towards the front, slightly right of centre. From anywhere else, it just wouldn't be the same, almost like trying to write with his left hand.

With all the patrons seated, he settled down to enjoy *California Suite* from a new vantage-point – the usher's seat at the back of the auditorium. Not ideal, but it was free. Better than that, he was being paid to sit on it. Once he discovered that his classmate Dave Kelly was sitting on the corresponding seat upstairs, watching *The Cat From Outer Space* and smelling of disinfectant, he would end up being paid a hell of a lot more.

6

Their paths finally crossed at six thirty when they were getting changed to go home.

'Zymanczyk, what are you doing here?'

'I was about to ask you that.'

'Well, that Maureen's a friend of my mum's. How do you know her?'

'I don't. I just turned up, asked for a job and here I am.'

They looked at each other with a mixture of delight and dismay: delight because both were pleased to have found a friend in what would otherwise have passed for the geriatric ward at St Mary's hospital; dismay for Andy because the fact that another boy in his class had secured a job at the place he worshipped somehow took away a little of his own achievement, and for Dave because he felt like a person on holiday who meets someone he half knows from home and isn't sure whether it's a good or a bad thing. Even after five years in the same class as Andy Zymanczyk, Dave hardly knew him. There had to be a reason for this.

They walked out on to Westbourne Grove for a much-needed shot of daylight and fresh air, not quite sure what to say to each other. The awkward silence was broken by a voice that neither boy recognised calling from across the street.

'Andy?'

Andy turned his head.

'Dave?'

Dave turned his. 'Who's that?' he said.

'God knows,' said Andy, whose mother had always told him never to talk to strangers. Especially if they weren't Polish.

It was a handsome if rather dishevelled-looking stranger in his late thirties who was calling them as he got out of his car.

'Blimey,' said Dave. 'It's Uncle Tony.'

Uncle Tony did not know either of them, yet he knew who they were. And, having called out their names separately, he now knew that the tall dark one was Dave and the smaller, fair-haired one was Andy.

Andy was confused. 'Uncle Tony? So he's your uncle?'

'No,' said Dave, with a grin, 'but a few years ago, he was everybody's uncle. Didn't you ever go to Saturday-morning pictures?'

Andy, with those years of Saturday-morning Polish school etched into his rueful expression, shook his head.

'Well,' said Dave, 'he was like the compère, introducing the films, organising the competitions, giving away the prizes. Great bloke.'

They looked across the road at the car he had just parked. It was supposed to be a Ford Escort 1.3L, but

Tony had politely declined the company car, which he viewed as insultingly modest, opting instead to provide his own means of transport in the form of a Mark II Jag. It was ten years old, which is always the age at which cars are at their least desirable: too old to be new and too new to be classic, ten-year-old cars litter the pages of local newspapers, like unwanted frumps litter the Lonely Hearts columns. In the late seventies, those pages were full of Mark II Jags going for a song. This was eight years before *Mona Lisa*, ten before *Inspector Morse*, a time when these cars carried villains rather than kudos and were considered flash, old-fashioned and thirsty. But, then, you could take one look at Tony Harris and remember that old saying, 'You are what you drive.'

His was an irrefutably fine example – immaculate coachwork in Old English white, red leather interior and 3.8 litres of grunt under its elegantly tapered bonnet. Tony claimed to need this power to 'outrun the Old Bill when I'm pissed'. He was only half joking.

Tony was lazy, irresponsible, had no time for book-keeping or paperwork and could often be found 'running' the cinema whilst buried under the weight of a colossal hangover. Yet he got away with it because he had one critical thing in his favour: charm. And if, like Tony, when you have a huge, self-replacing well of it, you need almost nothing else.

Though married with three small children, Tony was an Olympian flirt and not just with women. However, the Harris brand of man-to-man flirting was not remotely camp or effeminate: it involved a lot of firm handshakes and blokey banter. He could chat about anything with anyone in a relaxed, arm-round-the-shoulder way that would make whoever he was talking to feel like his oldest, most intimate friend. People loved him for it and no one more than Maureen Breslin – she'd do anything for him. Like, for example, his job.

The Gaumont was rather like a lake on which floated a fine-looking swan. Tony Harris was the top half, gliding serenely around, watched and adored by everyone, while Maureen was the bottom half, unseen beneath the surface, paddling furiously and efficiently to ensure that the swan remained afloat. She took care of everything, regularly administering the strong black coffee and Anadin that were often necessary to get Tony, to function. Sometimes, when things were particularly bad and the patient was showing no signs of responding, she would even take one of his trademark cigars from its box, and coughing and spluttering, would cut and light it for him before shoving it between his teeth in a final effort to get him started.

It was a combination that worked beautifully. Since her husband's sudden desertion. Maureen's life had been empty. With no children to care for, her maternal instincts had homed in on Tony. Moreover, she was eternally grateful to him for promoting her from cashier to assistant manageress and her Catholic conscience would never allow her to let him down.

Maureen usually did the day shift. At around seven

o'clock she would head home, having handed Tony the reins along with one of his hand-tailored tuxedos, fresh from the dry cleaner's, so he could stand resplendent in the magnificent marble foyer ready to greet his public. This was the part of the job he took most seriously, the part Maureen could never adequately perform.

Tony was tolerated by head office because of his love of cinema and his passionate belief in its social function. He knew that the Gaumont was a place where people came to be entertained so he'd always put in a little extra effort to make them feel special. Hence the tuxedo, the warm welcome for regulars and the fact that he was afforded the rare privilege of almost total autonomy in the selection of programmes. He knew his audience better than anyone and Head Office were smart enough to realise that.

He strolled over, smiled broadly and introduced himself, 'Hello, boys, I'm Tony Harris, your guv'nor. Maureen phoned me this afternoon, told me all about you. Welcome aboard. How was your first day?'

'Fine, thanks,' said Dave.

'You like films?'

'Oh, yeah,' Andy replied earnestly. 'Absolutely love them.'

'Even *The Cat From Outer Space*?' asked Tony, with a grin. 'No, seriously, it's a great place to work. I should have moved on years ago but, well, I'm too attached to the place. Anyway, you probably won't see much of me. I tend to do the evenings while Maureen does the afternoons, but thanks for helping us out in the holidays.' He looked at his watch. 'Now, if you'll excuse me, I'm a bit late. She likes to get home for *Coronation Street* and I don't want to get told off.'

With a wink and a smile, he was gone, leaving both boys struck by his amiability and flattered that he had taken the trouble to say hello. As everyone did after meeting Tony for the first time, they felt better for having done so. He had unwittingly banished any traces of the dismay that they may have been feeling.

'Well,' said Dave, 'I'll tell you one thing.'

'What's that?'

'He's a hell of a lot better than Johnny Mac.'

7

'Johnny Mac' was well aware of his nickname though he had never heard it uttered in his presence. Who would dare? Father John McLafferty was addressed only as 'Father' or 'sir' and had been Kelly and Zymanczyk's headmaster for five years. The very mention of his name united them in the way it would unite any current or ex-pupils of St Bede's Roman Catholic Grammar School for Boys who had experienced the terror of his tutelage.

As Dave pedalled towards Kilburn and Andy headed for Shepherds Bush, their minds rippled back five years to the first time they had ever seen him. They were callow, nervous eleven-year-olds, and had been invited with their parents to attend a school open evening for pupils joining the following September.

They remembered how the evening had begun, with McLafferty, the big, craggy-faced priest, standing on the stage, wearing a flowing black robe. He was in his mid-fifties with a shock of thick, unruly hair the colour and consistency of steel wool. There he had stood, in almost omnipotent silence, an expression of inscrutable stillness on his face. He hadn't even needed to clear his throat politely because, within a few seconds, the whole hall had fallen silent. He'd waited a few more, just to be certain that it would remain so, then had opened his mouth and spoken. 'Let me make it perfectly clear,' he began, in an even, rather menacing Scottish burr, 'that you have absolutely no say in what happens to your son once he enters this school. We have his best interests at heart but if you have a problem with that, please leave now.'

Having heard McLafferty's opening gambit, every one of the ninety-six boys in the hall began to dread September. McLafferty, powerfully silent again, let the truth and severity of his words sink in while sweeping the hall with a slow, stony gaze. Each boy was silently imploring his parents to get up and leave. Not one of them did. They were all very proud of their sons. To be offered a place at St Bede's was a great privilege. The school was in Wembley, less than a mile from the stadium, yet pupils from as far away as Paddington and Watford competed for places. They were mostly from working-class Catholic families and it was hoped that the education St Bede's could provide would be a passport out of the Irish enclaves of Kilburn, Wealdstone and Wembley.

McLafferty continued, 'We have a motto at this school: "Work hard, play hard, pray hard."'

Dave was praying very hard indeed. He realised that 'playing hard' probably didn't mean going out on the lash seven nights a week. It was more likely to involve blood, sweat and toil on various football, cricket and rugby pitches.

McLafferty went on to spell out the terrifying manifesto of academic and sporting excellence, religious fervour and iron discipline that awaited all new entrants.

Dave's heart had sunk at the thought of spending the next five years here. He didn't know a soul. Oh, God, he'd have to wear one of those ridiculous green blazers too. There would be peals of pejorative laughter from all over the estate. He was torn up inside. He knew how proud his parents were but it wasn't them who would have to go through it. Kids from Kilravock Street did not go to St Bede's. He consoled himself with the thought that there must have been some mistake, that he'd be released at any minute and allowed to attend the local comprehensive with his friends.

Sitting three rows behind, Andy Zymanczyk was marginally less fazed. Religious fervour and iron discipline had been part of his life ever since he could remember, and at least this McLafferty bloke wasn't Polish.

When September came round, Dave was racked with fear and apprehension as he checked off the list of items that every pupil at St Bede's was required to possess.

> One Platignum Varsity fountain pen
> One bottle of navy blue Quink
> One copy of the *Pocket Oxford Dictionary*
> One copy of the *Phillips Modern School Atlas*
> One Helix geometry set (Dave never did discover
>   what a set square was for)

He placed them carefully inside the black PVC briefcase for which his mother had proudly exchanged five books of Green Shield stamps. Then, on went the stringently stipulated uniform: white shirt, school tie, grey socks, itchy black trousers, shiny black shoes and, of course, the bright green blazer. Pupils from the 1973 intake could count themselves lucky: their older brothers had been forced to wear caps. He came downstairs, awkward, uncomfortable and terrified. His mother was almost tearful with joy 'Just look at you – so smart.' She'd sniffed. 'Good luck, now. We're so proud of you.'

He opened the front door and stepped out on to Kilravock Street, expecting, at the very least, to be pelted with rotten tomatoes. Instead, he found that quite a few neighbours had also opened their doors and were standing on their doorsteps proudly waving him off. It was as though he was going to get an education for them too. Something in which the whole of Kilravock Street could share. He was flattered but cringing with embarrassment. On balance, he'd have preferred the rotten tomatoes.

Jerzy and Ewa Zymanczyk had been equally proud of Andy. He'd be at St Bede's from Monday to Friday, Polish School on Saturday and mass on Sunday. They were delighted that their son would be receiving such sound academic and spiritual guidance seven days a week. Perhaps Jerzy's dream would come true: his son would go on to the place he referred to as 'The Cambridge University' infinitely superior, in his view, to 'The Oxford University'. Cambridge, he believed, was the home of fact rather than opinion. After 'The

Cambridge University', he could train as a dentist. Father and son could work side by side, drilling and filling Polish teeth before Zymanczyk Junior took over the family practice. Even at eleven, Andy knew he was stuck between a rock and a hard place. Far from offering him an escape from 'Little Warsaw', St Bede's would merely entrench his position there. If he gained the requisite qualifications, it would be impossible not to accede to his father's wishes. If he failed to gain them, he would spend the rest of his life serving *nalesniki* in his uncle Krzys' delicatessen.

Perhaps this was why Andy hadn't felt that Father McLafferty's welcoming address on the first day of term applied to him, although the other boys had found it inspiring. Their headmaster had told them they could be anything they wanted to be. Anyone of them could become prime minister, governor of the Bank of England, anything – it all started with a good education and there was no finer place than St Bede's to provide it. He was playing a role that the boys would rarely, if ever, see him in again: the kind, genial man of the cloth, attempting to put his newest, most nervous charges at ease. It worked very well. It always did. The boys emerged feeling relaxed, happy and proud of their new green blazers. It was a fairly short-lived feeling, lasting only until they were introduced to the other members of staff.

8

'Morning, boys, I am Father Ignatius Doyle. Now, it may seem unusual for a priest to be a PE teacher. I'm sure that priests in your experience have been kind, benign and holy. I, on the other hand, am a religious maniac and violent with it. Had I not taken Holy Orders, I could have played rugby for Ireland. My nickname is Pug – short for pugnacious. Fuck with me, boys, and you'll find out why.'

This was not how Father Doyle had introduced himself but it would have been a candid self-appraisal. He might have gone even further.

'One of my favourite punishments is to say, "Good Friday," to anyone I suspect of misbehaving. This is a coded order for the miscreant to hang motionless from the wall-bars. Very quickly his arms will be searing with pain but he will have to remain in agony until I say, "Easter Sunday," and he can come down. If, as is highly likely, he drops before I say, "Easter Sunday," he will be slippered. I have no qualms about wielding the slipper. In fact, in about two years from now, that poster over there, Blu-tacked to the wall, will simply fall off. I will ask who tore it down. Nobody will own up because nobody will be guilty so I will slipper the whole year. Every one of you will go running into the shower with a huge red weal on your backside. I am very particular about boys taking showers. It's unhygienic not to. However, this may lead to conflict with my colleague here.'

'Yes. Good morning, boys. I am Father Fergus Mitchell. I teach Latin which is immediately after Games. I am irritated by boys arriving late from the gym so I have instituted a simple policy. The last boy in gets four strokes of the cane, regardless of whether he is late or not. Unfair, I know, but the sooner you become accustomed to life's little injustices the better.'

'Morning, boys, I am Father Thomas Ryan. I teach RE. If I catch you talking during my lessons, you will be made to sit with your nose approximately one inch from your desk top. I will then drop a heavy, hardback edition of the *New English Bible* on to the back of your head, causing you great pain and, in some cases, a profuse nosebleed. If I catch any of you fighting in the playground, I will not bang your heads together, I will force you to do that yourselves. "Come on!" I'll roar. "You wanted to kill each other a minute ago! What's the matter with you?" I will watch quite happily while your heads then collide with a series of sickening cracks.'

'Good morning, boys. I am Mr Herbert Cooper. I teach history. I am the most miserable teacher in the school. And, believe me, that's saying something. I frown upon any display of mirth in my lessons. Any boy caught laughing will be subject to a rather peculiar punishment. He will be made to stand at the front of the class with a small stack of books on his head. If he laughs, the books will drop. For every book that drops, he will receive one vicious stroke of the cane. His classmates, of course, will do everything they can to make him laugh and after five minutes, his arse will look like a map of the London Underground.'

'Good morning. I'm Dr George Lacey. I teach mathematics. Believe me, you don't want to know what I'm going to do to you.'

9

Dr Lacey was mad. Not the zany, crazy, bit-of-a-character type of mad but properly mad – mentally unstable. However, like many other similarly deranged people, he possessed a calm, frightening intelligence that made him very adept at hiding it. 'Doc', as he was known, did not teach first-formers. This was not considered wise. These poor boys, cruelly snatched from the warmth and cosiness of their primary schools, had enough to contend with in their first twelve months. Exposure to Doc at such an early, impressionable stage would have inflicted psychological wounds that would probably never heal.

Gradually the new boys had settled in. It was a painful process, both literally and metaphorically, but you can get used to anything and they found themselves slowly getting used to St Bede's. Yet, like the sword of Damocles, their first lesson with Doc hung over them. Naturally, they'd seen him around the school but had never spoken to him or been addressed by him; they had scattered like frightened sparrows whenever he approached.

Dr Lacey had been a tall, commanding figure – at least six foot three, judging by the old school photos that hung along the corridors. Now, sitting in the wheelchair to which he was permanently confined, he had an even more sinister and imposing presence. He was about sixty, thin, bald and evil. All his lessons took place in room twenty-six, which was situated at the end of a particularly long corridor on the ground floor. Dave had noticed him struggling into his specially adapted car and thought how vulnerable he seemed. Surely his lessons couldn't be that bad.

Oh, but they could.

'Face the cross,' was his first command. Every boy in the room faced the cross while Doc, eyes closed and countenance severe, led them in a barking rendition of the Hail Mary. This was how each lesson began unless that lesson started at noon when they recited the Angelus. On opening their eyes, the boys noticed that every desk was spotless and covered with a sheet of clear plastic, secured by a drawing-pin at each corner. They already knew that if they spilled so much as a drop of ink on a desk, they would have to return at lunchtime to sand it off.

Thirty-two terrified twelve-year-olds stood ramrod straight in the immaculate classroom while Doc wheeled himself around, letting his malevolent gaze fall upon each one of them in turn. The flooring was a shiny crimson linoleum with a random white pattern in it. 'Do you know what that is?' their teacher roared, pointing at the dark red of the floor.

Silence.

'Blood. And the white bits?'

More silence.

'Trodden in bits of gristle and bone.'

They were ordered to sit down and their induction into the mysteries of trigonometry, algebra and logarithms was under way.

It was well known that Doc was a decorated war hero, having served in the RAF and fought in the Battle of Britain. Many people assumed that his paralysis was the result of a Douglas Bader-style wartime tragedy, but it had happened a lot more recently than that. He had been on a school trip abroad about ten years earlier at a time when polio was rife. Doc, adhering to some insane notion about never allowing drugs to pass his lips, had refused to be vaccinated. Then, having contracted the disease, he refused to be treated at a foreign hospital. By the time he got home, of course, it was too late: his principles had cost him the use of his legs. Doc's rabid Catholicism was all the more astonishing since, in an ironic reversal of fortune, this had all happened on a trip to Lourdes. He retained a level of religious zeal unmatched by any of the priests. Every year, for example, he banned the phrase 'Merry Christmas'. 'There's nothing merry about it,' he would boom, before delivering an unseasonally bitter and morbid lecture on the reality of the Nativity – impoverished Virgin, shunned by society, forced to give birth in a stable.

Nobody dared to point out that the reality of the Nativity was that it probably wasn't reality at all. We only had St Matthew's word for it, and in Matthew's case the word 'Gospel' was a bit of a misnomer. The Gospels of Mark and John make no mention of the Nativity and Luke merely goes into scant detail. It is only Matthew who provides us with the most famous story ever told. In another era, Matthew might have made a handsome living writing romantic fiction for Mills & Boon. He alone mentions wise men bearing gifts of gold, frankincense and myrrh. His tales seemed conveniently concocted so that a number of Old Testament prophecies could be neatly fulfilled. Doc, as a brilliant scholar, must have known this yet his belief was unshakeable.

In this respect, Andy found his maths teacher and his father remarkably similar. Doc had met Jerzy Zymanczyk at a number of parents' evenings and, in the old Pole, had found a kindred spirit. He admired Jerzy's religious mania and the fact that he, too, had served in the RAF. Andy hadn't the heart to tell Doc that his father had spent the war taking out teeth rather than Messerschmitts. The two men had fine, logical minds both impeded by the same illogical flaw. Doc's attraction to mathematics was like Jerzy's attraction to dentistry. It was the certainty or, in the case of mathematics, the perfection, that had appealed to them. Two plus two equals four. There can be no argument. It is not a matter of opinion, it is a matter of fact. Yet here he was, swallowing Matthew's highly improbable stories. He was no different from those poor demented *Coronation Street* addicts, who believed that Ken Barlow and Emily Bishop were real people. To question Doc's faith, to attempt a calm, rational theological discussion, would have been inviting trouble. Trouble on a scale only witnessed in room twenty-six because punishments inside that room were unlike any others anywhere else in the world.

'Come here, O'Mara.'

John O'Mara had shuffled nervously to the front where Doc slowly crossed his phenomenally strong arms, inserted one hand into each of O'Mara's lapels then shook and screamed at him violently enough to strike terror into the hearts of every one of his classmates. When he'd finished, O'Mara, bruised and battered, had been sent snivelling back to his desk and Doc had resumed the lesson as though nothing had happened.

'Come here, Clancy.'

Chris Clancy had been ordered to bend very low with his head beneath one of the spotless, plastic-sheeted desks. Doc had produced a cane from his desk drawer, then delivered six crisp ones with chillingly controlled savagery to the seat of Clancy's pants. Naturally, the agony of each one made the poor wretch jolt up and crack his head on the underside of the desk.

'Kennedy, fetch the toybox.'

Peter Kennedy, visibly quivering with terror, had been forced to fetch a brown cardboard box. Inside were a cane, a leather strap, a long metal ruler and an old plimsoll. He then had the honour of choosing the implement with which he would be beaten. Toybox beatings were carried out with the victim splayed across

45

Doc's wheelchair so that the blows were delivered from brutally close range.

One of his favourite little sayings was, 'I've killed people for less than that', and on one occasion when Doc had been in a (reasonably) good mood, Dave had asked him why he always said that when it couldn't possibly be true. 'Oh, but it is, Kelly. It's perfectly true,' Doc had replied gravely. 'I was a Lancaster pilot during the war and went on several bombing raids over Dresden and Cologne. We killed hundreds of men, women and children. And they hadn't got their sums wrong.'

Doc taught very few pupils beyond the fourth year because, at fifteen or sixteen, most boys had become too big and unafraid to be bullied, assaulted and humiliated in this way. The other reason was that his lessons were so intense, his pupils so frightened of not paying attention, that they were all primed and ready to take their Maths O level a year early. And, without exception, they passed.

10

So, after five years of this sort of schooling, it was understandable that Dave and Andy should feel such a bond. Ex-pupils of St Bede's invariably felt the same way if their paths ever crossed outside the confines of the school. Two complete strangers could meet in Whitefish, Montana, or in an anonymous suburb of Sydney and, once it was established that each had served time at St Bede's and the scars were shown to prove it, they would find the nearest bar and compare horror stories until long after closing time.

With thirty other classmates to separate them, Dave and Andy's lives had never become intertwined at school. At the Gaumont, however, with their class comprising just a handful of old-age pensioners, they were brought closer together. In this new class, they had expected to be on constant best behaviour, never swearing or making lewd remarks, but they soon realised that coarseness and profanity were practically *de rigueur*.

Old George's conversation was peppered with phrases like 'bugger awf,' and 'saucy little bleeder'. 'Tarts these days ain't 'alf skinny,' he observed to Dave one afternoon, as a sylph-like creature walked past outside. 'Time they get their stays awf, there's fuck-all to get 'old of.'

Lily, the seventy-two-year-old senior usherette, was almost as bad. Andy had initially thought that Gary, the projectionist, was being disrespectful with his frequent requests to the old girl – ''Ere, Lil,' he'd say, 'show us your susses.'

After a while, Andy realised that Lily, who still believed she had a pair of legs to rival Cyd Charisse's, loved nothing more than to hitch up her skirt and show her suspenders. As for Doris, they were still talking, six months on, about the striptease she'd performed at the Christmas party. Add to this the drunken, cigar-chomping manager and the almost saintly manageress, and you had a collection of characters off the screens who were even more extraordinary than the ones who appeared on them. They were real people, neither Polish nor Catholic, the like of whom Andy never encountered before, and he loved them all.

All except one. Neither he nor Dave felt any warmth towards Guy Patterson, the area manager. If you ever meet a man called Guy, you can almost guarantee that Guy will not be his real name, it will be something rather more staid, like Arthur, Graham or Eric. Guy is a sobriquet frequently adopted by the dull in a vain attempt to make themselves seem a little more racy and interesting

This particular Guy had been christened George Ronald Patterson and could be described as a triumph of ambition over talent. The Guy Pattersons of this

world infect every area of society. They compensate
for a lack of natural flair with an unhealthy desperation
to reach the top of whatever greasy pole they've chosen
to climb. They were the class swots, the teachers' pets,
the ones who believe that if you do things by the
book, suck up to those above you, don't bother with
those below, your elevation will be that much more
direct. They're not necessarily bad people: they just
don't know any better. Put them in any situation and
they are genetically programmed to try to come out
on top.

Ambition, like acne, is something that even these
people tend to grow out of, but at nearly forty, Guy
Patterson was still metaphorically covered in spots. He
played golf with his boss, not because he enjoyed it but
because he felt it might further his career. In his tartan
trousers and ridiculous sweater, he had to remember to
keep that rabid competitiveness in check because this
was his boss he was playing with, so he ought to let
him win.

As Guy's youth began to recede slowly into life's
rear-view mirror, he'd started to dye his greying temples
and had compounded this folly by investing in a cheap
home solarium to honey up his rather pallid complexion. The idea was to look like an all-conquering
plutocrat, who spent his summers in Anguilla and his
winters in Gstaad. Instead, with black hair and orange
face, he looked like a Jaffa Cake. As area manager
for Gaumont Leisure, he was responsible for 'sites',
as he liked to call them, from Westbourne Grove to

PAUL BURKE

Slough. He'd done a stint as a cinema manager but, unlike Tony, had not paused to enjoy it. It had been just another rung on the ladder. The Escort 1.3L had long gone, and he now sat proudly at the wheel of a Cortina 1.6GL and, who knows, within a few years he might be spending Sunday mornings polishing a new Granada Ghia.

He revelled in the unseemly deference shown to him by the daytime staff, who were from a generation brought up to kow-tow to authority. When 'Mr Patterson' came to visit, it was like a state occasion. However, if Tony happened to be there during one of Patterson's afternoon visits, he showed his boss no deference at all. As he explained to Maureen, 'I shook hands with him once and my whole right side sobered up.' Tony had nothing but contempt for Patterson, and his relaxed, easy-going charm made the area manager bristle with insecurity. Tony knew of his plans, Patterson made no secret of them, but as long as Maureen kept this particular site running so smoothly, he would have great difficulty in implementing them. Those plans could be summed up in one word: bingo.

'Come on, Tony, you must admit,' he'd say, with not-quite-ironed out northern vowels. 'Admit' was one of the giveaway words. Patterson, while affecting an educated Home Counties accent, couldn't help saying '*add*mit', over-pronouncing the first vowel as he did with '*con*servative'. Tony always let out a gentle chuckle when Patterson did this, just to let him know that he'd noticed, just to make him feel even worse.

'Come on, Tony, you must admit, bingo is the way forward. Cinema is on its last legs. Television sounded the death knell years ago and now these new video-recorders will see it off once and for all. This place would make a great bingo hall and, sooner or later, it will. Whether you like it or not.'

Over the last few years, Tony had watched in horror as some of the country's finest cinemas, including the Kilburn State and the Tooting Granada, had been closed down and disembowelled for this very purpose. 'Bingo's a game for morons,' was the only counter he could offer. 'Morons motivated by nothing but greed. That's not entertainment.'

Then it was Patterson's turn to chuckle, 'You try telling that to the thousands of punters who flock in every night of the week. Over in Kilburn, for example, or at Shepherds Bush Green. Try telling them they're not being entertained. They absolutely bloody love it.' Then he'd make a patronising attempt at empathy: 'At the end of the day, Tony, we're all human. We all have families to feed, we all want to improve our circumstances. Bingo offers the punters a chance to do that. It would go down a storm round here. Not exactly rolling in it, are they? I don't care how sophisticated people reckon they are, the moment that caller says, "Eyes down for a full house," you're hooked.'

Tony had never been hooked. He'd been in dozens of bingo halls and had failed to see the attraction. He deplored the lack of skill involved, the slim chance of winning and the paltry little prizes even if you did. But, most of all, he hated the petty greed and resentment he saw in every other person when one of their number shouted, 'House.' The cinema was fun, entertaining, often edifying; it brought people together. Bingo, on the other hand, seemed to pull them apart.

He didn't answer Patterson. Even if he did, the depressing fact was that Head Office weren't committed to cinema: they were committed to profit and were turning cinemas into bingo halls all over the country. If he couldn't somehow prove that his 'site' would make more money if it were left untouched, he would soon find himself calling, 'Two fat ladies – eighty-eight,' to a hall full of greedy pensioners.

11

'Bob – hello, mate, it's Tony Harris. What have you got for me?' Tony leaned back in his chair, feet on the desk, took a puff of his cigar and blew the smoke skywards while he listened to what Bob Stannard had to say. Bob was film scheduler for BBC Television, and every few months he would receive this call from Tony.

'Right, let me see. *True Grit*, *The Anderson Tapes*, *Some Like It Hot*, *And Soon the Darkness*, *The Great Escape* . . .'

'Not again?'

'Yes, again – *High Plains Drifter*, *Spring and Port Wine*, *The French Connection*—'

'Oh, you bastard! I was going to do that and the sequel as a double bill.'

'Never mind. *Whistle Down the Wind*, *The Man Who Fell To Earth* . . .'

'The Man Who Failed To Act.'

'Very funny.'

'Any Bond?'

'*From Russia With Love*.'

'Okay. I'll do *Goldfinger* and *Thunderball* as a double-header.'

The cigar was balanced on the edge of the ashtray as

the conversation went on. Bob was giving Tony a list of all the films to be shown during the BBC's autumn season. He never minded giving Tony this almost classified information, neither did Malcolm Green at Thames, who would be receiving an identical call the following day. Both admired Tony's love of film and his desire to show his patrons the best ones possible. It was almost unheard-of in a cinema manager, outside the independents anyway. With prior warning of the films to be shown on TV, Tony could compile a list of those he should not book for the Gaumont. And, by default, a much longer list of those he should. He drew a line, however, at subtitled films because, as he put it, 'People don't come to the pictures to read.'

In 1978, very few households had videos. The only way to see a film was either at the cinema or on TV, and if a good but not necessarily current one was going to be overlooked by both channels, Tony would revive it in Screen Two. A quick call to *Time Out* would alert movie buffs from all over London to make their way over. Andy had taken up almost permanent residency in Screen Two and was delighted to spend his eleven-week summer break watching a selection of films he never thought he'd see: *Saturday Night Fever*, *Apocalypse Now*, *Easy Rider*, *Cool Hand Luke*, *Midnight Cowboy* and *The Godfather*, Parts I and II. He had sat alone on the usher's seat and, like so many before him, he had lost himself in the magic of the movies. He had been engulfed by laughter, sadness, thrall, captivation and terror as he'd never experienced them before. Here, he was a million miles from the twin stringencies of Catholicism and all things Polish. Here, he could forget all about dentists' drills (he hadn't seen *Marathon Man*). He felt liberated by Hollywood, by his first tiny taste of independence, and by the easy-going friendship of Dave Kelly, a classmate he'd never really known until now.

Dave, perhaps because of repeated exposure to *The Cat From Outer Space*, wasn't quite so besotted. *Grease* wouldn't be released until late September so if he wanted unlimited access to Olivia Newton-John in her skin-tight pants he'd have to extend his employment beyond the summer holidays. And that would all depend on Derek, the gay postman.

12

No one ever called Derek gay. One reason was that, in the late seventies, certain words still clung to their original meanings. The word 'gay' still meant 'brightly coloured'. Tom Robinson may have sung 'Glad To Be Gay' but his message would have been more readily understood if he'd declared himself 'Glad To Be A Bit The Other Way'. Also, there was no evidence to prove that Derek *was* gay, although he was forty-nine, unmarried and, while not quite Larry Grayson, camper than your average postman. He lived with his mum in Marne Street, two turnings from Kilravock Street, and had done since the day he was born. His father had been dead for thirty years and his mother, now practically housebound, was wholly dependent on Derek to look after her. He had no real quality of life yet was perennially cheerful, even with a full sack of mail on his back. He whistled while he worked and said good morning to everyone, even the curmudgeonly souls who never replied.

He was also fantastically indiscreet. People's whole lives came through his fingers. If they were in trouble, hadn't paid their bills, hadn't paid their rent, were about to be sent to Trellick Tower, Derek would know.

And by lunchtime so would everyone else.

For Dave, Derek was a chilling reminder of everything he didn't want to be. Derek had never had a girlfriend, had never managed to escape and now, let's face it, he never would.

On this particular morning, knowing that his O-level results were somewhere in Derek's sack, Dave found himself listening out for the trademark tuneless whistling. It wasn't long before his ears picked it up and, with it, the cheery but still indistinct salutations. Gradually he was able to make out what Derek was saying. 'Morning, Frank,' he called to Frank Sheehy at number forty-two. 'Just come off the night shift?'

Pause.

'Yeah, that's what they all say.' Big, hearty chuckle. 'How's your Tina? . . . Is she? Oh, smashing. Well, give her my love when you see her.'

'Morning, Peggy,' he said to Mrs Blundell at number forty-eight. He was getting closer, and Dave began to hear the theme from *Jaws* getting louder and louder as Derek approached. 'Gas bill, I'm afraid. I think you ought to pay it. Looks like a final reminder . . . Yeah. Mind how you go.'

'Well, hello,' Derek said, in his biggest, friendliest voice as he reached number sixty-four. The theme music was louder than ever now: the shark was in shallow waters. 'Whose birthday is it today, then? How old are you? . . . Six? My, you are a big girl. Well, let me see what I've got for you.'

Dave could see him now, producing a little stack of

cards and a couple of small packages from his mailbag. The little girl was jumping up and down with delight, Derek picking her up, holding her high, planting a big kiss on her forehead and handing her back to her mum.

'You have a lovely day, now, and eat a big piece of cake for me.'

Dave knew he was next. Oh, shit. He needed to know whether he could continue to dig the escape tunnel from Kilravock Street and Derek had the vital information.

'Morning, Davey,' Derek trilled, waving the envelope that contained Dave's results. 'Your whole future is in my hands.'

What a grisly thought.

'Morning, Derek,' said Dave, with a nervous smile. He knew that the postman would not move on to next door until that envelope had been opened, so he was faced with two unpleasant scenarios. If the results were bad, he'd have to break down in tears in front of Derek. If they were good, he'd have to leap up and down, embrace Derek and plant a kiss on his cheek. He must have been the only boy in the country praying for indifferent exam results.

His wish came true. Five O levels from a possible eight. Two Bs, three Cs. Add to this the Maths he already had and that was a grand total of six. Not brilliant but not bad, and on the Queens Park Estate, the equivalent of a Nobel Prize.

Dave's reaction was one of satisfaction but Derek was almost delirious with delight. 'So, Einstein,' he beamed, 'what are you going to do next?'

'Well,' said Dave, 'if you get five O levels, you can go into the sixth form and do A levels, so I'll probably do that.'

'Oh, that's marvellous. So, at least you won't end up like me.'

Suddenly Dave felt sorry for him: he didn't like the idea of the kindly postman putting himself down. 'Being a postman's all right, isn't it?' he said. He knew exactly how Derek would reply.

'Well,' Derek smiled, 'it's better than walking the streets.'

Oh, God, if he had a pound for every time Derek had said that, he wouldn't need those six O levels – he could retire now.

Over in Shepherds Bush, Andy's envelope had been pushed through the letterbox. He picked it up, and suddenly noticed that both of his parents were standing behind him. Such was their knife-edge anticipation that they both seemed to be holding their breath. If he delayed the opening long enough, Andy wondered, would they would both fall down dead on the doormat?

Andy's cold, sweaty palms pulled out the slip. Eight out of eight – six As, two Bs. Andy's reaction was one of relief rather than pride and joy. To have disappointed his parents with anything less would have been unimaginable.

'Well, done, son.' Jerzy's old face creased into a smile

as he enveloped his son in a warm embrace. Then his mother hugged and kissed him, but every silver lining has a cloud.

'You have done very well,' said Jerzy. 'But now, of course, is when the work really begins.'

Andy's relief and relaxation had lasted approximately eight seconds. He'd better enjoy the next couple of weeks at the cinema because, although the doors to St Bede's were open for him, the doors to the Gaumont were about to swing shut.

Oddly enough, it was Father McLafferty who suggested that they didn't. As soon as he received the boys' O level results, McLafferty phoned their parents to see how many would be returning to the sixth form. When he dialled the Zymanczyks' number Jerzy picked up the phone. '*Slucham.*' After more than thirty years, it still never occurred to Jerzy that the person calling might not be Polish. So '*Slucham*' or 'I am listening' was how he always answered the phone.

'Mr Zymanczyk?'

'Yes.'

'Hello, it's Father McLafferty from St Bede's. Congratulations. Andrzej's results are excellent. You must be very pleased – six As and two Bs, plus the one he already has.'

'No, no,' insisted Jerzy. 'The *two* he already has. Father, you are forgetting the A grade he received for Polish.' All Andy's other results paled in comparison with this one.

'Of course,' said McLafferty with all the patience he could muster. 'So I was just checking that we'll be seeing him back for the sixth form in September.'

'Oh, yes, he will be there.'

'Good, good. And how is he?'

'He is very well. He is working at the moment. Just a summer job, you understand, in a cinema. He will, of course, be stopping this as soon as he returns to school.'

McLafferty was well aware of the stifling atmosphere in the Zymanczyk household. Yes, it had helped produce these excellent results, but in the Lower Sixth the pressure eased and it might do Andy good to establish a life outside that tight-knit Polish community. 'Well, it's up to you, of course, Mr Zymanczyk, but in the Lower Sixth, the academic timetable isn't so demanding. We feel that the boys should be allowed to develop socially as well as academically, that they should be allowed a little more independence. If it's a job he enjoys and it is not to the detriment of his studies, perhaps he should be allowed to continue with it.'

'Very well, Father, I will speak to him.'

Tony Harris also wanted to speak to Andy. He liked the boy very much and saw in him the same passion for cinema that had gripped him as a teenager. He liked the other one too – Dave. He had less interest in films but more of an interest in the Gaumont itself, its history and in the stars who had performed there.

This was true. Dave was fascinated by the sad,

neglected dressing rooms, hidden behind Screen One, forgotten and unused for years. If ever he went down there, he could almost feel, even in the cold, musty silence, the long-dead music-hall stars like Max Miller and Robb Wilton, nervously waiting to go on. He could hear the screams of a thousand teenage girls as John, Paul, George and Ringo bounded out on to the stage. He could see Sid James and Dick Emery, dressed as the Ugly Sisters for the Christmas panto having their makeup slapped on at those mirrors surrounded by lightbulbs. How he wished it was still one huge cinema, theatre and live-music venue. These feelings were amplified when he saw Ted Hogarth give one of his occasional Sunday-afternoon recitals on the magnificent Wurlitzer organ. Coachloads of organ enthusiasts would descend upon the Gaumont to hear Ted, a shy little man with glasses, suede shoes and a greying goatee, run through his repertoire of wartime and showtime favourites. His podgy little fingers could instantly evoke a lost era of which Dave would have loved to have been part.

Tony did not want to say goodbye to either boy's charm, industry and enthusiasm. He had them ushered into his office, where he greeted them with a warm, expansive smile. 'So, boys, back to school next week?'

''Fraid so,' said Dave, with a rueful smile.

'And have you enjoyed working here?'

Andy nodded. He looked like he was about to cry but the regular thrashings at St Bede's had taught him how to hold back tears.

'Good. Because we've enjoyed having you.' He paused. 'So I was wondering if you'd like to become night boys.'

It sounded as though they were being offered careers as juvenile prostitutes but Tony simply wanted them to work one or two evenings a week and maybe at weekends.

'It's a bit more fun. You don't have to put up with those old cackers either,' he said, jerking his head towards the foyer and the senior citizens who worked there.

'Let me know tomorrow, eh?

Andy couldn't bear it. He was returning home, a place where Our Lady of Czestochowa was now going head to head with His Holiness the Pope in a battle for pictorial supremacy, where only Polish was spoken, where instead of this wonderful cornucopia of films there were just the eighty-eight keys of Chopin and the dreary stanzas of Adam Mickiewicz for entertainment. His parents would now be pushing him down the home straight towards 'The Cambridge University'. The genie would have to be forced back into the bottle.

When he got home, however, he was in for a shock. Far from forbidding him ever to set foot in that fleapit again, his father was almost reasonable. 'I feel,' he said slowly, trying to remember his lines, 'that you should be allowed to develop socially as well as academically. Carry on at the cinema if you want to.'

My God, this was a cataclysmic change of attitude.

Whatever next? Surely it was only a matter of time before his old man started saying, 'Hello,' when he answered the phone.

13

The Zymanczyks' number was, naturally enough, the last that John McLafferty had dialled. Good, they had all accepted. As he replaced the receiver with an air of satisfaction, the phone rang again. 'Hello?'

'John, hi, Pete Roberts.'

The caller had said only four words but had managed to offend McLafferty with three of them. *John?* Father McLafferty to you, laddie. *Hi?* The correct form of salutation is either 'Hello' or 'Good morning'. What sort of sloppy Americanesque greeting is *hi?* We're not in a cowboy film. You may as well go the whole hog and say, 'Howdy'. *Pete?* That's not a proper abbreviation. It may be worth truncating Christopher into Chris, or William into Bill, but Peter into Pete? Hardly worth it. Was that one letter really too much to bear? Just wanted to display your own brand of matey individualism, did you, *Pete?* Roberts? Well, he'd let him off with that one.

'Mr Roberts,' said McLafferty, with a forced smile and an unforced sigh, 'what can I do for you?'

Pete Roberts was 'chair' (God, what if McLafferty knew that Pete also liked to be referred to as a piece of furniture?) of the local education authority. McLafferty had never met him but had visions of a corduroy jacket and desert boots. Pete was bright, idealistic and, to use a word not yet in everyday use, 'focused'. You didn't get to become chair without being focused.

The Comprehensive Education Act had been passed a couple of years earlier. Antony Crosland had started it and Shirley Williams, with Pete's help, was determined to finish it. St Bede's was the only school in the borough that hadn't yet fallen into line. They had been given a little leeway. It was a Catholic school, very much tied to the Order of St Bede, so they'd always had a different way of operating. Also, their academic results had been among the best in the country for as long as anyone could remember. However, it would appear that they were simply ignoring the Parliamentary Act as though it didn't apply to them. The way Pete saw it, St Bede's was still a state school, funded by the borough and governed ultimately by the local education authority of which he was chair. They had to sign up for the programme. They were out of touch, this was the future, this was progress, and everyone would benefit.

Pete had an almost missionary zeal for comprehensive education. It was a wonderful idea. Equality of opportunity for all. Wasn't it grossly unfair that a child's life could be blighted simply through failing to pass an exam at the age of eleven? The eleven-plus system fostered élitism. Children who might have been having an off-day on the morning of their exam would then be consigned to life's scrap-heap with no possible chance of escape.

McLafferty would beg to differ. In his view life, unfortunately, was selective. It always had been and it always would be. As a young boy in the tenements of east Glasgow, he had emerged as a gifted footballer. He'd augmented that natural talent with years of practice, long cold hours of slog. He had a burning desire to play for Celtic. The green and white hooped shirt had been his Holy Grail. He progressed through the ranks and finally signed schoolboy terms at Parkhead. He made it into the youth team, then into the reserves, but when it finally came down to it, although he was good – brilliant, even – he was not quite good enough. No matter how hard he tried or how deep he dug, he could not produce that final 5 per cent, conferred upon the very few, that would have seen him worshipped by half of Glasgow.

What if Celtic had adopted a 'comprehensive' approach, inviting anyone who lived in the catchment area to come and play for them? How could they have maintained their standards? The once-mighty football club would have shrivelled up and died. And what if every other club had followed suit? They would have become a bunch of undistinguished, indistinguishable Cowdenbeaths and the whole country would have been adversely affected.

It would be a waste of time to try to explain this analogy to 'Pete'. He probably called football 'soccer' and regarded it as a game played by yobbos and watched by hooligans. It would be at least a dozen years before Pete, from the comfort of his hospitality box, would suddenly start claiming to be a lifelong Arsenal fan.

Pete knew he'd have to tread carefully. He was aware of opposition to the council's plans to turn St Bede's into a comprehensive. Most of the school's teachers were dull old reactionaries who lacked his bright, quixotic ambitions. Nonetheless, there was no sense in upsetting them. 'I just thought you'd like to come up and see the plans for St Saviour's,' he said.

This was the brand new sixth-form college to which pupils from St Bede's, St Angela's Convent across the road and other Catholic schools in the borough would be sent to do their A levels. It was due to open the following September and Pete was very excited. He'd thought of the college's name himself, and although he knew nothing about saints, he liked the word 'Saviour'. He saw himself as one of the saviours of Britain's education system.

McLafferty however had little faith in St Saviour's. He would have called it after St Philomena, the patron saint of lost causes. He felt like Captain von Trapp in *The Sound of Music*, unable to turn a tide of tyranny that looked set to engulf his country. He could procrastinate no longer. 'Very well. When would be convenient for you?

'Well,' said Pete, 'how about next Thursday – about eleven thirty?'

The response was stone cold. 'Mr Roberts, I have a school to run.'

'Yes, yes, of course. Er . . . four-thirty? Would that be okay?'

'Four-thirty will be fine.'

'Okay, John, see you then. Goodbye.'

'Goodbye, Mr Roberts.'

McLafferty stared down at the list of names, due to start in the sixth form in a week's time before being transferred up the road – or in this case, down the river – to St Saviour's the following year. He looked at them all, from Aherne to Zymanczyk, and hoped to God that they wouldn't feel too betrayed.

14

From Aherne to Zymanczyk, they didn't feel betrayed at all: they felt almost privileged. For gaining the requisite five O levels and surviving all those years in a green blazer, they were rewarded with a black one. They were entering the sixth form. The long, hard stint in the prisoner-of-war camp was over and its legacy was a great sense of camaraderie among those who'd survived. They'd all been in the same boat, united against the enemy.

Having done the five years, they were, of course, free to go. And while some were only too glad to have their sentences commuted and to be released back into society, others were happy to sign up for a further two years and change the colour of their blazers. Secure in their new uniforms, sixth-formers were freed for ever from the brutal regime that their old ones had guaranteed. Never again would they have to endure the dreadful punishments and the bowel-loosening fear of punishment visited upon them by almost every member of staff. No more would they experience that awful little mechanism in the throat that always threatened to fall either one way or the other: one way would make you burst into uncontrollable tears, the other would make

you lash out with an equal lack of control and beat
your tormentor viciously with whatever he had chosen
to beat you. Somehow, you had to keep that mechanism
centred. Don't cry, don't react – take your punishment
unflinchingly and try not to get caught again.

Academically, it was a bit easier – three subjects
instead of nine. Dave had chosen English, Economics
and Political Philosophy. Or, rather, those subjects had
chosen him since they were the only ones he had the
slightest chance of passing. All forms of science were
unintelligible to him, and he was the only boy in St
Bede's so genuinely hopeless that he hadn't had to take
Physics, Chemistry or Biology beyond the third year.
Father Macken had summed it up a few years earlier
after a Chemistry test: 'Kelly, I felt rather sorry for you
so I've doubled your score: nought.'

Andy also shunned the sciences, despite having an
O level in each subject. He felt that the sooner he
distanced himself from science the less chance he'd
have of spending the rest of his life saying, 'Open
wide, please.' He'd opted for English, Economics and
History. He couldn't bear the thought of Political
Philosophy, a subject with which his father would be
only too keen to 'help' him. For this reason, he hoped
that History did not include the Second World War.
Like everyone else, Andy was far happier about putting
on the black blazer than he had been about putting on
the green one. The black one allowed you the privilege
of sauntering to the front of the dinner queue, which
was marshalled with some savagery by 'Bruv'.

Bruv's real name was Brother Aloysius. He was a monk, and since he was far too stupid to teach anyone anything, he had been given the job of school caretaker. His impenetrable Irish accent was exacerbated by a stammer like a Bren gun. Bruv was excused pastoral duties like saying mass because, unfortunately, had he ever been allowed to do this, early-morning mass would have lasted well into the afternoon. He didn't let the fact that he wasn't a teacher and therefore had no legal right to discipline the pupils, stop him assaulting them on a daily basis.

He was a huge, heavily built monster of a man and had never been seen without his blue nylon warehouse coat, grubby old trousers, socks and sandals, which would have required major surgery to remove. He would have waltzed home with the first prize in any contest to find Britain's Greasiest Hair but, as if this weren't bad enough, he plastered bucketloads of Brylcreem on top of his own natural supply. Shampoo and general hygiene were unknown to Bruv, so every few days he applied a fresh slathering of Brylcreem without bothering to wash out the stale one.

He favoured a swift approach to mindless violence, often wading into a hapless pupil for no reason at all. In the depths of Bruv's psyche, there was probably a reason for the attack, which he sometimes tried to convey, but the combination of violence, stammering and spittle meant that the recipient would go to his grave without ever knowing what he was supposed to have done.

As caretaker, Bruv was never without his enormous bunch of keys, which he would hurl with devastating inaccuracy at any boy he suspected of misbehaving. This lethal missile invariably caused grievous injury to an innocent bystander while the culprit got away scot-free. It didn't matter: that boy's turn would come. And, almost certainly, for something he hadn't done.

Worse than anything was Bruv in a good mood. Then he would get you in a playful headlock in which your face met his armpit, affording you an olfactory experience that made you feel ill for days.

Once you entered the sixth form, though, his attitude changed completely. Unnervingly, he would address you politely by your first name. Dave wondered who he was talking to when he said, 'Morning, D-David,' after years of hearing, 'K-K-K-K-Kelly, you're a l-l-l-lout,' as blows rained down on his head.

Bruv was probably quite relieved to say, 'Morning, Andy,' as he had never quite mastered 'Zymanczyk'.

15

'Pa pa-pa pa-pa-pa-pa-pa-pa pa . . .'

This could be one of two things: it was either Bruv trying to say 'Patrick' or, in this case, Pearl & Dean's famous signature tune, which preceded the commercials before every programme at the Gaumont. The first was an artfully shot, rather surreal epic for Benson & Hedges.

That reminds me, thought Andy, sitting with his torch at the back of Screen Two. I must give up smoking.

This was not quite the response that Benson & Hedges had been hoping for. Hugh Hudson had not been hired at huge expense to direct this ground-breaking masterpiece so that teenagers would decide to stop smoking rather than start. However, for the boy in the Crimplene jacket, cigarettes had served their purpose.

Smoking was cool – stupid, pointless and a fast track to lung cancer, but cool. Countless practitioners from Bogart to Bowie had somehow made it the zenith of sophistication. Andy had been particularly impressed by French movie stars' effortless use of the lower lip to smoke and talk simultaneously. On the rare occasions that he'd seen *The Sweeney*, he'd loved the way Jack Regan would stomp into the interview room and slam twenty Piccadilly on the table before giving some 'lowlife slag' a particularly belligerent grilling. He loved the various ways in which a cigarette could be smoked: between forefinger and middle finger, between forefinger and thumb, or hidden between middle finger and ring finger, the cigarette smoked secretly through an almost clenched fist, just in case a teacher happened to be passing 'The Corner'.

As the first-formers at St Bedes grew into spotty teenagers, voices half broken, bodies half built, more and more of them, at break time, began to prefer fags to football and gravitated towards 'The Corner'. Football had been fine. Indeed, in the infants' playground it had been the most important thing in the world. It was probably the first real activity in which a five-year-old voluntarily immerses himself. This was not a game of Cowboys and Indians. Nobody was pretending. This was a real football match, every bit as valid as the FA Cup final. However, after eight or nine years, its attraction palled in comparison with the iniquitous clouds of smoke drifting up from 'The Corner', a little recess at the far end of the playground, which had a language all of its own.

'Chip it', in Cornerspeak, meant 'Extinguish your cigarette immediately. A member of staff is approaching.'

'Gis a lug' meant 'Please may I have a drag of your cigarette.'

'Fuck off' was the same in both languages, as was 'Oh, come on'.

'All right, but I'm driving' translated as 'Very well, but I must insist on holding the cigarette while you take a drag for fear of you running away with it.'

Player's No. 6 was the most popular brand, especially since Ravi Patel, an enterprising local newsagent, had begun selling them loose. 'Looseys', as they were known, were 5p each, and guaranteed to tempt the keen-to-be-cool fourteen-year-old away from the more mundane pleasures of Mars Bars, Revels and Opal Fruits. For a shy Polish boy looking for acceptance among his peers, 'looseys' were perfect. And although Andy hated the taste and was unsettled by the giddy rush he always felt after the first three drags, it was worth it. Fag in hand, Andy Zymanczyk was one of the boys.

The Corner was a portable concept: as long as at least two like-minded smokers were together, each with a loosey about his person, it could be set up in temporary premises almost anywhere.

Oddly enough, Dave and Andy felt no need to set it up in the cinema. Here, where it was not forbidden, it had somehow lost its edge. Andy's slowly burgeoning confidence had released him from the need for nicotine. What's more, the sight of Doris with twenty Kensitas stuffed down the front of her pinafore or of old George sucking on a disintegrating matchstick-thin roll-up meant that suddenly it didn't seem cool any more.

Drinking was terminally uncool. It was something middle-aged people did, like going to mass every Sunday and believing the ludicrous liturgy. Andy had grown up seeing his father and an assortment of other old Poles sitting in the front room under the baleful gaze of Our Lady of Czestochowa draining tiny cut-crystal glasses of revolting Polish vodka in one gulp with the cry '*Na zdrowie*' or 'To your health'. After a few of these, there would be some dewy-eyed reminiscences about the old country followed, in really dire circumstances, by a little Polish folk music.

Dave was even less attracted to alcohol since the pub – or at least those within staggering distance of 76 Kilravock Street – embodied everything he wanted to escape. The Grey Horse, round the corner, the William IV, on the Harrow Road, or the Neeld Arms, a little further down towards Paddington, were all depressing examples of the great British pub – shabby décor, balding carpets and maroon plastic banquette seats, split in places with the stuffing spilling out. Sitting on them or standing at the bar you'd find a collection of miserable old men either talking to, or studiously ignoring, other miserable old men and being served brown lukewarm beer by a miserable old landlord. But worse than any of these places was the Cobden Working-men's Club, just across the canal. The working-men's club was a northern concept, which had never really taken root in London, and it wasn't hard to see why. There, you'd find 'members' who were mean as well as miserable: they drank at the club primarily because the brown lukewarm beer was fourpence a pint cheaper. Even in 1978, the Cobden was a relic of a long-dead and unlamented era. You almost expected a Bernard Manning-style compère to waddle out and introduce a 'comic' whose opening gag would begin, 'There were these two poofs in a lift . . .' Every now and again, Bernard would come back, blow into the microphone, and announce that the meat pies were ready or that the bingo was due to start in ten minutes.

These weren't places for a young man looking for a laugh. Very few pubs were. The under-age drinkers so desperate to get served were the ones almost guaranteed to be miserable old men themselves before they were thirty.

Far more appealing was the disco. And for most sixteen-year-old boys, going out regularly for the first time, this was the choice they had to make: pub or disco? And the path you took at this tender age was often a reliable indicator as to your downfall in later life: drink or women.

For Dave, it looked like it was going to be women. He was instantly seduced by the heady scent of Charlie, the sound of soul music and the ever-present threat of a punch-up afterwards. He usually played in midfield, lurking just behind the front two, sometimes breaking forward at the crucial moment just in time to score. That was how the boys at the St Joseph's Youth Club Friday night disco unwittingly organised themselves – like a football team, usually a 4-4-2 formation.

Up front would be Paul Cronin and Adrian Harte. There is a Cronin in every class, the boy hit by puberty before his tenth birthday. Cronin's voice had broken and he was well acquainted with a Gillette GII by the time he arrived at St Bede's. He wasn't the only one: between his first and second years, Neil Feeney had come back from the summer holidays about six inches taller, two stone heavier, his hormones having exploded out of his pores in a mass of unsightly acne. His classmates had to ask who he was. Feeney would be all right in a slow dance until the lights came up: then, on seeing that he had a face like a badly iced birthday cake, his partner would run sobbing back to her friends. Cronin had been more fortunate. He was big and handsome with a man's physique and a dark, swarthy complexion. Even if he shaved in the morning before school, he could usually squeeze out a full beard by lunchtime. He was the fastest runner, the finest footballer and the hardest bloke in the year.

His strike partner could hardly have been more different: Adrian Harte was a fey, fop-haired Leif Garrett lookalike. He had that slim, pretty femininity combined with rampant heterosexuality that was lethal to women. Harte danced to his own tune. Literally. This was a time when it was practically illegal for teenage boys not to like either punk, heavy metal or fifties rock 'n' roll. Dancing, unless it was 'strolling' to rock 'n' roll or 'pogo-ing' to punk, was a capital offence. Yet, Harte would be in among the girls grooving exuberantly to 'Boogie Nights' or 'Dancing Queen'.

The entire female half of any disco would fancy either Harte or Cronin, usually both of them. Towards, the end of the evening, when the opening bars of 'I'm Not In Love' or 'If You Leave Me Now' oozed out of the speakers, the pair had their pick of potential partners.

Dave wasn't too far behind. As an attacking midfielder, he usually found himself in a clockwise embrace with an equivalent female from the other side.

Andy could play in midfield at the Polish Youth Club discos, but with this sort of competition, he had to settle for a place in the back four alongside the likes of Feeney, whose sexual experience, unsurprisingly, did not extend beyond the shower-fittings page of the Argos catalogue.

Right at the back, however, in goal, was Fishy Wilkins, so-called because his dad had a fishmonger's shop in Burnt Oak and Fishy's filial duty was to put in a full day's work every Saturday. This meant that he was permanently permeated with an odour that no amount of soap and water could remove. He would scrub his skin red raw in the bath, then deluge himself in Brut 33 so that the truly foul aroma of wet fish mixed with Brut preceded him into a room. In comparison, Bruv's armpit was like the heavenly scent of jasmine. Even though he was a fat, greasy, unhygienic psychopath who had taken a vow of celibacy and had a personality disorder the size of Texas, Bruv's chances of pulling at the school disco would have been no worse than Fishy's.

After a while, Fishy slunk quietly off and joined

the pub contingent, where no almost-sexual conquests would be expected of him and the smell of stale beer and smoke could almost, though not quite, eradicate the stench of skate, halibut and cod.

Fishy Wilkins, like almost every other teenage boy, was stuck with those two options: pub or disco? Andy and Dave, however, as newly appointed 'night boys' were suddenly presented with a very lucrative third.

16

Dave explained it to Andy: 'The tickets come out of the machine in a strip, right?'

'Yeah.'

'So if there's two on a strip, I fold it in half and give them back two halves, right?'

'Yeah.'

It was then that Dave heard the dramatic drum roll in his head. He felt like Lord Caernarvon when he chanced upon the tomb of Tutankhamen. His eyes glinted and his palms moistened as he explained his pocket-bulging discovery. 'If I quickly tear off one ticket and hide it in my pocket, I can just tear the other one and give them back two halves of the same ticket. Then I'll bring the untorn ticket back to you and you can resell it. We'll be quids in. I mean, on a busy Saturday night, we can get a thousand punters in. We wouldn't have to do it very often.'

Andy knew it was wrong – he knew it was stealing. Suddenly he saw his mother, father and Our Lady of Czestochowa frowning at him as he searched his conscience for the reserves of Catholic guilt that would normally call a halt to this sort of activity. Guilt had prevented him, in the sacristy of St Andrew Bobola's, from helping himself to a percentage of the collection money as he transferred it from the plates to those long cloth bags to take it to the bank. He remembered the sizzling temptation. He was all alone: Father Lizewski had left him to it. Fistfuls of notes and coins were almost begging to be stolen. Who would ever find out? Yet every penny made it to the Midland Bank round the corner. Perhaps he felt that God was watching him in the sacristy. Now, though, it seemed unlikely that He'd be hanging around a place where, in Screen Three, they were showing *Snow White and the Seven Perverts*.

But it was more than that. Perhaps Andy was following his own guidelines now, rather than the ones that had been so strictly laid down for him. Whatever the reason, he could see the glorious, lucrative simplicity of his friend's plan. He took to grand larceny far more readily than he had ever taken to Polish dancing. Dave's lightning speed and sleight-of-hand would provide the untorn tickets. Andy's quick, arithmetical brain would make sure the figures all tallied before they divided the plunder at the end of each shift. Doc's torturous maths lessons were now proving invaluable.

Most evenings they were free to fiddle. Maureen had gone home and Tony, the Gaumont's very own *maître d'*, was far too busy greeting his public to notice Dave's digital dexterity. One night, however, he was standing a little too close for comfort. Once he had taken up his tuxedoed position in the foyer, Tony seldom needed to move. Everyone came to him for their own fix of personalised bonhomie. As he laughed and joked with a couple of regulars, Dave gradually moved a few paces further back towards the kiosk, where his eyes alighted on another way to augment his income.

On top of the counter was a big stack of red waxed-cardboard cups with Coca-Cola emblazoned on the side. If there were two hundred at the beginning of the evening and one hundred at the end, then the money for one hundred cups of Coke should be in the till. It didn't take a criminal mastermind to work out that if you went round the cinema collecting the empty cups, then washed them up and put them back on the stack, you could keep fifty pence for every one you returned.

And, of course, there was also the chance to indulge in the oldest and simplest fiddle of all: overcharging. Two Cokes, a bag of Fruit Pastilles, a bucket of popcorn and twenty Benson & Hedges, with no prices displayed and the till no more than a drawer under the counter – who knew what that little lot added up to? The person serving always did, and invariably added a few unnoticeable pence to the total. By the time the nightly stock-take was done, there was quite a surplus to be transferred from till to trouser.

On his next shift on the kiosk, Dave would put these little scams into practice. Unlike Andy, he was no stranger to dishonesty – which occurred to him a few weeks later when he got a faceful of his Uncle Patsy's buttocks.

Patsy Fagan had the finest example of a builder's

cleavage you were ever likely to see. No matter what trousers or jeans he was wearing, his enormous stomach would give them a self-folding waistband, which worked its way south over the course of a day to reveal the tops of two flabby white buttocks peeping over his Y-fronts. Patsy had the Raquel Welch of builders' cleavages, which, when he was bent over in the tiny hallway of 76 Kilravock Street, left little room for anything else. His buttocks were out in the hall but his head was in the cupboard under the stairs. Patsy was Dave's mother's brother, so Dave was well aware of whose buttocks he was looking at.

'Hello, Uncle Pat,' he said to them.

'All right, son,' came the breathless reply, which suggested that Patsy was in the throes of something difficult, intricate and almost certainly illegal.

Dave's mother was looking very ashamed,

'Oh, God,' said Dave, with a sigh, 'what's he doing now?'

'Er . . . just fixing the meter,' replied his mother, guiltily.

'What meter?'

'What is it with you?' she replied, a little too sharply. 'Questions, questions . . .'

Dave, intrigued, repeated, 'What meter?'

'The electricity meter.'

'And since when did Uncle Pat work for the Electricity Board?'

At which point, Patsy came into the kitchen, his big

round face flushed with triumph. 'C'mere, while I show you how it works.'

Dave looked at his mother and laughed. 'This I've got to see.'

Patsy had somehow acquired a job-lot of surgical needles, so thin that they were practically invisible. With the pinpoint accuracy of the surgeon who was supposed to be using them, he had inserted one into the Kellys' electricity meter and stopped it going round. Again, like a surgeon who had just performed a life-saving operation, Patsy was very proud of his handi-work. 'You can burn as much as you like, it won't cost you a penny. Just remember to take it out a couple of weeks before the fella comes round to read the meter, so it clocks up a little bit. Then put it back when he's gone.'

Patsy's surgical needles had paralysed electricity meters all over Kilburn and Queens Park, but Eileen Kelly was still ashamed of what she was doing. Though she was fundamentally governed by Catholic guilt and honesty, she didn't possess the upright moral rectitude of her husband. She was a little more stooped. Dave, in that respect, was bent almost double. Morally, his dad was such a hard act to follow that, he didn't bother trying. He'd only have felt like a struggling young actor whose father was Sir Laurence Olivier.

'For God's sake,' his mother said to him, 'don't tell your father.'

Dave had no intention of telling anyone. He looked at Patsy and realised that he had clearly inherited his uncle's dishonesty gene. And, with pockets bulging with stolen cash, he was in no position to take the moral high ground.

17

Like all Catholics, Dave could assuage his guilt by going to confession and having his spiritual slate wiped clean, so that he could spend the next few weeks sin-soiling it again. Apparently it didn't matter how many sins you committed as long as you confessed them to a priest, who had the power to absolve them. Even better, the priest was forbidden by his vows to tell anyone.

At first, Dave thought this was great: he could commit multiple murders and jewellery heists, confess them all to a priest and get away with it. In the eyes of the Lord, anyway. Of course, he soon realised that the more serious his sins, the less likely he would be to 'fess up – particularly when both Father Quigley and Father Curran would recognise his voice. Yet he still felt a soupçon of guilt about the money he was taking without its owners' consent. Maybe it was this that propelled him to mass every Sunday.

Ding, ding.

At the sound of the bell, Father Quigley, flanked by two candle-carrying acolytes, would emerge from the sacristy. The twelve o'clock mass had begun.

For Dave, the bell was like the one he'd heard so many times on the number fifty-two bus. 'Ding, ding

– hold tight, please,' and he was off on a journey, straight into a trance. He was sufficiently aware of his surroundings to stand, kneel, sit and burble his rhythmic responses, but otherwise he was having an out-of-body experience. He wasn't there. He was anywhere but the Church of the Transfiguration, Kensal Rise, London NW10.

People have spent years studying yoga, or trekking to Himalayan heights, in order to reach a level of spiritual Nirvana which Dave could effortlessly attain within seconds of hearing that bell. He might just hear Father Quigley say, 'The Lord be with you,' but after that he was gone. As a child, he would often float straight up the Harrow Road to Wembley Stadium and be Rodney Marsh scoring that magnificent goal for QPR in the League Cup final. On other occasions, he'd float down Scrubs Lane to BBC Television Centre and be Mick Jagger doing 'Brown Sugar' on *Top of the Pops*. Occasionally he'd be Terence Stamp in a black and white sixties film, leaping out of a droptop Lotus outside his swinging chick's Chelsea pad, in a London untroubled by yellow lines or residents' parking bays.

As he grew older, his fantasies ripened to involve Wendy Baker, Maria Flynn or Janice Shadbolt. Sometimes all three. Now and again he would float back into church, just to check what was going on.

'A reading from the letters of St Paul to the Corinthians.'

Oh God, he'd wonder, who the hell were the Corinthians anyway? Were they a family, like the

Kellys or the Shadbolts? Did they really want this constant correspondence from that weirdo who fell off his horse?

Dave imagined Mr and Mrs Corinthian sitting at the breakfast table when the postman arrived.

'Anything for me?' asks Mrs C.

'No, just the usual. Phone bill, bank statement, letter from St Paul.'

'Oh, no, what does he want this time?'

Mr C scans the letter. 'He says it's better to marry than be aflame with passion.'

'Oh, right,' says a bewildered Mrs C. 'Pass the sugar.'

Dave's parents always went to the nine o'clock mass, better known as 'the nine'. Once Dave was old enough to go by himself, he'd opted instead for 'the twelve'.

This later mass wasn't quite so earnest. It was for the less-committed parishioners, too lazy or hung-over to spring up for the nine. What's more, it was conducted by Father Curran who, unlike Father Quigley (nicknamed Father Slowly), would rattle through it in around forty-three minutes, a good twenty minutes faster than Father Quigley's personal best.

Dave was sitting alone at the back of 'the twelve'. As the bell rang and the congregation got to its feet, Dave decided to visit Wembley once again in Rodney Marsh's no. 10 shirt. As he prepared for astral projection, he suddenly realised that he had a bike outside and could visit Wembley for real. There was a huge market every Sunday in the stadium car park, officially opened a few years earlier by Bobby Moore. Dave had never been. Surely next week, his pockets loaded with stolen cash, he could pedal up there. Twenty minutes there, half an hour wandering round, twenty minutes back. As long as he'd grabbed a news-sheet on the way to provide documentary evidence of his attendance at mass, not a smidgen of suspicion would be aroused.

Wembley Market was a welcome oasis in a country where all sorts of arcane Sunday-trading laws were still in force. You couldn't buy a book, for example, but you could buy a magazine. So, on a Sunday morning, although it was illegal to buy the Bible, it was perfectly okay to stock up on porn mags. At Wembley Market you could buy anything you wanted, and Dave found plenty of stalls to part him from his cash, principally those selling records and clothes. As he wobbled home, feeling the wicked warmth of iniquity at buying all these things not only on the Sabbath but with stolen money too, he suddenly realised that they would have to be stashed away somewhere until the following Saturday. The twelve-inch singles could slot invisibly into his already enormous collection, but where the hell was he going to hide that white woolly Starsky cardigan?

On Sunday afternoons, most of Britain was dead. Nothing was open. Men disappeared into sheds or out on to allotments. Apparently some families went for a Sunday drive to Windsor Safari Park or Dunstable Downs, but for the carless Kellys this was never an option. Dave had often wondered whether the stultifying boredom of Sundays was a deliberate ploy by

God to make him look forward to Mondays when even double Physics with Father Casey would come as a welcome relief.

Now Sunday had been transformed into his favourite day of the week, filling him with anticipation and joy: a trip to 'mass' in the morning, followed by the challenge of secreting his purchases in places where they would never be found. The Starsky cardigan, for example, found itself double-wrapped in bin-liners to spend six days in the coal bunker.

At four o'clock, in Westbourne Grove, the Gaumont opened for business, sometimes earlier if Ted Hogarth was giving an organ recital. The Sunday shift, which paid double time, was the most sought-after, and since the programmes changed on a Sunday, the film buffs would already be queuing outside. One film buff, however, was denied the opportunity to see each new film on its first day of release. For the Zymanczyks, Sunday was a day of rest and Andy was strictly forbidden to work at the cinema. Even at sixteen he had to be grateful that he was allowed to work there at all. Since the election of a Polish pope, his father had felt that the Poles had now supplanted the Italians as the most Catholic nation on earth and this meant that the Sabbath was observed more strictly than ever.

18

'Quick! Help! He's trying to kill himself.'

That would have been the understandable reaction of a passer-by who saw an old man sitting in his driveway for several minutes in a stationary Austin Cambridge with the engine running. Anyone who knew Jerzy Zymanczyk, however, would have realised that this was just part of his normal Sunday-afternoon ritual. 'Just warming the engine,' he would explain. There was no point in suggesting that this was a futile exercise and that the best way to warm a car's engine was to drive it. Jerzy knew best. He always did. He knew, for example, that the pope was infallible; in fact, since the new pontiff was Polish, he was doubly infallible. After the requisite four minutes (five in winter), the Austin's engine was deemed sufficiently warm, Jerzy would don his black felt Homburg and hold open the passenger door for his wife. His son would be told to take his seat in the back and their Sunday-afternoon journey would begin. Slowly. Painfully slowly. The term 'Sunday driver' could have been coined for Jerzy, who proceeded to enrage every driver in west London with his inconsiderate dawdling. In the back, Andy would be crimson with embarrassment, knowing that

93

he would probably reach thirty before the car did. He wanted to hang a placard outside the window saying, 'I know, I know. Look, he's nothing to do with me,' to the stream of fulminating motorists who had the misfortune to get stuck behind him. Jerzy had perfected a signal known as the 'eventual left', whereby he put on his indicator at least three turnings before the one he intended to take. Traffic bulletins should have been broadcast every Sunday at around 2 p.m. – 'Long tailbacks westbound on the A402 Goldhawk Road. That old Polish dentist from Askew Crescent is on his way to visit relatives in Ealing. Please allow at least an extra half-hour for your journey.'

After what seemed like hours, the Austin Cambridge would pull up three miles away at the gates of Gunnersbury cemetery and Andy would have to join his parents on a pilgrimage he had made more times than he could count, to the Katyn Memorial, a brooding black obelisk, twenty feet high, erected in memory of fourteen thousand Polish prisoners killed by the Soviets during the Second World War. From there, they would walk fifty yards to the grave of General Komorowski, who had commanded the Polish Home Army during the Warsaw uprising of 1944. They would not be alone. On any given Sunday, the Zymanczyks would be joined by other Polish faces, set in granite-like solemnity, paying silent respects to their fallen compatriots and praying that their homeland would be freed one day from the yoke of oppression.

Jerzy's cheeks would often become wet with the grief

and emotion that he tried but failed to keep buried inside. He had known people who had died at Katyn and many others who, betrayed by the Russians, had been slaughtered by the Nazis in Warsaw.

'This is what it means to be Polish,' he would explain to his son. 'This is why it is important. These people died simply because of their nationality. We must never forget that. By taking pride in who we are and in where we come from, we keep their memory alive. We are only in exile here. We are forever indebted to the British for taking us in, but we are Polish. You are Polish. Never, ever forget that.'

Andy never knew how to respond to this. He knew that what Jerzy was saying was true. He felt great sympathy for what his father had experienced, but sympathy is very different from empathy. He felt no empathy at all. How could he? He hadn't been there. Although these atrocities were still relatively recent, the world had changed immeasurably since they had taken place. It had all happened in an alien country in a totally different era. He had always been moved by his father's tragically impassioned patriotism but, try as he might, he just couldn't feel the pain.

For Andy, this poignant duty was always followed by the relief of a trip to see his auntie Ania and uncle Krzys. Their house was no more than a mile from the Katyn Memorial and this was when Andy became most infuriated by the snail-like pace of his father's driving. He was always desperate to get there and erase the pain-by-proxy of the vigil at the cemetery. There, he could feel something close to normality, playing with his older cousins Adam and Jan. Jan had recently relinquished a tiny piece of Polishness – one letter to be precise. He had changed his name from Jan to Ian, which Andy found intoxicatingly rebellious. 'Ian! Ian!' he shouted to his cousin, as they played football in the garden.

Hearing this from the kitchen, Jerzy was nonplussed. 'Ian?' he enquired. 'Who is Ian?'

'Oh, that's Jan,' laughed Ania. 'He's changed his name. Teenagers, eh? I'm sure he'll grow out of it.'

Jerzy's sister-in-law was a lot more easy-going than he was. Most people were. He would have been appalled if his only son had renounced the Polishness of his name. He still had no idea that Andrzej was known to one and all as Andy.

Andy treasured his visits to Ealing. The house was always full of food, drink, people and laughter. Uncle Krzys was a warm, generous host, his house a natural extension of the delicatessen-cum-Polish-community-centre he owned on South Ealing Road. His round, smiling face was adorned by a magnificent Lech Walesa-style moustache, perfectly groomed and sleek with pomade. Like many Poles, Uncle Krzys seemed to have an elastic family. Into his house, he was forever welcoming a stream of 'brothers and sisters', who were, in fact, distant cousins and 'cousins' to whom he was no relation at all. For Andy, it was a joyous and comforting contrast to the silent piety of his own home.

Ania, although she admired and respected Jerzy,

couldn't help feeling sorry for her elder sister and her nephew, who, it was plain to see, had far too little fun in their lives. She encouraged her two boys to treat Andy like a brother, which was why he adored Adam and 'Ian'. With them, he could play football, listen to records and even watch TV in the back room. His father, relaxed into submission by Krzys and Ania's hospitality, never raised an objection. But most of all Andy loved his cousin Alison. She was six months younger than him and, in his view, her white-blonde hair, flawless complexion and sapphire-blue eyes made her the most beautiful girl in the world.

As a child, he was made to entertain the elastic family by dancing with her, which he loved and loathed in equal measure. He hated having to dance in the sitting room for the benefit of his relatives but adored the close physical contact with Alison, which gave him a peculiar, but pleasurable sensation, which took him years to identify.

As those years went by, the Sunday-afternoon visits to Ealing started to change. First Adam, then Ian disappeared to university, leaving Andy and Alison as the only two 'children' left. As Andy grew older, even he was allowed out to a few discos and parties. As he met more and more members of the opposite sex, he'd expected Alison to lose her crown as Most Beautiful Girl in the World, yet there she remained, growing ever more gorgeous and ever more unassailable. None of the girls with whom he had occasionally slow-danced at youth-club discos could compare. The ones who reeked of cigarettes and Charlie, who had slapped on their makeup with a trowel and would remove it with a blow-lamp, had given him a gentle shove towards mental turmoil. The feelings he had for Alison were wrong: she was his first cousin, for God's sake. All right, so it wasn't technically illegal for cousins to marry – in certain parts of the West Country it was almost compulsory – but he couldn't consider it. Their children would be born with three heads.

Finally, just after his O levels, Andy turned up with his parents in Ealing after a particularly sombre trip to the cemetery. He was in dire need of the fun he always had with Alison so he asked his aunt where she was.

'Oh, she's out with her boyfriend. I think they've gone to the pictures.'

Auntie Ania could never have guessed how her light remark had just sliced her nephew's soul in two, how sad, immature and inadequate it had made him feel, and how it had removed his main reason for wanting to visit his relatives. He'd have to find something to fill that void and weld his soul together again.

Who'd have thought that it would come, indirectly anyway, from the Harlequin Hippies?

19

Andy didn't know who they were but they had arrived in the foyer for the third time that week: three blokes and two girls, almost indistinguishable from behind, all of whom worked at Harlequin Records on Notting Hill Gate. They were enslaved to prog rock and couldn't believe their luck when Tony, in a rare lapse of taste, had decided to show *Genesis: A Band In Concert* for a week in Screen Two. It was a monumentally dreary documentary about the band playing a concert at the oh-so-glamorous Bingley Hall in Staffordshire. Even Andy couldn't be bothered to sit through the twenty-minute Phil Collins drum solos, but the hippies from Harlequin clearly could. As they queued once again to see their idols, Andy's Catholic compassion would not allow him to take their money. 'It's okay,' he said. 'You've paid twice already. Come in for free. Come in every night of the week, if you want to.'

And naturally, the hippies really 'dug' this cat's attitude.

'Man, that's really cool. Thanks,' said one.

'And, hey, look, right,' suggested another, 'if you want any, like, records for free, just come into Harlequin, you know, up on the Gate.'

'We all sort of work there and shit,' continued a third, 'so come in and say hi. We'll give you any, like, records you want.'

'As long as it isn't Genesis,' said Andy, with a grin, 'I might take you up on that.'

And so a lucrative and complex barter system was established, through which free entry to the cinema was exchanged for records, clothes, shoes, hamburgers, bargain buckets of Kentucky Fried Chicken and almost anything else for sale in Kilburn, Kensington or Notting Hill. Dave and Andy found themselves in the surreal position of having bundles of cash but practically nothing to spend it on.

Dave was just considering stuffing his ever-growing collection of banknotes under the floorboards when he remembered his old Post Office book. His auntie Delia had given it to him on his seventh birthday with a crisp green pound note inside to get him into the habit of saving. It was a hobby he had never taken up. Even now, with more spare cash than he knew what to do with, Dave had no wish to become one of life's savers. He didn't want to be one of those shabbily shod skinflints who took the same pride in the size of their bank balances as a market gardener would in the size of his marrows. He didn't want to feel the terror of ever seeing that balance diminish. He despised the way they put the money aside for that mythical 'rainy day' – though it never seemed to rain hard enough to make them fill out a withdrawal slip. Weren't they missing the point? No matter how much money you managed to amass, it will only ever have one ultimate purpose: sooner or later, it had to be spent. As his big fat, generous-to-a-fault, Uncle Patsy was fond of saying, 'There are no pockets in a shroud.'

Guy Patterson struck Dave as a saver, carefully planning every move and constantly searching for a better return on any investment he made, whether it concerned his career or his finances. He hadn't seen Guy for months – the area manager's visits only ever took place in the afternoons. Under cover of daylight, his plans for bingo seemed so much more feasible: the cinema was practically empty, the films often shown to a few lonely and impecunious pensioners, who weren't even watching them. They only scurried in on cold afternoons to save on their heating bills.

Guy also liked to get the assistant manageress on her own: 'You know, Maureen,' he would say, with an oleaginous smile, 'we think a lot of you at Head Office.' This compliment was supposed to make Maureen feel as though she was one step from canonisation. 'This place would collapse without you.'

'We all work as a team,' she would loyally insist.

'Yes, but we all know who the team leader is. You know, when this place is converted to bingo, you'd make a marvellous manager. I mean, Tony's not going to do it, is he?'

'I have no idea,' she would state coldly, 'but while it's still a cinema, he is still the manager.'

Maureen had never warmed to Patterson. She had

that Catholic lack of ambition in herself and concomitant mistrust of it in others. She had no wish to take over. She adored Tony and was quite happy to run things for him. She preferred the ultimate responsibility to be his rather than hers.

'I know it all looks a bit pathetic this afternoon, Mr Patterson,' she would say, 'but why don't you come back tonight? It's so different at night.'

And it was.

From being an innocuous daytime place, which showed Disney films to children, it was transformed around dusk into a nocturnal palace of pleasure. Tony Harris took the reins and suddenly Dr Jekyll had come out to play.

The floodlights illuminated the art-deco splendour of the exterior, and if you approached from Notting Hill Gate, you would catch the Gaumont in all its magnificence. The long queue of people snaking round the block only added to its air of desirability. On seeing that queue, you would find yourself gripped by some primeval urge to join it, and once you had, you would discover the reason for that peculiarly British love of queuing – that sense of fair play and real equality, which ensures that, no matter who you are and how great your importance in any other aspect of your life, you wait your turn. Also, you could enjoy looking over your shoulder from time to time and seeing how much the queue had lengthened behind you. That warm glow of achievement would seep through you as you saw more and more people who, in this context at least, were worse off than you. You would feel that within the equality of the queue there was actually great inequality. Each person was a tiny bit more important than the person behind, your own pre-eminence increasing as you inched your way forward until the sublime moment when you reached the front of the queue and no one in the world was more important than you. For a couple of seconds, you were master of the universe.

What's more, in a cinema queue you probably wouldn't be alone. You'd be with someone you loved or, at least, fancied. You might be with someone you fancied but hardly knew and therefore had very little to say to. That was why the cinema was such an ideal first date, infinitely preferable to 'going for a drink'. Sitting in a dreary pub, exposed by the cold light of sobriety. Those long awkward silences were even longer when one half of the date was standing at the bar, failing to catch the barmaid's attention, while the other sat alone at the table, thumbs a-twiddling – and it was still only ten past eight. At the cinema, silences lasting for an hour and a half were not awkward when both halves of the date were engrossed in the film. In the pub afterwards, you had something to talk about. This led effortlessly to other conversational topics, empty glasses and 'Same again?' By the time the landlord politely asked you to 'Drain your glasses and shift your arses,' you had established a rapport. It's 'Your place or mine?' or 'Are you coming in for a coffee?' And even if it wasn't, it wasn't too embarrassing or painful a way to find out.

Sometimes, as he tore the tickets of a canoodling couple, Dave would feel a cold pang of envy. He wondered whether, having worked in one, he could ever enjoy taking a girl to the cinema. When he had worked at the butcher's, would he have taken a date to the local abattoir? His twinge of self-pity seldom lasted for more than a few seconds, its ample compensation being the growing collection of untorn tickets in the pocket of his Crimplene jacket.

And, anyway, his employment at the cinema had led to the discovery of late-night venues he hadn't realised existed. A whole after-hours world, a subterranean subculture in which Tony Harris was a prime mover. After the night's programmes had begun, Tony would disappear into his office, change out of his tuxedo and hang it carefully on the hook behind the door. Emerging in more casual apparel, he would give Andy and Dave the trademark wink. 'Just off for a mooch about,' he'd say, with a grin. 'Any problems, call me. You've got the list.' And with that, he'd vanish into the Notting Hill night.

20

'The list' was a scrawled sheet of phone numbers of all the places that might be graced with Tony's presence. Many were not apparent to the general public – pubs, restaurants, drinking clubs, gambling dens, shebeens and blues joints, where both blues and joints were freely available. And now, as trusted 'night boys', Dave and Andy were often invited to join him.

Tony Harris was well known in Notting Hill. Born and bred in Treadgold Street, this was his 'manor'. The sharp suits and Mark II Jag would give the impression that he was a 'face', a gangster, a man to be feared, but nothing was further from the truth. He had no interest in criminal activity, not because of any moral objection but because he couldn't be bothered. He wasn't driven by money or status, he drank and gambled for fun. His only motivation was having a good time and, if you knew where to look, there was no better place than The Grove. This was the local term for the place otherwise known as Over There. Its unofficial borders were Westbourne Grove, Ladbroke Grove, Golborne Road and Chepstow Road. The grimy, insalubrious streets to the north and west of the cinema were a well-disguised playground.

Caribbean immigrants had begun to settle there in the early fifties and had colonised the neighbourhood ever since. Ironically, it was Peter Rachman, the notorious slum landlord, who had so cruelly exploited them whom they could now thank for its wild, hedonistic flavour. The new immigrants had been unwelcome in most of post-war Britain but not in this part of London. Rachman's racism had been outweighed by his greed, and he didn't care whose money he took. He knew that the newly arrived West Indians were finding it almost impossible to secure accommodation. Vacant rooms would suddenly be 'gone' once the landlord saw the pigmentation of the smartly dressed applicant on his doorstep.

At that time the Grove was one massive slum in which Rachman owned dozens of huge, dilapidated houses, most of which weren't fit for human habitation. Each had been divided, and dangerously sub-divided several times more, for multiple occupancy and maximum profit. He saw a gap in the market and charged these desperate people extortionate rents for Third World accommodation. One house, which had nine rooms, was home to twelve adults and twenty-one children. Mothers from four or five different families had to cook on two gas rings on the landing. With up to twenty people sharing a single lavatory with no lock, it was little wonder that they usually resorted to buckets.

Rachman had long gone but the vibe he had unwittingly created lived on, typified by places like the

Mangrove on All Saints Road, Fiesta One on Ledbury Road or the Globe in Talbot Road. After the cinema had emptied, the lights had been turned out and the huge, leather-sheathed chains and padlocks had been secured around the fire exits, Dave and Andy, at their manager's behest, would enter these places wide-eyed and excited. On the door of Fiesta One was a huge, fearsome-looking Barbadian known as Biscuit, but it was clear, as he welcomed them in with a glinting eighteen-carat smile, that any friend of Tony Harris was a friend of his.

Tony remembered the Caribbean influx very well. Yes, there had been problems, but he'd welcomed the arrival of colour, vibrancy and life in one of the dingiest parts of London at the dreariest time in its history. And sometimes, after a flagon of Dragon, he'd deliver a discourse on the social and demographic history of W10 and W11.

'I was probably about your age – maybe a bit younger – when they first came over. They used to say that Notting Hill was about the only place they felt safe. Anywhere else it was a fucking nightmare, unless you were behind locked doors. Thing is, because there were so many of them round here, they could open little clubs, play their music and that, a bit like the Irish over in Kilburn a few years before. It was great in the summer – they'd all be sitting on those crumbly old steps that led up to their front doors, shooting the breeze with the people next door. They still do. Isn't that how it should be?

'I'm not saying that these people were angels. I mean, to be honest, a lot of them were right fucking herberts on the run from the Old Bill or other gangs back home, especially the flash ones from Trinidad. But they were fun. And, at the time, what this place badly needed was fun. It was such a fucking dump, nothing to do, nowhere to go. They breathed a bit of life into it. And as long as you weren't looking for trouble, you generally wouldn't find any. You just had to go with the flow. But some of the people round here didn't like it one little bit – and the crap they used to come out with! I remember there was a few of us in the Bramley one night and Billy Elsom, ugly little fucker, started on about 'the coloureds', as he called them.

'"They're taking our homes," he says, and we all start pissing ourselves.

'"Well, they ain't taken your house, have they, Billy? More's the pity. And since when have you wanted to live in a slum that's well known to every rat and cockroach in the area?"

'But he wouldn't let it go. "They're taking our jobs," he says.

'"Oh, leave it out, Billy," says someone. "I didn't notice you queuing up to clean the bogs or work on the buses."

'Then, in desperation, Billy has one more go. "Well, they're taking our women." What a load of bollocks! Nobody can "take" your woman unless she wants to be taken. And if she does, whose fault is that? It was always the ugly ones who said this. Billy Elsom couldn't have pulled if he'd wandered naked into Wormwood Scrubs with two hundred Rothmans.'

It wasn't always the Caribbean clubs that had the pleasure of Tony's company. One or two of the area's more traditional pubs often had his drink waiting before he reached the bar. At the Eagle on Ladbroke Grove closing time was an alien concept. The Princess Alexandra in Portobello Road was also famous for its lock-ins. However, Tony usually headed a little further west, just beyond Latimer Road tube station, to the Bramley Arms. They didn't bother with lock-ins: they just kept on serving until the guv'nor, Big Eddie Dempsey, decided it was time to close. Since most of the illegal imbibers had just come off their shift at Ladbroke Grove police station, prosecution was unlikely.

Many nights ended with Dave and Andy politely excusing themselves. As long as it was after midnight, Tony never objected – 'No civilised man,' he always maintained, 'goes to bed on the same day he got up.' They would leave him, laughing, drinking and holding court in whichever underground blues club he had summoned them to earlier.

As they staggered up on to the street, giddy from the effects of passive ganja-smoking, one sobering and incongruous thought would float towards them. *Shit, we've got to be up for school in the morning.*

21

'Here's a good one, listen to this. "Shul Gabbai, 28. I take out the Torah Saturday morning. Would like to take you out Saturday night."'

Rachel Harvey and Suzy Minkoff were sitting in Rachel's house on the lush velvet sofa. A copy of the *Jewish Chronicle* was spread across the gilt-edged coffee table and Suzy was reading from it. Both had emerged into the world and straight into ready-made social lives seventeen years earlier. There were parties, youth clubs, weddings, bar mitzvahs, discos, summer camps and trips to Israel with the Federation of Zionist Youth. They'd both had lovely, happy, secure lives, and Rachel was just about sick to death of it.

'How about this one?' said Suzy. '"Jewish man seeks partner to attend shul, light shabbos candles, build Sukkah together, attend brisses and bar mitzvahs. Religion not important."'

'Well, that's just it,' said Rachel, with an exasperated smile. 'Religion *is* important. It's always so bloody important. That's why they're advertising in the *JC* in the first place. Don't you get fed up with it?'

'I know what you mean, but we're not like the

Hasidim. We don't have to wear wigs and start reproducing the moment we leave school. And can you imagine reproducing with a bloke with a long beard and ringlets? Ugh.'

'Yeah, but at least they're honest about it,' said Rachel. 'The pressure on us may not be as obvious but it's every bit as strong. I mean, how many people do you know, *really* know, who aren't Jewish?'

'Hardly any,' Suzy had to concede, but it didn't bother her. She was quite happy to have been born in the London Borough of Barnet, which was said to have the biggest Jewish community in Europe She revelled in its warmth, its affluence and its clearly defined parameters. Plus, of course, the limitless line of suitable young men. Rachel's feelings were slightly different. She didn't really regard herself as a Jew, more sort of 'Jew-ish'. She craved the freedom, just for once, to go out with someone whose parents were not acquainted with hers. She could never understand why Bjorn Borg would be completely unsuitable yet either Mike or Bernie Winters would be fine. She didn't want to go out with a boy simply because he wasn't Jewish: she just wanted it not to be an issue.

Suzy had thought this herself, but had decided that it was a lot easier to stick with your own. 'It's just less hassle, isn't it?' she concluded.

'What? You mean hassle from your parents?' said Rachel.

'Well, not just that. Becky Adams went out with a *yok* – total nightmare. He just didn't understand.

111

You know, Friday-night *shabbat*, not eating this, not eating that.'

'Well, perhaps he was right. It *is* all a bit daft. What's that old poem – Does any man of common sense think ham and eggs give God offence?'

'It's not a matter of whether it's right or wrong. It's just that he was brought up one way and she was brought up another. It was never going to work. It's the oldest story in the world. It's *Romeo and Juliet.*'

'Or *West Side Story.*'

'Exactly. I mean, she found it hard to take him to parties and that. Nobody was horrible to him but they'd all known each other for ever so he always felt left out.'

'That's what I mean. It's so cliquey.'

'Well, the way I look at it, either you go the whole hog and turn your back on all of it, say goodbye to everything you've ever been and start again – and I think that's a very heavy price to pay – or you look at all the benefits, like Melanie's party on Sunday night. You *are* coming, aren't you?

'Yeah, maybe later. I've got to work.'

'Work?'

'Oh, didn't I tell you? Wait there.'

Rachel left the room and returned two minutes later. 'And this,' she announced, doing a little twirl, 'is what I'll be wearing.'

Suzy burst out laughing. 'Bloody hell! Not exactly Yves Saint Laurent, is it?'

Rachel, also laughing, looked down at the shapeless red nylon pinafore dress and had to agree.

22

'Dave, this is Rachel,' said Maureen, with a smile. 'She'll be helping you behind the kiosk. Rachel, Dave here will show you what to do.'

Dave looked at his new colleague and was struck by one thought: Christ, if you can look sexy in a red nylon pinafore dress, you can look sexy in anything. Never before had he entertained an impure thought involving a Gaumont standard-issue red nylon pinafore dress, but such was the allure of the figure inside it that he was fast discovering its erotic potential. His thoughts were now so impure that he couldn't even bear to look at the image in front of him. Instead his eyes sought refuge by staring down at the marble floor of the foyer. In those eyes, Rachel Harvey had a head start simply because she was Jewish. Dave had always had a thing for Jewish girls. They were like girls, only more so. Always feminine, with a judicious use of perfume, makeup and jewellery to provide the icing on an already gorgeous cake. He'd often looked longingly at them on Saturday mornings when he'd seen them fresh from Willesden synagogue, beautifully dressed and walking home with their families. He'd ignored the blokes in their stupid hats and homed in solely on the women: stylish, glamorous, slightly exotic. They had a panache he seldom saw in the Catholic congregations that stumbled out of mass the following day. Most of his fellow parishioners would be cheaply attired and either wreathed in sanctimony or just relieved to have fulfilled their dreary weekly obligation and desperate to get into the pub.

If heterosexual attraction is a celebration of differences, Rachel's position right at the other end of the scale was what made her so alluring. She wasn't classically beautiful – the truly sexy never are – and Dave's infatuation with her intensified if she sometimes turned round and looked a bit ugly: that gave him the feeling that her beauty was something that only he, as a connoisseur of such things, could see and appreciate.

Lifting his blue eyes from the floor, he locked them on to her chocolate brown ones and decided that the kiosk was his domain: he was in charge. He would use his red Crimplene jacket to his own advantage, and draw from it a confidence he didn't usually possess. He hoped that Rachel wouldn't realise this, and would assume that he was like this all the time. He ran through the prices with her, finishing with a vital piece of advice: 'If in doubt,' he explained, 'just make it up, but always make the price higher rather than lower. The punters don't know and they don't care. A bloke trying to impress his bird is not going to quibble over the price of a packet of peanuts.' And with that, he winked in the conspiratorial way he'd seen Tony wink so many times before for so many different reasons.

That was what Rachel tried to convey to Suzy: this boy was different – confident, laid-back and sassy.

It was a while before Dave realised that this had been his lucky day. She was as attracted to him because he wasn't Jewish as he was to her because she was.

It didn't take her long to learn the ropes. She was very bright and also, when a bag of Rowntrees Fruit Pastilles is 'about' 45p and a hot dog 'about' 70p, there wasn't much for her to get wrong.

Dave knew immediately that he could trust her, so he began to collect the Coke cups from around the foyer and, wash them under the tap,

'What are you doing?' she asked.

'Oh, just a bit of washing-up,' he grinned. 'I do love washing-up.'

As he replaced them on the pile on top of the counter, Rachel suddenly worked out why he was doing it. When they finished the quick stock-take, he gave her exactly 50 per cent of the usual surplus, which she took without hesitation. It wasn't that she was dishonest, it wasn't as though she even wanted the money, she just thought that Dave was the acme of cool and her participation in the scam would bring them together like quick-drying cement.

'Whereabouts do you live?' he enquired.

'Willesden.'

Dave was ecstatic. All right, so he had his bike tonight but next week he'd come on the bus and they could go home together. His ecstasy, however, was short-lived.

'It's only about ten minutes in the car.'

Car? What car?

Rachel had a little red Mini parked outside.

He was crestfallen and emasculated. She'd passed her test. He hadn't. She wouldn't be interested in him. Shit, shit, shit. Girls who didn't have cars were often attracted to boys who did. It seldom worked the other way round.

As he unlocked his bike from the railings outside, he saw her driving off up Chepstow Road. It began to rain as he pedalled in the same direction at a mere fraction of her pace and he watched helplessly as the tail-lights of the little red Mini disappeared towards the Harrow Road. 'Oh, God,' he asked rhetorically, 'how the fuck am I ever going to catch up with her?'

23

Dave had always thought he fancied Olivia Newton-John. And Kate Bush. And Debbie Harry. Yet, within seconds of seeing Rachel, he realised that he didn't. He felt no attraction to the saucy sirens he'd seen in all the soft-porn delights in Screen Three any more than he did for the genital apertures displayed every week in *Playboy*, *Penthouse* and *Mayfair*. It wasn't that he disapproved – far from it: if people found the pull of Mr Patel's top shelf irresistible, good luck to them, but those girls were not for him. They weren't girls anyway – just pieces of celluloid, sheets of paper or cardboard album covers. He couldn't fancy them because he'd never met them. He had no first-hand experience of the light behind their eyes, the scent of their skin and, most importantly, whether or not they laughed at his jokes.

'Chemistry' was a word he'd always detested, because it was redolent of Father Macken, Bunsen burners and hydrogen sulphide but, in this context, chemistry was exactly what it was. A violent rush of dopamine flooded straight into his brain whenever he clapped eyes on Rachel. Then came the shot of norepinephrine, which gave him an energy boost, heightened his attention and improved his mood. If Father Macken had explored this aspect of chemistry, perhaps Dave would have taken it for O level. If he had explained that a genuine chemical reaction caused the wit, vivacity and sex appeal of one person to engender the same qualities in another, every boy would have paid attention. And when, years later, Rachel made him feel, one Sunday evening, like a cross between Sean Connery, James Dean and Oscar Wilde, he might have nodded to himself and thought, Ah, yes, we did this in Chemistry.

Dave knew that Rachel was the sexiest human being he'd ever seen, but at seventeen, he wasn't quite sure why. He hadn't had the time or experience to create the mental filing cabinet into which his emotions could be neatly categorised. The skill of ascertaining why one person is so attractive while another, though better-looking, isn't takes time to acquire – helped and hindered by haywire hormones.

Rachel had managed to work out that part of Dave's attraction lay in his desire to talk about her and not him. She had been out with other boys who had bored her to sobs with their world-conquering plans to become doctors, lawyers or clothing entrepreneurs. She knew that their parents often put them under a lot of material pressure, but that didn't make their ambitions any less dreary. She therefore found Dave's genuine interest in her life, her background, her views and opinions, an unexpected joy.

'How come you decided to work here?' he asked.

'I just fancied it,' she replied. 'My grandmother used to live round here.'

'Really?'

'Oh, yeah. This is where my mum was brought up. There used to be a big Jewish community in Notting Hill. There's still that synagogue on Kensington Park Road and Barnett's toyshop a bit further up, but that's about all that's left. I remember my grandma taking me and my sister to that toyshop to choose our birthday presents. I'd be almost sick with excitement.'

Catching a flash of those gorgeous brown eyes, Dave knew exactly how she'd felt.

'Just the anticipation of finally getting my hands on something I'd been lusting after for ages,' she explained.

Yep, he knew exactly how she'd felt.

'My grandma was lovely,' she went on. 'She used to bring us here as well.'

'What?' said Dave, without thinking. 'Saturday-morning pictures?'

'Hardly,' said Rachel, with a grin. She admired his lack of forethought and easy-going attitude – the way he felt that the things he had so far acquired had come to him through good fortune and not because it was his divine right to have them. He was clearly going to enjoy his life because wherever he ended up would be better than where he had started out.

Dave, for his part, loved everything about her. Her turn of phrase amused him, especially two phrases that never seemed quite finished.

'Going back to mine,' she would say.

Going back to your what?

The other was, 'Are you coming with?'

With what? With whom?

Rachel, in turn, was quietly amused by the fact that Dave always said 'indoors' when he meant 'at home' – 'I've left it indoors' was a throwback to when people never went far from their front doors, which, in Dave's case, still wasn't a million miles from the truth. She knew that it was his second-generation Irishness that made him say *anny*way rather than *enny*way.

He'd never thought to analyse why he found her so gorgeous: he was just happy to be pulled along by those haywire hormones. He loved her company, respected her quick intelligence and, of course, fancied her more than he had known it was possible to fancy anyone. This, when he finally did stop to think about it, was like getting three lemons in a line on a fruit machine. And how often does that happen?

Despite their disparate backgrounds, they found enough common ground to make the hours they spent together feel like minutes. Through their conversational explorations, they discovered that their different backgrounds were, in fact, remarkably similar. They began to compare what they saw as the idiocies of the faiths they were supposed to follow.

'Do you eat bacon?' Dave asked her, one Sunday evening

'No.'

'Why not?'

'I don't know. I just never have. I suppose to me it would be a bit like eating dog. Do you eat meat on a Friday?'

'Not supposed to.'

'Why not?'

'God knows.'

'I don't think He does.'

'Me neither.'

She laughed. 'It's just rubbish, isn't it? On Yom Kippur, we're not supposed to do anything. Between sunrise and sunset no eating, no drinking, we're not even allowed to clean our teeth. I always do, though, but I have to do it in secret. I mean, what sort of religion makes brushing your teeth wrong?'

'Do most people stick to it?'

'Oh, yeah, it's disgusting. You go to *shul* and have to be kissed by a load of herring-breathed relatives. Orthodox Jews take it very seriously. They don't do anything at all on the Sabbath. They won't even switch on a light.'

Dave imagined God looking down on them every Saturday, shaking His head in despair. Why were they doing this? For whose benefit?

As he went to tell her about his Uncle Michael, he hesitated. She might think he was making it up, just trying to outdo her in the 'my religion is sillier than yours' stakes. However, it was true so he went ahead. 'My Uncle Michael, my dad's brother, is a Cistercian monk in Ireland. It's a completely silent order. He's not allowed to say a word.'

Rachel was fascinated. 'What's he like?'

'I've never met him. He's been in the monastery for about thirty years. My dad hasn't seen him in all that time. He says he was always very quiet.'

'Just as well, really.'

'I can't help thinking, though,' said Dave, 'that it's a terrible waste of a life.' He imagined his mysterious Uncle Mick arriving at the Pearly Gates and getting a shock. He imagined God staring at him in disbelief and saying, 'Now, run that past me again. I gave you two arms, two legs, a heart and, most importantly, a voice. And you did what? You shut yourself away in a remote monastery for your entire adult life and never said a word? You deliberately wasted the things I gave you? Think of the good you could have done. Think of how your voice could have brought comfort to those who needed it. Instead, you devoted your life to prayer, the main purpose of which was to get yourself into heaven. Well, I'm sorry, mate . . .'

They realised that their respective faiths were both weighed down with bewildering layers of guilt and hang-ups. Dave preferred the Jewish approach to hang-ups, which often involved frequent trips to an analyst. The Catholic approach involved frequent trips to the pub.

They realised that they were in the same boat, and every Sunday they sailed off in it. Rachel, keen to keep one particularly enjoyable voyage going, offered Dave a lift home. He desperately wanted to accept, just to spend more time with her, yet he declined. The thought of her as the driver and him as the passenger only widened the gulf between them that he still hadn't managed to bridge.

'It's all right, thanks,' he replied, rather coolly. 'I've got my bike.'

As Rachel drove back to Willesden alone, she didn't know what else she could do. She found herself muttering, 'We get on so well. I really fancy him. More and more, in fact. He's so nice, so funny. If only he'd ask me out, we'd have such a good time. Why the hell isn't he interested?'

24

'John, hi, good to see you, come in.'

Pete Roberts was all smiles as he ushered the fly in his ointment into the faceless civic-centre meeting room.

McLafferty shook his hand with a tight smile. Pete looked exactly as he had sounded on the phone. He was perhaps a little taller, but the narrow, rounded shoulders and almost concave chest fitted the image McLafferty had conceived. He was no more than thirty-five, sandy hair just a little too long at the back, compensating for the fact that it was rapidly becoming a little too short at the front. Shirt and tie beneath a V-necked jumper, slightly flared trousers and, yes, desert boots. McLafferty, in his long black cassock and highly polished black brogues, could hardly have presented a greater contrast.

Pete gestured towards an unprepossessing creature with glasses, waist-length hair and a pinafore dress that failed to disguise a pair of remarkably sturdy calves. 'This is Jools, the deputy chair.'

Jools? Deputy chair? McLafferty had no idea what Pete was talking about but shook the young lassie's pale, freckled hand anyway. Jools would not have looked out of a place in a church folk group, and as she sat down, McLafferty half expected her to produce a guitar and start singing 'Kum by Yah'.

Pete, the chair, sat on the chair's chair and chaired the meeting. In an attempt to break the ice, he managed to freeze it even further. 'John, look, I'm so glad you've become a convert to the cause.'

McLafferty's complexion changed dramatically, as though someone had shot purple dye into his veins. He fixed Pete with the sort of glare usually reserved for recalcitrant first-formers and curdled his voice into a snarl. 'Mr Roberts, I remain as opposed to your plans as I did on the day they were first presented to me.'

This was not in Pete's script. 'Well, anyway,' he smiled, 'you're here, aren't you?'

'I had very little choice. You are determined to force comprehensive education upon us whether we like it or not.'

'We're not forcing anything on you. You had the option to turn St Bede's into an independent, fee-paying school but you've already ruled that out.'

'Of course we have,' said McLafferty, with a weary sigh. 'Our pupils, as you well know, do not come from wealthy families. Their parents are almost all working-class and predominantly Irish. They can't afford to pay for their children's education. They believe, as I do, that a good free education is every child's birthright. Schools like ours were the only chance these children had of receiving one, the only chance they'd ever get to compete on level terms with those from more privileged homes. And now you're going to take that away.'

'We're not taking anything away.' Jools had entered the fray. 'We just believe in greater opportunity for all.'

McLafferty turned and gave her a bewildered and-who-asked-you? stare, before addressing them both. 'Tell me, do you believe in private education?'

'Absolutely not,' asserted Jools. This was page-one stuff. How could McLafferty be asking such a daft question?

'Well, that's odd,' said McLafferty, still affecting bewilderment, 'because your plans are going to give private schools the biggest boost they've ever had.'

'I'm not quite sure what you mean,' said Pete, both wearily and warily.

'I'm not talking about places like Eton and Harrow. Generations of what you might call toffs have always sent their children there and they always will. I'm talking about the minor fee-paying schools. They were almost dead and buried, but now you're going to revive them.'

Pete gave his best patronising smile. 'We have no intention of helping the private sector.'

'I'm sure you haven't,' said McLafferty, 'but that's exactly what you're going to end up doing. When you've abolished all the grammar schools, parents who can afford it – and, sadly, many who can't – will start sending their children to fee-paying schools because the academic standards will be so much higher.'

Jools was outraged. 'Says who?' she demanded. 'There's no reason why there should be any difference in standards. Our aim is to provide a good education for all.'

It was McLafferty's turn to be patronising. He took a quick look at the unadorned third finger of her left hand. 'If I may say so, Miss . . .'

Jools was about to say 'Jools' but, realising that McLafferty was not one for informality, replied, 'Lockyer.'

'If I may say so, Miss Lockyer, you're being very naïve. Pupils will be admitted regardless of ability so of course standards are going to drop.'

'On the contrary,' Jools insisted, 'a good teacher should be able to raise standards.'

'Up to a point. But you have to have the right basic material. You cannot make a silk purse out of a sow's ear. Especially without reasonable discipline.'

'By reasonable discipline, I suppose you mean corporal punishment,' said Pete unctuously, 'which in our view has always been immoral and now it's going to be illegal.' The unction became tinged with a sneer. 'Are you saying that a man of your experience cannot control a class without resorting to six strokes of the cane?'

At that moment, McLafferty, would have loved to punish Pete's impudence by exactly that method. 'I'm not saying that at all,' he replied. 'But once disruptive pupils realise that you are forbidden by law to touch them, they will be unassailable. Believe me, there'll come a day when they'll start threatening to sue you if you so much as lay a finger on them.'

'That's absurd,' said Jools

'Oh, is it?' asked McLafferty, letting Jools feel the laser-like force of his glare. 'Sooner or later, probably sooner, some of the better teachers won't want to be threatened, abused and unappreciated. They'll switch to the private schools and be lost to state education for ever. The private sector will get stronger and stronger, the state schools weaker and weaker.' He turned back to Pete. 'Is that what you want, Mr Roberts?'

'Of course it isn't and it's not going to happen,' Pete replied, with an attempt at a reassuring chuckle. 'Grammar schools are outmoded. They foster élitism. As a committed socialist, I am against that.'

McLafferty was silent for a moment, then countered quietly, 'I, too, am a socialist. I've spent my whole life trying to help children from less-privileged backgrounds. I'm no fan of the middle classes. I've generally found them to be pushy, ambitious, always wanting their money's worth. They'll look on these revitalised private schools as service providers. They'll be paying good money to send their children to them and they're going to want results. In twenty years' time, you'll have a two-tier education system. The gulf between the haves and have-nots will grow wider and wider. It's not me who is fostering élitism, Mr Roberts, it's you.'

Pete and Jools looked at each other, each expecting the other to provide a cogent counter-argument. Neither could. McLafferty concluded, 'However, I realise that if I refuse to go along with your plans I will be breaking the law. Where do I sign?'

Jools produced the relevant document, to which McLafferty applied his moniker with a swift, disdainful scrawl.

Pete, pleased to have won the battle, attempted to extend the olive branch. 'Hey, look, it's going to be fine,' he smiled. 'Would you like to have a look at the scale model of St Saviour's sixth-form college?'

Once again, he had hit a bum note. McLafferty stared at him in disbelief before replying, 'Would *you* like to see the desecration of *your* whole life's work?'

He saw himself out. Pete and Jools looked at each other again. Although there had been two of them and only one of him, they somehow felt that he had ganged up on them.

Despite finally having secured the most reluctant signature of them all, Pete felt he had to justify his failure to put up a more impressive performance. McLafferty had an excellent record, but he and those other despots over at St Bede's ran that school with a reign of terror. Yes, he got results, but that was not the right way to go about it. He was a reactionary, a Luddite, completely out of touch. He was. Wasn't he?

25

Pete Roberts and Guy Patterson had never met and never would. If they had, each would have felt an instant and unconditional loathing for the other. Guy would have regarded Pete as a wishy-washy lefty, who was damaging the country's education system; Pete would have regarded Guy as a vulgar, thrusting little man, who was damaging the country's entertainment system. And they'd both have been absolutely right.

Yet that was not what each man saw when he gazed into the mirror. Both Guy and Pete saw a visionary, a man of purpose, an architect of change with the intelligence and prescience to know what was best for people, even if those people didn't necessarily agree. In different ways, each believed he knew what was best for Dave Kelly and Andy Zymanczyk. Both were determined to have a profound effect on those boys' lives, but neither boy was remotely aware of this.

Dave was depositing yet more filthy lucre at the Post Office and Andy was on his way to empty his own overstuffed wallet at the Abbey National Building Society. However, the latter decided that, *en route*, he would make his first trip to see the Harlequin Hippies and take them up on their kind offer. The detour eventually ensured that little, if any, of his earnings ended up with the Abbey National.

Andy knew nothing about music. With no TV and a radio invariably tuned to the BBC World Service, the fripperies of popular music had no place in the Zymanczyk household. So how could he know what he liked? He only knew what he didn't like: the weighty pomposity of Pink Floyd, Genesis and Yes, for example, and the insubstantial sweetness of disco. As for punk, forget it: the very sight of an album entitled *Never Mind The Bollocks* would have had his parents begging Father Lizewski to come at once and exorcise the radiogram.

He left Harlequin Records with the first album he had ever owned – *Quadrophenia* by the Who, which one of the hippies behind the counter had assured him was 'like, cosmic' adding, in reverential tones, that the Who had 'played at Woodstock, man'.

'Oh,' said Andy. The only thing he knew about Woodstock was that he was supposed to be impressed that the Who had played there, but the album had appealed for two reasons: he knew that a film based on it was the most eagerly awaited release of the year, and the album's title seemed to sum up his own emotional state. He could feel four wholly separate sides to his personality: at school, he was English; at home, he was Polish; at the cinema, he was a movie buff and part-time thief; and at family gatherings he was a filthy pervert who wanted to have sex with his cousin.

He placed side one on the turntable and tried his

best to get into it. It was, apparently, a seminal work, brave, challenging stuff. This was Pete Townshend at his creative peak. He knew he was supposed to identify with the story – a disaffected west London teenager trying to come to terms with the hopelessness of his situation. It was hard, gutsy, true to life, but by side four, Andy realised that it was having no effect on him whatsoever. He felt as though he were at a hypnotist's and, after several minutes of gazing at the fob watch swinging back and forth, still wide awake. The music was of no interest to him; he wasn't even listening to it. However, the story inside the gatefold sleeve and the big booklet with its gritty black and white shots of the seamy side of London had him in its thrall. Andy was intrigued by the central character, the Shepherds Bush Mod. He found himself coveting the boy's scooter, his parka, his whole persona. And it struck him that no real Mod would be listening to stuff like *Quadrophenia*, which, despite its cover, had turned out to be yet another turgid, seventies concept album. He was looking for escape, he was looking for fun, and he knew he wouldn't find it here.

So, what sort of music would a real Mod listen to? He had no idea. But tomorrow, after school, he would ask the 'music teacher'.

26

Mr Birdsall was the music teacher for many of the sixth-formers at St Bede's. He wasn't a teacher and hadn't been inside a school since he was expelled from Wembley Grammar at the age of fifteen, but he owned and ran Johnny B's record store, three streets from St Bede's. It was where the cooler kids hung out every lunchtime – a dusty, musty little place, crammed with thousands of old 45s in their original paper sleeves. They were simply categorised: Soul, Reggae, Rock, Punk, Country and, by far the biggest section, Rock 'n' Roll. Johnny Birdsall would greet his customers from beneath a quiff so big, shiny and immaculate that, in order to construct it, he must have got up almost before he went to bed. Outside was an equally big, shiny and immaculate 1958 Vauxhall Velox, custard yellow and white. For Johnny, the clock had stopped in 1958, the day Elvis joined the army, and it had all been downhill since then. In his check shirt, old jeans, and black suede creepers, many people would have described Johnny as a Ted, but if he'd heard them, he would have taken great exception: there was nothing remotely Edwardian about him, no drape, no bootlace tie. Johnny Birdsall, you would be informed, was 'rockin''.

Having to support a wife and four children meant that he couldn't survive solely on the sale of fifties records, so he'd had to expand his stock to encompass the sixties and seventies too. And, despite appearances to the contrary, he had developed a love for, and a phenomenal knowledge of, the music from all three decades.

Johnny was friendly and passionate, and ran his shop more for love than money. Nonetheless, a sign above the counter warned the light-fingered, 'Shoplifters will be beaten to a pulp.' Having undergone too many similar punishments at school, no pupil of St Bede's was keen to find out whether or not this was true.

Andy had never felt quite cool enough to be a regular at Johnny B's. Although the banter in there was always friendly, far from intellectual and anyone was welcome to join in, Andy found it hugely intimidating. Of course he knew who Elvis Presley, the Beatles and the Rolling Stones were, but if things got any more esoteric than that, he would find himself on the edge of the conversation – the loneliest place in the world. His knowledge of Polish folk music would be of little use there.

'What are you doing lunchtime?' he'd asked Dave, after double English.

'Going down Johnny B's,' said Dave, giving his friend the answer he was hoping for. 'Coming?'

'Yeah, all right.'

Dave gave a surprised smile.

Their friendship was obviously strengthening, Andy thought, if Dave had invited him to join this exclusive little club. He felt he needed Dave's sponsorship for his first trip. When they got there, Wilbert Harrison was singing 'Kansas City' and a few of the boys were already up at the counter, chatting and smoking. It was clear to Andy that Johnny B's was to some sixth-formers what the Corner had been a couple of years before.

'Johnny,' said Dave, after a while, 'have you got *New Boots & Panties*?'

'That's a very personal question, young man,' replied Johnny, with a grin.

'No, I mean Ian Dury.'

'I know what you mean,' said Johnny, with a sneer, 'but Ian Dury? Do me a favour. He's just Chas and Dave with attitude.' He turned to Andy. 'Hope you've got better taste than your friend. What can I do for you?'

Andy explained his *Quadrophenia* problem and his quest for real Mod music, whatever that was.

'*Quadrophenia*,' scoffed Johnny, eyes rolling up to his quiff. 'Jesus Christ, don't you get enough of that sort of thing at school? It's too much like hard work. Popular music should be simple. Otherwise, you know, it stops being popular. You wouldn't catch Mods listening to double albums. You want the Tamla, the early soul, maybe some ska.'

It was clear to Johnny from Andy's quizzical expression that the boy had no idea what he was talking about. 'Tell you what,' he suggested, 'have a sort through those sections over there. Pull out anything with a black Tamla-Motown or Stateside label, a red Atlantic one or a yellow Stax one, and bring them all up here.'

Ten minutes later, Andy placed a huge pile of singles on the counter, from which Johnny removed a select few. On black labels, he picked The Temptations' 'Get Ready,' Martha and The Vandellas' 'Nowhere To Run' and Marvin Gaye's 'Can I Get A Witness'. On the red Atlantics, he pulled out Wilson Pickett's 'Land Of 1000 Dances,' and Otis Redding's 'I Can't Turn You Loose'. From the yellow Stax stack, he chose Johnnie Taylor's 'Who's Makin' Love' and 'Soul Limbo' by Booker T and the MGs. Completing the line-up were Tammi Lynn's northern soul smash 'I'm Going To Run Away From You' on Mojo, the Kinks' 'You Really Got Me' on original pink Pye and a Blue Beat reissue of Prince Buster's 'Al Capone' with 'One Step Beyond' on the other side. 'There you go, my friend,' said Johnny. 'Try that little lot. Let's call it a Mod starter pack. If you like them, there's hundreds more.'

Andy had an old Dansette record player in his bedroom. His cousin Adam had given it to him but it had seldom seen active service. It seemed too old a contraption on which to play new records (not that he had any), but for this little pile of sixties treasures, it was ideal. He stacked them up on the long spindle. As soon as he heard the opening piano chords of 'Can I Get A Witness?' he froze. He'd never heard it before yet something deep inside him recognised it. It was the call he hadn't known he'd been waiting for, and it made him move. He found he had no control over his actions. Suddenly he was like an electric toy that had never been plugged in until now. And as each new discovery clattered on to the turntable, another few thousand volts zapped through him. Although he was doing no harm, just dancing alone in his bedroom, Andy felt decadent, liberated and bad. Understandable for a teenager whose idea of domestic insurrection would have been boiling the contents of a tin of soup and impairing the flavour.

Johnny's selection had been impeccable. Andy would ask him to sort out another pile tomorrow. This was what he wanted. He didn't want the angst and the gritty realism of *Quadrophenia*. He needed the healing power of music to escape. He wanted to discover joyous new feelings, not wallow in the misery of the ones he already had. However, the acquisition of that double album had not been in vain. He still loved the whole Mod image depicted in the booklet and had decided that what he didn't spend on records he was going to spend on clothes.

27

Wembley Market, even if he'd known where it was, would have been no good to Andy. He wasn't looking for tank tops, loon pants or cheesecloth shirts. He wasn't even looking for leather jackets, Wranglers or Dr Martens. He was looking for a sartorial world that had vanished without trace. What he needed was a time machine to take him back to the Carnaby Street of 1964, to His Clothes for Italian suits and button-down shirts, and to Raoul for hand-made, almond-toed shoes.

With Carnaby Street now a cheap, tacky tourist trap, where would he find such style and elegance in the decade that taste forgot? He'd have to start with the casual stuff. An old army-surplus parka from Laurence Corner just off the Euston Road, a couple of Fred Perry T-shirts, one white, one red, from Lillywhite's in Piccadilly. A couple of pairs of Levi's from Dickie Dirts, and a pair of Hush Puppies.

Now for the hair. For the first time in his life, he was not going to Leslie Daruk, the Polish barber in Hammersmith. For a barber, Leslie had one rather vital thing missing: his left eye. The left lens of his glasses was blacked out and even his 'good' eye wasn't particularly good. However, because he was Polish, 'Blind Leslie's' loyal customers were willing to ignore this. They would emerge out on to King Street, hair cut rather wonky, all looking as though they were wearing badly fitting wigs. In the early eighties, when the Human League first appeared, Andy was convinced that Phil Oakey must be Polish.

At last, Andy was going to have his hair cut by somebody with no ocular deficiency. He was venturing into unknown territory: a unisex hair salon. This one had the obligatory unfunny pun of a name, Head Masters, which made him wonder whether it would be McLafferty administering the cut, wash and blow-dry. Fortunately, as he leaned backwards over the little sink, it was a Saturday girl called Tracey who massaged his scalp with shampoo before applying conditioner, an indulgence he felt almost guilty about receiving. He was then introduced to Justin, his stylist, who clipped and snipped with a care and precision unknown to any client of Blind Leslie. Justin carefully re-created the classic Mod look: short-half parting with hair combed in opposite directions to give Andy the desired appearance of having a 'two-tier head'.

When he arrived at the cinema, Tony greeted him with great enthusiasm. 'I don't believe it – a Mod. Christ, I thought they'd died out for ever. You look fantastic.'

Those last three words were all that Andy had needed to hear. His growing but still brittle confidence would have been shattered by even the slightest suggestion of a snigger. Instead, those three words had lifted his self-esteem to a new level where it was solid and untouchable. His courage and independence had paid off. If, in later life, he would remember the defining moment when he started to wriggle out from his parents' shadow, then it would be the one in which Tony Harris had told him he looked fantastic.

Tony looked at him again. 'Wow, this takes me back,' he said

'Were you a Mod, then?' asked Andy.

'Sort of. Most of us were round here. It was quite a London thing. You know something? Pete Townshend modelled himself on me.'

Andy knew Tony well enough now to realise that this would be no idle boast. 'Really?'

'Oh, yeah. You see, I had a mate called Danny Klein, Jewish kid, lived over in Wembley. Even at fifteen, sixteen, he was wearing beautiful handmade suits and shoes. The very first Mods were mostly Jewish boys whose families were in the rag trade. Well, I started getting seriously into clothes. My first job, which I fucking hated, was in the bank just opposite Ealing Common tube and I had to wear a suit so I thought I might as well make it a really nice one. I had three or four, handmade. Each one would take me at least six months to pay off. Anyway, Pete Townshend's family owned the greengrocer's two doors down, and every time Pete came into the bank and I was on the till, I used to see him looking at me – admiring the threads.'

Andy was enthralled. After the initial disappointment of *Quadrophenia* he'd discovered the more primal
delights of 'My Generation', 'I Can't Explain' and
'Anyway Anyhow Anywhere'. Pete Townshend was a
god, and Tony Harris knew him.

'And I'll tell you how you can look exactly like him.
Wait there a minute.' He disappeared into the office
and came out with a spoon. 'Just stare into the back of
that,' he laughed, 'and no matter who you are, you'll
look exactly like Pete Townshend.'

'So what happened to all those suits?' asked Andy.
The long, lugubrious face staring at him from the back
of the spoon was laughing because the trick really
did work.

'Well, fashions change and so do waistlines,' said
Tony, patting his stomach. 'Believe it or not, I was
as thin as a pin in those days. At school, if I turned
sideways, they used to mark me absent.' He looked at
Andy's new image and smiled. 'You know what really
killed off the Mods, don't you?'

'No?'

'The crash helmet. Ruined the whole image. How
can anyone look cool in a fucking crash helmet?'

'So where can you get suits like that now?'

'Well, nowhere, really,' said Tony, shaking his head.
'I mean, it's all wide lapels and flares, nobody wants
the old stuff any more. And, anyway, they wouldn't
be prepared to pay for it. I mean, there are still tailors
around who can do the old styles, but if you asked
them for HP, they'd think you wanted a bottle of brown

sauce.' He paused for a moment. 'Are you serious about all this?'

'All what?'

'Being a proper Mod.'

'I suppose so.'

'Well, if you are, I suppose I could have a word with Vaughan.'

'Vaughan?'

'Vaughan Robinson – he's got a tailor's about five minutes from here. Me and him go back years. He used to have a blues club in the basement. I've had some nights there, I can tell you. Brilliant tailor and cutter. And his wife's even better. Go round and see him later. Tell him I sent you.'

It was about four o'clock when Andy went on his break and walked round to a shabby little shop on Talbot Road. As he entered, it actually had one of those little bells at the top of the door-jamb that you hear all the time in sitcoms but never in real life. On hearing its jangle, Vaughan emerged from the back room smiling broadly. 'Well, well, well.' He grinned. He was a small, wiry Jamaican with a deep, double-bass voice almost bigger than he was. 'I've been waiting years for you.'

'For me?'

Vaughan nodded. 'For a guy smart enough to revive the old styles. Tony's told me all about you.' He let out a big, throaty chuckle and put an avuncular arm around Andy's shoulder. 'Come here, let me show you the cloths.'

After he'd looked at dozens, Andy took Vaughan's

advice and chose two mohairs, one navy, the other a sort of mustardy-gold.

Vaughan, familiar with the fickle finger of fashion, had kept all his original sixties patterns. The two suits would be identical: narrow lapels, three buttons, six-inch side vents, and trousers with a tapered leg.

Leaving his wife to take Andy's measurements, Vaughan disappeared into the back room and returned with half a dozen dusty old cardboard boxes. Inside were original button-down shirts, one or two others with the buttonless 'Billy Eckstine' collar and unsold ties in perishing Cellophane wrappers. Half buried treasure that had lain forgotten and unwanted in Vaughan's stock room since the early sixties.

Hang on a minute, there was more. From their zip-up protective covers, Vaughan unveiled two hand-tailored jackets – one in white linen, the other, high-collared, in grey herringbone – and a beautiful Prince of Wales check suit, all made to measure for customers who had never come back to collect them.

As Andy tried them on, Vaughan explained, 'You see, after the work that had gone into them I could never quite bring myself to throw them out. This suit was made for a guy called Clyde from Port of Spain. Man, he was a snappy dresser. Always plenty of cash, paid in advance. I never asked where he got it. One day, he just disappeared. All sorts of rumours – some say he went to Miami, others that he went back to Trinidad. Another guy said he'd seen him in Harlesden. All I know is he never came back for his suit. Hold your arms out.'

Andy did as he was told while Vaughan walked pensively round him. 'Sleeves are a bit long, bit big on the shoulders, but that's no problem. Few alterations and you'll look sensational.'

Vaughan was only too pleased to see these precious garments finally going to a good home and let Andy have them for a fraction of their true value. His complete new wardrobe would be ready for collection in two weeks. Having dealt with many a cash-strapped Mod, Vaughan then began to work out the HP terms. Andy was just about to say that, like the mysterious Clyde before him, he was more than able to pay cash up-front but suddenly thought again. What if word got back to Tony that Andy had an enormous disposable income? Where had he got that kind of money? Far better to sign Vaughan's little chit and agree to pay in modest instalments of eight pounds a week.

28

Dave had never wanted to kiss a man in his life. Particularly a man as unattractive as R.J. Hargreaves. RJ was in his fifties, overweight, balding and wearing an anorak. He gave off a smell of pipe tobacco and stale, unwashed hair, and was a taciturn and unappealing character. Yet Dave was seized by an overwhelming desire to give him a big fat juicy kiss simply because he had uttered the following words: 'Well, that's the end of the test, Mr Kelly, and I'm pleased to tell you you've passed.'

Dave felt his tear ducts swell with disbelief and joy. These tears would be different from the ones he'd shed two months earlier when R.J. Hargreaves had told him he'd failed.

Or, rather, 'hadn't passed'. RJ never liked to use the word 'fail'. Dave had wanted to pass so much it made him feel ill, made him desperately nervous, made him hit the kerb doing his three-point turn and mount the pavement while reversing round the corner; things he never usually did, but R.J. Hargreaves wasn't to know that. Dave had gone home and sobbed, disgorging so much salt water that he began to think that he'd shrivel up like a prune and die. Still, at least he hadn't told anyone he was taking it. The relief of not having to contend with well-meaning friends and family saying, 'Well? Did you pass?' was the only consolation he had.

While other small boys, when playing alone, had pretended to be footballers, pop stars, cowboys or Indians, Dave had been different kinds of car, mimicking the engine sounds of each one: the gentle hum of a Mini, the air-cooled clatter of a Beetle, the throaty throb of an E-type Jag. Almost from the day he could walk, he could tell a Triumph Herald from a Vitesse, an MGB from an MGC, and explain why the Rover P5 was better than the P6.

The fact that his family had never owned a car was the gun that had started the race. The race that would only be over when his provisional driving licence could be exchanged for a full one. His seventeenth birthday couldn't come soon enough. Seventeen was all he ever wanted to be. He'd never need to be any older. He wasn't bothered about getting served in pubs, not that he had any trouble anyway. He'd seen more X films in six months than most people see in a lifetime, and had no desire to put his own X on a ballot paper for either Jim Callaghan or Margaret Thatcher. All he wanted to do was drive. He wasn't a natural, more like a member of the Amish working at Dixons. He'd never had a car in which to practise around a disused airstrip or deserted car park. The inherent clumsiness and lack of co-ordination that had made him such a danger to himself with a meat cleaver had made the simultaneous mastery of clutch, gears and steering inordinately difficult at first but it didn't take long to click.

For Dave, this raging desire to drive was not about being flash or being able to pull, it was about mobility. It was about having the means to escape from wherever he happened to be if he suddenly didn't want to be there. And if you'd spent your life shivering in the rain waiting for buses that never turn up, this was a powerful incentive.

At last, a great chunk of the four-figure sum that had been burning a hole in his Post Office savings book could be withdrawn. At last, he had something to spend it on. A justification for his crimes. At last he could banish the anguish felt by so many sixteen-year-old boys who have to stand impotently aside as all the best-looking girls are seduced by the jangle of car keys. At last, he could start looking for a set of his own. He began to scour 'the boards' outside newsagents on which second-hand goods were offered for sale. As he scrutinised each one, it occurred to him that many seemed to be selling dead children's clothes: 'School blazer – aged 11–12, hardly worn'. 'What happened to the kid?' he wanted to scream. 'What happened to the kid?'

The kid would be alive and well. It was just that, in an era before charity shops appeared on every high street in Britain, people rarely gave things away. Not if they could get three quid for them.

The boards proved useless. Around Kilburn they

usually did, unless you were looking for a council-house exchange with a family in Rotherham or a second-hand Holy Communion dress. He turned his attention to the *Exchange & Mart*. This great British institution was a weekly microcosm of all human life. Within its pages, you were bound to find someone somewhere who wanted to sell what you wanted to buy. A Mirror dinghy, perhaps, the uniform of a Japanese admiral or a stuffed grizzly bear. Fortunately, there was a separate motor section, which would be far more fruitful than 'the boards'.

Dave's eager ballpoint circled the cars he wanted to look at. He had been rehearsing for this day for years. He knew exactly what to do. Always take cash and, when you make an offer, show it in real money. If they decline and you turn to go, very often the thought of that thick wad of notes walking away with you will be enough to change their minds. When phoning, never say, 'I'm phoning about the Ford Escort,' always say, 'I'm phoning about the car.' If the reply is 'Which car?' you know it's a dodgy dealer posing as a private vendor and you hang up immediately. If you arrange to call at three thirty, go round at three fifteen so that the vendor will not have had a chance to run the car round the block to get the engine nice and warm. Most importantly, before you even look at the car, have a good look at the person selling it. If you wouldn't buy the vendor, then don't buy the car. All of which meant that in order to buy a second-hand car you didn't necessarily need any mechanical knowledge. A sound understanding of human nature was far more valuable. This was especially vital for Dave because, despite his obsession with cars, he had no interest in knowing how they worked. To a child brought up without a car, the idea of being whisked along at a hundred miles an hour, being in a different place every second, able to take off on a sunny day to Brighton, Bournemouth or Bognor was pure sorcery. It was *Bedknobs and Broomsticks*. It was *Chitty Chitty Bang Bang*. He didn't want some mechanical bore expounding on pistons, valves and tappets, letting daylight in upon magic.

If his magic carpet needed fixing, he'd do what everyone else on the Queens Park estate did and get Denis round. Denis Byrne was a mobile mechanic. He and his little van lived round the corner in Huxley Street. It was said that Denis did not have blood in his veins, he had Castrol GTX and he was as important and respected a figure as the doctor or the parish priest. If he went into the Prince of Wales, the Grey Horse or the William IV, he never had to put his hand into his pocket. Regulars would be queuing up to buy him a drink in return for all the holes he'd dug them out of. Denis hated the idea of people trying to fix their own cars, not because he wanted their money but because he was genuinely concerned for their safety. 'Fixing your own car is illegal in Norway,' was his favourite piece of European law. 'You have to go to a registered mechanic. Bloody right an' all. What if you get some clown putting on a set of brake pads and he doesn't put them on right? Then the brakes fail and he knocks down a kiddie on a zebra crossing. What then?'

He had a point.

Cars on the estate were always in need of new brakes, clutches and head gaskets because most of them were like ex-heavyweight champions long past their prime. They were always big – tail-finned Zephyrs and Zodiacs were particularly popular, as were Vauxhall Crestas, Austin Westminsters and any sort of Jag. These once-mighty machines had fallen out of favour after the oil crisis of the early seventies. Their prices had plunged, bringing them well within a Kilravock Street budget. In some cases, the cars were bigger than the houses they were parked outside.

Dave had set his heart on a Ford Capri, Britain's answer to the Mustang. Behind the wheel of a Capri, he would feel like Steve McQueen in *Bullitt*. However, as Andy the film buff pointed out, McQueen's was an unusual Mustang: in the famous car chase through San Francisco, he changes gear upwards no fewer than sixteen times.

Before heading over to Harlesden to see a yellow Capri, Dave decided to nip out to Kingsbury to see a Cortina. He'd formulated a little trick for which he needed Andy as his accomplice. If a car was up for seven hundred, Andy would call first. Even if it was worth every penny, he would only offer four. The offer would be declined and twenty minutes later Dave would call. He might offer five. The vendor, remembering that the previous caller had only offered four, would be far more inclined to accept.

All very well in theory until Dave and Andy turned up outside the neat semi-detached house and saw HUR 747G resplendent in the driveway. This was a Ford Cortina 1600E, a car Dave had adored and coveted since he was a small boy. Just seven or eight years since the last one had left Dagenham, they were already becoming collectors' items. For seven hundred quid, Dave had been expecting a rotting wreck with a knackered engine belching tell-tale blue smoke from the exhaust. He had not been expecting what he saw in front of him. This one was metallic gold and, despite its decade on the road, was perfect, every original feature intact: the chrome Rostyle wheels, twin front spotlights, black vinyl roof – all present and correct. Inside, not a mark besmirched the toffee-coloured seats, the rally steering-wheel or the handsome wooden dash. Dave's heart raced with excitement: he wanted this car so much that it hurt. He knocked at the door. It was answered by a kindly-looking man in his sixties. Dave asked him the first question: 'Why are you selling it?'

'Well, I had a heart-attack, see, only a minor one but the doctor says I've got to take it a bit easy. Now, this is a lovely car. I've had it since new but the steering is very heavy. Fit young man like you won't have a problem, but I can't really manage it any more. I'm going to get one of them little Fiestas. It'd be a lot easier to nip around in.'

Almost before the man had finished his sentence,

Dave was counting twenty-pound notes into his hand. He wasn't going to insult this charming old gent by haggling over the price of his pride and joy. He just wanted the reclining seats, the wooden dash with its clocks and dials, and the Lotus sports suspension.

But, most of all, he wanted one particular person in the passenger seat.

29

Andy was in no hurry to drive. The driving test, after all, was yet another examination. Having spent his whole life being examined, he was unwilling to take any sort of test that wasn't absolutely necessary. Besides which, his favoured mode of transport did not require a test. This was a time when any kid, at seventeen, could legally roar off on a 250cc motorbike, despite having no idea how to ride it. The result was that quite a few failed to make it to eighteen.

Andy's ambitions weren't quite so perilous. Speed (well, this sort of speed, anyway) had never been important to Mods. He just wanted a scooter, but by the late seventies the classic Vespas and Lambrettas had all but disappeared from Britain's roads. However, persistent perusal of the *Exchange & Mart* had finally unearthed one. 'Vespa GS160 1964. All original. Needs work. £50.' This was followed by an unfamiliar dialling code, which turned out to be Barking, and led to the front door of a small terraced house, which was opened one Sunday afternoon by a man in his thirties named Kenny.

From inside the house, Andy could hear the yelling of Kenny's twin baby daughters, whose double buggy meant that there was no longer room for the Vespa.

'It'll happen to you one day, mate,' said Kenny, with a smile that was both happy and sad, before removing a mouldy old canvas cover from the emblem of his youth. 'I don't mind,' he said wistfully. 'You've got to settle down sooner or later and I left it later than most. As long as you have plenty of fun first. That's the main thing. Too many people don't.'

Andy looked at the scooter. It had been a truly beautiful machine but one glance told him that it had lived a bit. It was a veteran of countless run-outs to Brighton, Clacton and Margate. It had stood parked outside the Scene, the Ad Lib and the Flamingo Club, waiting faithfully for Kenny to ride it back to Bethnal Green with a beehived pillion passenger whose legs, so cruelly exposed by her mini-skirt, would have turned to corned beef long before she got home.

After six years at St Bede's and many more spent sitting on the pews of St Andrew Bobola's, Andy had long ago mastered the art of listening without listening. This particular skill came in handy as Kenny explained, in completely unfascinating detail, about the mechanical superiority of the Vespa GS160 over the Lambretta TV200. Having nodded thoughtfully at what he guessed to be appropriate junctures, Andy then exchanged five ten-pound notes for the keys, which he then tried in the ignition. He'd bought an old crash helmet for the occasion but was still a little embarrassed at having to ask, 'So, how do I ride it, then?'

'Ride it?' Kenny laughed. 'This thing ain't been ridden since 1969. When I said it needed work, I meant it. Do you know anything about scooters?'

Andy shook his head and Kenny felt rather sorry for him. Still, he'd finally unloaded the scooter and fifty quid would buy a hell of a lot of nappies. 'Most of the old scooter places have gone now but there's still one on the Edgware Road run by an Italian bloke called Claud. There's nothing he don't know about Vespas. Shouldn't take too much to get it going again.'

From inside the house, Andy again heard the plaintive cry of four little lungs yelling for their feed.

'Good luck, mate,' said Kenny, with a wink. 'I'd better go back indoors.'

Andy was stuck. He had neither trailer nor Transit, and even the Olympic Committee would have deemed the Pushing a Vespa from Barking to Shepherds Bush event as too tough for inclusion in the Games. With some discomfort, he realised that there was only one way to transport it across London: he'd have to go back the way he had come – by tube. He wheeled it to Barking station and then, with a strength and balance he hadn't known he possessed, managed to bounce it gingerly down a long flight of stairs to the platform. As he waited for the train to pull in, he was approached by an officious-looking guard. 'You can't take that on the train,' he insisted.

Andy pointed to the stairs down which he had just wheeled his new acquisition and explained that he couldn't now wheel it back up again. 'Not my problem,' said the guard, with that very seventies militant and self-satisfied fold of the arms.

'Well, what am I supposed to do?'

'You can do whatever, you like, chummy, but you're not taking that scooter on the train.'

The station was deserted except for one man sitting reading the *Sunday Times*. Having heard this brief exchange, the man piped up quietly, politely but with the certainty of knowledge behind him, 'I know what you can do.'

Andy turned round. 'I'm sorry?'

'I said, I know what you can do about your scooter.'

Andy was bewildered. 'What?'

'Go and get a copy of the *Sunday Times*,' the man said. 'There's a newsagent just outside the station. Oh, and a roll of Sellotape. Go on. I'll look after the scooter.'

Andy returned two minutes later to find the guard glowering at the mystery stranger, who had simply carried on reading his newspaper.

'Ah, right,' he said, putting down the paper. 'All you have to do is wrap your scooter in newspaper. There are enough sections to wrap a 747. Now wrap it up so that not an inch of metal is showing and there will be nothing our friend here can do to stop you taking it on to the train.'

'What are you playing at?' asked the guard, confused now, as Andy began to do as the man had suggested.

'I'm not playing at anything,' the man replied, acknowledging the guard's existence for the first time. 'By wrapping that scooter in newspaper, it becomes a parcel – it technically becomes "goods" – and as long as it fits comfortably inside the carriage and doesn't obstruct other passengers, then . . . I'm sorry, what's your name?'

'Andy.'

'Then Andy here is legally entitled to take it on to the train.'

The guard was left with only the stock response to fall back on. 'Right, I'm going to fetch the station supervisor.'

The man was unimpressed. 'You can fetch whoever you like, but I suggest you have a quick flick through your own rules and regulations first and you'll find that what I've told you is true. And, anyway, the train will be almost empty – what harm is he doing?'

'That's not the point,' the guard snapped,

'No,' the man replied, with ill-disguised disdain, 'I don't suppose it is.'

Andy was now applying the finishing touches to a Vespa-shaped parcel when he saw the Hammersmith train approaching. He was awestruck. 'Thank you very much,' he said to the stranger. 'I don't know what I would have done.'

'Not at all,' the man replied. 'It was a pleasure.'

'Are you getting this train?'

'No, no. I'm waiting for the District line.'

'Well, before I go,' said Andy, 'how did you know all that?'

'I'm a lawyer,' the man explained. 'I know all sorts of useless things. Mind you, ask me to change a fuse and I wouldn't have a clue. 'Bye now. And good luck. I hope you get it going.'

'Thanks again,' said Andy, as the man helped him heave the scooter into the carriage. At that moment, he'd made up his mind what he was going to do with his life. He was going to be a lawyer. How cool was that bloke? He'd be like Petrocelli, star of the eponymous TV series. Without a TV, of course, Andy had never seen *Petrocelli*, but in Screen Two, he had seen *The Lawyer*, the film on which the series had been based. Like Petrocelli, he would use his expertise to help those in need. He'd say nothing until nearer the time. His father could hardly object. A lawyer – what could be more noble and respectable than that? It wasn't as though he was threatening to renounce Catholicism, join the British Nazi party and try to reinvade Poland. He just wasn't going to be a dentist. He'd never wanted to from the moment he'd discovered that the training involved removing teeth from dead people's heads.

Fired by this new purpose in his life, he wheeled his parcel along the platform of Goldhawk Road tube station, down another steep flight of stairs to the street. In his excitement, he'd forgotten one critical thing: where the hell was he going to keep the scooter? Unlike his new old records and his new old clothes, his mother might notice him trying to hide a new old Vespa in his bedroom.

30

Andy had never been one for sport. He had a vague interest in football, which had been sparked off on one of the rare occasions that he had been allowed to watch TV. At the age of eleven he had gone with his father to Tomek Zlotnicki's house to watch that now famous World Cup qualifying match between England and Poland. As everyone now knows, England needed a win to qualify and, in perhaps the most one-sided match any of those watching had ever seen, they should have won 5 or 6–0. Instead, the ball refused to go into the net, thanks largely to the heroics of Polish goalkeeper Jan Tomoszewski, whom Brian Clough had dismissed as 'a clown'. The final score was 1–1. Poland went through; England failed to qualify. On the way home, Andy had been surprised by his father's reaction. His joy at Poland's triumph was marred because it had been at the expense of the nation he loved, the country that had taken him in. Why did it have to be the English? Why not the Germans or the Russians?

Andy wasn't a great footballer; he wasn't a great athlete. He was, well, average. In a race of ten boys, he would come fifth. There was glory in being really good and a certain comic value in being really bad, but no point at all in being average. The new latitude offered to the sixth-formers meant that they could choose what they did for games. Andy and Dave had both eschewed football and rugby in favour of golf. This involved unsupervised practice at Greenford golf course. Neither of them had ever been there – Andy didn't even know where it was – so Games usually meant buying records at Johnny B's or working the afternoon shift at the cinema.

However, on this particular afternoon, Andy was volunteering for physical exertion far more rigorous than anything he had attempted before. He would be pushing his scooter from Shepherds Bush to Paddington. He started well enough, but within minutes the pain had begun to seep down through his shoulders and arms to the front of his thighs. An hour and a half later, his whole body wobbling like jelly, his face bathed in sweat, he arrived at Claud D'Urso's scruffy premises on the Edgware Road. There were dozens of old scooters and bits of old scooters everywhere. Not one appeared to be complete or in working order. It smelt exactly like the metalwork room at school and, on seeing Andy, Claud poked his head out from behind an old Lambretta. 'Can I help you?'

'Er . . . yeah, I'm Andy Zymanczyk, I phoned earlier—'

Claud took one astonished look at the Vespa and cut him short. 'Where did you get this?'

'Um . . . from a bloke over in east London.'

'How much did you pay for it?'

'Fifty quid.'

Claud looked at him in amazement, and started to laugh. Andy felt a bit of a fool, just as he had when he'd wheeled the fucking thing down the stairs at Barking station. Fifty quid? That Kenny must have seen him coming.

Claud inspected the scooter carefully. Andy noticed he was wearing gossamer-thin surgeon's gloves, which were covered in oil. He then switched back a generation from his native Clerkenwell to the Neapolitan parlance of his ancestors. '*Meraviglioso*,' he whispered, before calling, 'Franco, Mario, *viene a veder questo*.'

Two overalled, gossamer-gloved Italians scuttled out of the back, covered in crankcase oil. They, too, seemed awestruck at what Andy had just pushed in. '*Stupendo*,' said one, whistling through his teeth.

Claud reverted to Cockney. 'I've been looking everywhere for one of these in original nick. It's perfect.'

Andy looked at it, sad, rusty and rattling. It looked far from perfect. 'But it's all rusty,' he said.

'That's only the chrome,' said Claud, with a chuckle. 'You can get that off with a cloth and a can of Coke.'

'But it doesn't go.'

'It might need a new engine, clutch, gearbox and brakes. The whole lot's probably seized up. And look at the tyres – totally bald. But this is a Vespa GS160 in original condition. Whatever it costs to restore it, it will be worth it.'

Andy looked worried. All those clothes and records had meant he was spending his money almost faster than he could steal it. Still, he feebly tried to convince himself that this would be an investment, you know, a bit like putting money into an Abbey National savings account. 'How much is it going to cost me?' he asked nervously.

'Well, that depends,' said Claud. 'Either . . . well, who knows? But we're talking hundreds, or alternatively . . .' He paused. 'I'll do it for nothing.'

'For nothing?' Andy didn't know what to say. Since he'd first seen the scooter and come into contact with Kenny, the stroppy guard at Barking station, the lawyer with his newspaper and now Claud with his gossamer gloves, his world had gone mad.

'Nothing,' confirmed Claud. 'I want to make it the best-looking Vespa ever, and I'll do it for nothing on one condition.'

'What's that?'

'When it's finished, I'll need to borrow it for a couple of weeks.'

'What for?'

'Well, that's just it. I can't tell you at the moment, but if you don't ask, I'll restore it for nothing. Deal?'

Andy knew he'd be a fool to turn this down so he nodded resolutely and thrust out his hand. 'Deal.'

Claud gave Andy one of the disposable gossamer gloves and motioned for him to put it on. Only then did he shake him firmly by the hand. Then Andy saw that his glove was also now covered in oil. Claud smiled. 'If you're going to be a proper Mod, son, the last thing you want is oil on your hands.'

31

Top button undone, collar pulled wide apart and a tie knot so big there was virtually no tie left to poke through it. From around 1972 to 1977, that was how most pupils at St Bede's tended to wear their ties. With the advent of punk, it had all changed. Buttons were done up, ties pulled straight and skinny, hair cut short and spiky. Andy Zymanczyk, however, was probably the first and only pupil to have his blazer professionally altered by a tailor – lapels narrowed, shoulders taken in, six-inch side vents inserted. And he was certainly the first to have three pairs of narrow black trousers handmade in the same barathea cloth as the blazer, with four-inch inside turn-ups so they would hang just perfectly. McLafferty raised no objection, largely because uniform rules, like all other school rules, were not so strictly enforced for sixth-formers and also because Zymanczyk was, without doubt, the cleanest, smartest-looking pupil St Bede's had ever produced.

It was stealth rebellion. Andy's new look filled his parents with pride. As he walked between them to mass every Sunday, in one of Vaughan Robinson's beautifully tailored suits, they assumed that he was enthusiastically embracing the noble tradition of Sunday Best, treating the Sabbath with due respect and deference, acknowledging its place as the most important day of the week. The simple truth was that, having to wear his – albeit wonderfully customised – school uniform from Monday to Friday, the tasteless red Crimplene of the Gaumont on Saturdays – Sunday was his only chance to enjoy the clothes on which he'd lavished so much of his money.

His whole image might have undergone drastic change, but his family's Sunday-afternoon rituals remained set in stone. On this particular Sunday, he was spared the morbid trip to Gunnersbury cemetery because it was the Zymanczyks' turn to play host to the Gomoulkas. Uncle Krzys and Auntie Ania were welcomed with warm hugs and double kisses, and behind them, Alison was wondering, who is that cool-looking bloke in the gold mohair suit? After an incredulous blink or two, she realised it was her cousin, the nice boy whom she had always regarded as 'sweet'. Fortunately, she had never told him this. Andy was male, and males, without exception, hate being called 'sweet'. Though meant as a compliment, it cuts like a knife, being the polar opposite of 'sexy', 'hot' or 'raunchy'. It's like being described as a Fondant Fancy, and who'd want to shag one of those?

Whether he liked it or not, Andy had always been 'sweet' but now, Alison had to concede, he was intriguing. She'd known him all her life but clearly didn't know him at all. Ever since he'd gone to work at that cinema he'd become a lot more interesting. Suddenly he seemed to know everything about films and music, and he was now the best-dressed boy she'd ever seen.

After they had all finished a hearty lunch of *barszcz* and *bigos*, Jerzy had thought himself very benign and enlightened by suggesting that 'the young people' might like to go into the back room and 'play some pop music' while the adults gave the vodka a serious caning and had an animated discussion about the unrest in the Gdansk shipyards. Andy and Alison slid quietly away, and Andy went upstairs to fetch a stack of Johnny Birdsall's finest. He started her off with familiar Mod anthems like '1-2-3' by Len Barry and 'The In Crowd' by Dobie Gray before introducing her to the aural delight of Doris Troy's 'Whatcha Gonna Do About It' and Arthur Alexander's original version of 'You Better Move On'. To this wonderful backdrop, they began to talk. Alison found herself treating him as if he were a cool and enigmatic stranger.

'So what happened to your boyfriend?' asked the 'stranger', affecting a tone of brotherly concern, which so belied his true feelings that his performance was worthy of an Oscar.

'Oh, him,' she replied dismissively. 'Well, it all went downhill because of the Krooklok.'

'The what?'

'Krooklok – you know, those stupid things like umbrella handles that you lock round your steering-wheel to stop your car getting nicked.'

Andy was having trouble working out how a Krooklok could have led to the break-up of his cousin's relationship unless, of course, the ex-boyfriend had bashed her over the head with it.

'We only had to stop for five minutes and out would come the bloody Krooklok, as if anyone would want someone to steal his poxy Austin 1100. It really got on my wick. Such a turn-off. That and the way he drove – so slow, so careful like—'

'My dad?' suggested Andy

'Even worse.' She laughed.

'Not possible,' said Andy. 'So where is he now, this bloke?'

'Bangor University doing Marine Biology. I hope he bloody drowns,' she said, still laughing. 'Anyway, how about you? Going out with anyone?'

'Well, there are girls I see,' explained Andy, not technically lying, since there were female members of the public whom he saw every day, 'but nobody special.'

'Oh, right,' she said. 'And are you going to college?'

Andy gestured towards the front room and his education-obsessed father. 'I don't think I'll have much choice. Anyway, I do want to go – I'm going to be a lawyer.'

'What?' she gasped, covering her mouth in mock-horror. 'Not a dentist?'

Andy shook his head.

'Well,' she giggled, 'I wouldn't want to be in your shoes when you tell him.'

'How about you?' he asked.

'Well, I quite fancy Edinburgh – about as far away as possible from K. Gomoulka's delicatessen. I'll do English, as long as there's no Chaucer. I mean, it's just rubbish, isn't it?'

Andy agreed. 'Just because something is six hundred years old doesn't make it worthwhile, relevant or even good.' He warmed to the theme. 'It's like a horse and cart. I mean, a marvellous piece of engineering in its day but nowadays it doesn't really compare to a brand new BMW.'

'Even when you translate it out of that gobbledegook, it's just Benny Hill.'

Andy had never seen Benny Hill but he knew what she meant.

Alison jerked her head towards the record player where the Miracles' 'Shop Around' was emitting from the original London 45. 'These records,' she said, 'they're not good because they're old, they're good because they're good.'

To Andy's ears, her words were even sweeter than Smokey's. Next up was John Lee Hooker's 'Boom Boom' on Stateside, so rare he didn't like to play it too much. He whacked the volume up so that Alison could fully appreciate its driving bluesy rhythm. There were no complaints from the front room. The vodka had taken hold, Polish bread and a selection of cold meats were being served and the health of Lech Walesa was being loudly and lustily toasted.

'I don't think they'll miss us for half an hour,'

said Andy. 'Come with me. I've got something to show you.'

They walked round the corner to a row of shabby lock-up garages in Percy Road. Andy's key unlocked the second from the end. Inside, restored and customised to jaw-dropping perfection, was TBY 964B, the finest example of a Vespa GS160 the world had ever seen. Every plate and panel had been resprayed and buffed to its original glory. It was a symphony of metallic ice blue and gleaming chrome, with tiny whitewall tyres completing the effect. Claud D'Urso was as Italian as Michelangelo and this had been his Sistine Chapel. You didn't need to know anything about scooters to realise that you were in the presence of something very special.

'Well,' he said, smiling broadly, 'what do you think?'

'God, it's gorgeous,' she gushed. 'Where did you get it?' And Andy was then cued up perfectly to regale her with the tale of Kenny, the guard, the lawyer and Claud.

'So why does he need to borrow it?'

'Wouldn't tell me. Just said that he'd ring me when he needed it and I was to take it to his workshop. He'd let me have it back after a couple of weeks and then I could keep it.'

There was only one word to do justice to that story and naturally Alison said it: 'Wow.' She threw an eyeball around the rest of the garage. 'What are all these other things?' She was looking in particular at about half a dozen large plastic containers.

'Records.'

Her eyes then came to a halt on an old oak wardrobe in the corner.

'Clothes,' said Andy. 'I haven't got room in my bedroom. Besides, my mum would wonder where all these things had come from. I just swap them round every now and again. As long as I don't have too many in the house at any one time, she won't suspect anything.'

Alison opened the wardrobe and saw suits, trousers, shirts, jumpers and wonderful old jackets in leather and suede, all assiduously arranged. She looked askance at her cousin. 'Where did you get them all?'

'Don't worry, nothing's stolen. It's all bought and paid for.'

'Blimey.' She whistled. 'That cinema job must pay well.'

'Yeah,' said Andy, looking down, 'er . . . you could say that.'

Her gaze again fell upon the centrepiece. 'But this,' she said, running her middle finger delicately along the paintwork, 'obviously your mum and dad don't know about it.'

'Are you joking?' He laughed. 'You know what they're like. They've only just let me go out on a pushbike. My old man would do his nut. Anyway, do you want to go for a quick spin?'

'I'd love to, but I haven't got a helmet.'

'Container number seven.' He grinned, pointing to one of the plastic boxes. 'And you'll find a spare parka in the wardrobe. Not really *haute couture* but even on a sunny day, it can get a bit nippy.'

As Alison swamped herself in the big green parka and buckled on her helmet, Andy pushed the scooter out into the sunshine. The sun danced off its glittering chrome and Alison just stared at it again. He kick-started it. The engine fired at once. Well it would – almost every moving part was brand new.

Alison straddled the bike and nestled into the rider. Andy was struck by simultaneous delight and horror. Her arms clung tightly around his chest as the Vespa swung swiftly round the Holland Park roundabout. Andy was doing this on purpose, just to make sure she noticed the difference between him and that creep with the Krooklok. As they went faster, it felt better and better, but at the same time worse and worse. She was gorgeous, she was interesting, they had so much in common – but she was his cousin, for fuck's sake.

Alison, meanwhile, filled with admiration, excitement and more than a tingle of fear, was starting to feel exactly the same way.

32

Dave had a different dilemma, but his thoughts were similar. She's gorgeous, she's interesting, we have so much in common – but she's Jewish, for fuck's sake, and how often do they go out with gentiles? He felt like Ed Moses taking his place on the blocks for the 400-metre hurdles. First hurdle was the Jewish one; if he could get over that, he was in with a shout. Next one was the fact that they worked together: if he asked her out and she said no, their hitherto happy relationship would become unbearably awkward. Next hurdle was the reason she might say no. To Dave, there seemed to be a huge gulf between them in experience and sophistication. She had ten O levels to his six, she'd been driving for months rather than days, she had been abroad – to Israel, America and her family's second home in Marbella. He'd never been on a plane, never even made an Airfix one.

Then there was his own insecurity. He could see that she liked him, but wondered whether it was simply as a friend. He could understand her thinking that he was good company, a bit of a laugh, but short of her signing a written declaration that said, 'I find you sexually attractive, please ask me out,' this was a difficult one to call. Perhaps, somewhere deep within him, there lurked that potent and reproving form of Catholicism, which still regarded sex as immoral and solely for the procreation of children. Add to this his two elder sisters, seemingly put on this earth to stop him from ever regarding himself as a sex god.

Worst of all, he hoped, just hoped, that Rachel didn't view him as 'sweet'.

Legs leaden and lungs bursting for air, he came round the bend to face the most difficult hurdle of all: how was he going to ask her out? What exactly was he going to say?

'So, do you fancy coming out for a drink, then?'

He'd always vowed he would never utter these words, opining that any bloke asking a girl out for 'a drink' simply wasn't trying hard enough and deserved to have his invitation declined.

But if they weren't going for 'a drink', where were they going to go? They both worked in a cinema so he could hardly ask her out to the pictures. At seventeen, you don't ask a girl out for dinner – far too grown-up. He thought about asking her to come with him one night to watch QPR get beaten at home but, in the days when hooligans still went to football matches, he thought that he, too, might end up getting beaten at home. A club or a party was out of the question. That was where you went to get off with a girl whom you might then ask out. It would be like going to a restaurant and taking a packed lunch. So he was reduced to that tried and tested request: 'So . . . er . . . do you fancy coming out for a drink, then?'

Rachel felt something inside her go 'ping' as the norepinephrine hit her like the snort of cocaine it so closely resembles. At last, at long last, everything inside her exclaimed, 'I was beginning to think that he was gay or I was as ugly as sin.'

'Yeah, okay,' she said, with a coy smile that seemed to hit Dave somewhere between his waist and his upper thigh. 'When?'

Yes! There had been no hurdles after all: it had been a flat 400-metre race and he was now Alberto Juantorena, breathless and triumphant, sprinting across the finishing line. 'Well,' he gasped, 'we're both off on Wednesday. How about then?'

'Yeah, great.'

'I'll pick you up at eight.' Dave had waited years to say those words to somebody. 'I'll pick you up.' It felt wonderful.

He spent most of Wednesday afternoon wondering what he should wear. His wardrobe, while not quite on a par with Andy's, still housed an impressive selection. Since discovering the Kings Road and Kensington Church Street, he now shuddered at the thought of ever having bought a single stitch at Wembley Market. When he got home, he pulled out almost every item of clothing he possessed, some so far back in the wardrobe that they were almost in Narnia.

He still couldn't make up his mind. Jumping out of the bath, he had a ball of cotton wool in one hand and his sister's Anne French cleansing milk in the other when he wondered what the hell he was doing. Rachel had only ever seen him in a red Crimplene jacket, slacks and a clip-on bow-tie and had still wanted to go out with him. Did it really matter what he wore? His mind wandered back to the last occasion on which he had purposefully gone out 'on the pull'. Thoroughly scrubbed up and shampooed, he'd put on all his best clothes, his cooler than cool but cripplingly uncomfortable Solatio basket-weave shoes, gone off to a party and left empty-handed. He wondered whether he had given off the whiff of somebody trying too hard, somebody who was tense with expectation, not relaxed and therefore not attractive.

Then he thought back to the times when he had got lucky and they had almost always been when he was least expecting to, when he wasn't overdressed and over-splashed in Blue Stratos. With this in mind, he put down the cleansing milk. He'd had a bath, washed his face and behind his ears. He was clean enough. He opted for the clothes in which he felt most comfortable: a battered brown leather jacket that was older than he was, a crisp white American T-shirt, a pair of Levi's and his favourite brown suede Shelly's shoes.

At eight o'clock he hooted, as instructed, outside a big thirties semi in Egerton Gardens and Rachel came running out. She hadn't lied to her parents: she had said she was going out tonight with a nice boy called

David. She knew that, since David was a popular name among Jewish boys, it wouldn't occur to them that this particular David had managed to hang on to his foreskin.

He wasn't like any other David she had ever met and neither was the pub he took her to. The chairs inside were toffee-coloured and they reclined. It had a wooden dash and a sports steering-wheel and, unlike any other pub in the world, it moved. Along the back seat, the landlord had neatly arranged miniature bottles of vodka, gin, Scotch, brandy, Bacardi and Southern Comfort. There were bottles of red wine, white wine and cans of beer, plus soft drinks, juices, mixers and a soda siphon. The jukebox was the radio-cassette player he'd had fitted that very afternoon. 'Welcome to the mobile pub,' he said. 'Where do you want to go?'

'Well, out of Willesden for a start.' She laughed, and the driver headed off towards the Harrow Road and Paddington.

'It's a self-service bar,' he told her, and she served herself a gin and tonic, while the driver had to be content with a Britvic orange.

He'd taken a risk with the music. He'd made a tape entirely at random, pulling out any old single and taping it on the premise that if he'd bought it it must have been good, but gave no thought to the order. So James Brown, Lou Reed, Blondie, Tom Jones, Steely Dan and, inexplicably, David Essex all found themselves together on the jukebox of the mobile pub.

They headed through Lancaster Gate and into Hyde

Park. It was a warm, balmy evening so he parked the pub just by the Serpentine. Rachel loved the Cortina. Most of all she loved the fact that it was his car, not his parents'. He'd paid for it with the money he'd earned (all right, stolen) but, unlike so many other cars she had been in, this one had not been a seventeenth-birthday present. They gazed out of the window of their own little world.

'So,' she smiled, 'why did it take you so long?'

'What?' said Dave, knowing exactly what she meant but trying to play for time.

'To ask me out.'

'Well, I'm very shy.'

'You're the least shy person I've ever met.'

'All right,' he said. 'Do you really want to know?'

'No. I just ask questions for the hell of it. Of course I want to know.'

It never takes much to make a Catholic confess. Dave, as well he might, had an almost permanently guilty conscience and, if stopped by the police for a routine check, would happily own up to the Great Train Robbery, so Rachel's simple question elicited an instant unburdening of the soul. 'Well,' he explained, 'you'd passed your driving test and I hadn't.'

'So?'

'So I just felt that I couldn't take you out until I had.'

Rachel didn't know quite what to make of this. 'Are you saying that I wouldn't go out with you unless you had a car?'

'No, the other way round. *I* wouldn't go out with *you* unless I had a car.'

'It wouldn't have mattered.'

'It would to me. I could hardly have set up a mobile pub on the back seat of the number twenty-seven.'

'So when did you pass?'

'Last Thursday.'

'And you asked me out immediately.'

'You should be flattered.'

'I am,' she said.

She thought this was endearing and odd. So weird it had to be true. What was all the fuss about? The driving test hadn't mattered to Rachel. Her parents had always had a car. It was just another domestic appliance, like a fridge or a washing-machine, so when the time had come, she'd learned how to use it. It hadn't bothered her whether she passed or failed so, naturally, she'd passed first time. Dave sensed this so spared her the full story of his pathetic and irrational obsession. This was a pity because a genuine display of heartfelt underprivileged passion was something she had never encountered and would have made him even more attractive.

Dave had spent countless days out with his mates during the school holidays on Red Rover tickets, jumping on and off buses all over London, so he knew his way around fairly well. As long as he stuck to the bus routes. He'd only been driving for a few days and was wary of becoming trapped in the maze of no-right-turns, one-way streets and general pitfalls that are planted like landmines all over the West End to separate those who knew from those who didn't. And, in Dave's view, there were few things in life as uncool as a man who didn't know where he was going.

Luckily, he remembered that route thirty-two offered the chance of a world tour. After a gentle stroll around the Serpentine, he suggested this to her.

'A world tour?'

'Yep,' he said, starting the engine, and heading towards Marble Arch. 'Who needs to go abroad when you can just go up the Edgware Road?'

As they approached Marble Arch, Dave began to explain. He wished he'd had Ronnie Hilton on his tape singing 'Around the World', though Jonathan Richman's 'Road Runner' was a fairly apt substitute.

'This end is like the Middle East,' he said, pointing out the well-dressed Arabs having coffee at pavement tables outside Lebanese cafés. 'Further up in Maida Vale, it's quite mixed: a lot of Jewish people on the right towards St John's Wood, more Irish and West Indian on the left towards the Harrow Road. Into Kilburn, completely Irish. Cricklewood pretty much the same. Then over the flyover into West Hendon and Colindale where it becomes very Asian – sari shops, those funny sweet shops and great curry houses. Next up is Burnt Oak – very London, very Cockney. They cleared out the slums around the East End and Kings Cross just before the war and moved thousands of people out there. It's still cockles and whelks, "Knees Up Mother Brown", and "Ain't the Queen Mum got a lovely smile?" Finally you get into Edgware and it's very Jewish, but you'd know more about that than I do.'

'Oh, God, yeah. Funny enough, my mum and dad are looking for a house up there.'

'Really?' said Dave. The fact that people moved house seldom occurred to him. Most Kilravock Street tenants felt reasonably fortunate that the council had placed them there and, knowing they'd never have the money to buy a place of their own, were quite content to stay put.

'So you're moving?'

'Sooner or later, yeah.'

'How about your job? Edgware to Westbourne Grove would be a bit of a schlep.'

'Well, I'll probably have to pack it in anyway, once my A levels get nearer. There's only my sister and me so, as far as my dad's concerned, I'm the eldest son and he wants me to go to university. How about you? Do you want to go to university?'

'Dunno.' Dave shrugged. 'Never really thought about it.'

'No,' said Rachel, with a smile. 'I don't suppose you have.'

'I'm starving,' said Dave. 'I wonder if there's a McDonald's up here.'

'Better than that,' said Rachel, and she directed him to the B&K salt beef bar and introduced him to the low end of Jewish cuisine – the salt beef beigel. 'Jewish hamburgers,' she explained. The generous splotch of mustard on his beigel had given Dave an eye-watering prickle at the bridge of his nose that brought tears of laughter to Rachel's eyes before they floated back towards Willesden. Still dabbing his eyes, he said, 'I must introduce you to the delights of bacon and cabbage.' And, on realising that, as far as the Old Testament was concerned, his suggestion was tantamount to asking her to have sex with a goat, she laughed again.

Presently, as the mobile pub's maiden voyage neared completion, Dave was surprised to discover that this was the bit he was really looking forward to; dropping her off. Not because he was bored of her company – on the contrary, he couldn't remember enjoying himself so much on a date. It wasn't because he wanted to launch himself at her in a clumsy and ill-judged quest for carnal gratification, he just wanted to drop her off. He'd passed his driving test, he was a man. He'd looked after his girlfriend – if that's what she was – and had brought her safely back to her front door. Just pulling up the handbrake and saying goodnight filled him with braggadocio.

As for carnal gratification, he wanted it more than anything else in the world, but you wouldn't have thought so. First of all, he still wasn't one hundred per cent sure that she fancied him and that his attempt to kiss her wouldn't be met with an embarrassing rebuff. Also, his ingrained Catholicism made him feel that he had to ask permission to do anything – especially something as important as this. So he kissed her chastely on the cheek, said he'd see her at work as usual on Sunday and disappeared down Chamberlayne Road.

As Rachel let herself in she knew she would have to tell Suzy that her wonderful night had ended a little disappointingly. What's the matter with me? she wondered, the tears in her eyes not put there this time by laughter. Why, why, *why* doesn't he fancy me?

33

'So, are you going out with him, then?' asked Suzy.

It was a simple enough question, but one that Rachel found impossible to answer. How do you know when you're 'going out' with someone? What does it actually mean? Some couples are 'going out' but never go anywhere. Others go out together all the time but aren't actually 'going out'. Rachel and Dave had only been out once but the time they had already spent working together had put them on a sort of accelerated promotion scheme, already further ahead than some couples who had been 'going out' for months. Except, of course, that he hadn't tried to kiss her, so Rachel was convinced that he wasn't very keen.

Dave had gone home that night with the scent of her perfume still in his nostrils. He tried desperately to hold it there, breathing only through his mouth, so that the fragrance remained on the back of his throat. As long as it was there, he could imagine she was still with him and he couldn't wait until the next time she was. Hardly the behaviour of someone who isn't very keen.

The following Sunday, they worked their shift again but, for some reason, neither mentioned the previous

Wednesday. Dave was wondering whether his elabo-
rate mobile-pub routine had been a bit too weird and
that she had gone along with it just to humour him.
Had he blown it? He had to find out soon because the
minutes were ticking away. The kiosk had been closed
up, the hot-dog machine cleaned out, the stock-take
done and the surplus split fifty-fifty. As Rachel put on
her jacket to go, Dave said one word, 'Wednesday?'

'Yeah, all right,' she replied, and shot him one of
those coy, sultry smiles. The five seconds it took her
to leave seemed like hours, and as she disappeared
through the swing doors, Dave once again became
Rodney Marsh in the League Cup final. He ran the
length of the foyer, sprinted up the grand staircase and
leaped into the air on the landing outside Screen One,
arms aloft, shouting, 'Yes! Yes! Yes!'

On the second date, his approach was rather different. He hooted outside her door and she got into
the car. No mobile pub this time – funny once, a bit
stupid twice – and they drove up to Hampstead for
a stroll over the heath. As they got out of the car, he
leaned over and kissed her. Properly. Passionately. He
had seen thousands of kisses in the hundreds of films
he'd watched in the course of his work. He selected the
Paul Newman and Faye Dunaway version as performed
in *The Towering Inferno*, and went straight ahead and
did it. Twenty-four seconds later, they came up for
oxygen.

'Right,' said Dave, with a grin. 'That's that out of
the way, now let's have a nice time.'

Kissing someone properly for the first time can be a far more significant step than having sex. It immediately moves the relationship up several notches to a completely different plane, where touching, grabbing, hugging and stroking are all suddenly permissible. They wandered deep into Hampstead Heath, got completely lost and couldn't have cared less. He could put his arm round her now, giving their relationship a loving, informal warmth to replace the slightly awkward tension. Dave remembered Tony Harris telling him that the prostitutes around Bayswater were quite happy to let you shag them senseless but would never let you kiss them. That was deemed too intimate, reserved strictly for the person you were 'going out' with. Having crossed that threshold, Dave and Rachel now found themselves officially 'going out'.

Rachel might have been attracted to Dave initially because he wasn't Jewish and was therefore 'forbidden fruit'. It was an almost clichéd act of teenage rebellion but, very quickly, it had gone way beyond that. She loved the effort he put in to making sure she had a good time. He refused to take her either to the pub or to the pictures so each time she got into the Cortina she never knew where she'd be when they got out. It was as though Dave, delirious with his new-found mobility, was trying to make up for all those Sunday-afternoon drives he'd never had.

They were out all the time, largely because they had no desire to stay in. Dave couldn't bring her back to Kilravock Street: there wasn't room, she'd have to sit on the floor and then her head would be blocking the telly. She couldn't bring him back to her house. Although her parents would not have disapproved – not openly, anyway. How could they? He was a kind, intelligent, handsome young man, who adored their daughter and treated her very well. They might not have objected but they would have worried. He wasn't Jewish and, should the relationship continue, all sorts of problems would arise. Had they known about it, they would have hoped quietly that this 'friendship' would fizzle out in its own time. What did the pair know about love? What did they know about life? They were still so young. They had so much to learn.

But did they? It was hard to imagine two people happier in each other's company. You'd be unlikely to find two human beings so hopelessly attracted to each other – youth had nothing to do with it. Inexperienced golfers have scored holes in one, teenage strikers have hit hat-tricks on their first team débuts, the first film Orson Welles made was *Citizen Kane* – it does happen. Rachel had now overtaken Dave's Cortina as the most precious thing in his life. And by suggesting one night that they stayed in instead of going out she was about to become more precious than ever.

34

The sixth form at St Bede's was a great leveller. It brought pupils together who, previously, had hardly ever spoken to each other. Every year always had its hard boys and its more studious ones, and Dave had qualified as one of the less-hard hard ones. Nonetheless, after the fifth year, most of his mates had gone into the initially well-paid but subsequently poorly paid world of manual work, leaving him to make friends with the more studious types, with whom he wasn't expecting to get along. He'd been pleasantly surprised, particularly by the quiet, almost timid boy whom he'd only ever known as Zymanczyk and who was now his best friend.

He could confide in Andy – after all, they now shared enough secrets for each to send the other to Borstal. He felt able to tell Andy exactly how he felt about Rachel – how all the clichés were true. How the soppiest songs seemed to be written just for you. Andy nodded thoughtfully. He knew exactly what Dave meant. Only last week he'd discovered Elvis Costello's first album. He thought it best not to ask for it in Johnny B's, sensing that the very mention of the artist's name would provoke a terrifying rage in the proprietor, who thought that the 'specky little twat hijacking his idol's name was an act of unforgivable heresy. Instead, he 'bought' it at Harlequin simply for the track entitled 'Alison'. He played the plaintive paean over and over again and could never work out whether it made him feel better or worse.

On hearing Dave's tales of bliss he was consumed with envy. Not jealousy, envy. He wasn't jealous because although he could see how attractive Rachel was, he didn't fancy her. In his mind, no one could compare to Alison and this, of course, was what he could never admit. He thought about admitting it. Dave, of all people, would have understood, but Andy's shame was too great. For him, it wasn't only contemporary songwriters but seventeenth-century metaphysical poets whose words seemed particularly apposite. He recalled a line from John Donne, 'I was two fools, I know, for loving and for saying so' and decided that being one fool was quite enough.

He envied the fact that Dave's affections were reciprocated while his own never could be – but, then, he and Dave were very different creatures; you only had to look at their modes of transport. Dave's car, and indeed his whole life, was designed to carry passengers – he was voluble and gregarious, far more relaxed in those late-night shebeens than Andy could ever be. Andy's scooter was more suited to solo transport and his life had always been solitary. Despite his cool and immaculate appearance, he wasn't vain: his obsession with clothes was just a hobby and, like stamp-collecting, one that needed no other participants.

When he went out, he was accustomed to the attention that his clothes, and particularly his scooter, would attract. Just pulling up at the lights on such a magnificent machine made him feel like a busty blonde in a mini-skirt walking past a building site. People, especially dewy-eyed ex-Mods, now driving estate cars full of kids, actually wolf-whistled. It happened so often that he hardly noticed it now. However, the whistles he received one morning as he whizzed along South Africa Road caused him consternation and dismay. They came from two youths of about his own age, both wearing parkas, Levi's and Clark's desert boots. Oh, no, he thought, I'm not the only one. Please don't tell me there's going to be a full-scale Mod revival.

Gradually, it started to happen and Andy didn't know whether he wanted to be part of it or not. Out of curiosity, he and the Vespa had ventured into uncharted territory. He went over to east London one night, to a pub called the Bridge House in Canning Town to see a new Mod band called the Purple Hearts. On another occasion he crossed the river to the Thomas à Beckett on the Old Kent Road to see The Chords. The following week, he found himself in Islington to see The Beat at the Hope and Anchor, where he wasn't sure whether to love or loathe their ska version of 'Tears Of A Clown'.

As he stood among a throng of like-minded loners, he couldn't work out why he wasn't enjoying it, but on the way home on the scooter, the cool night air clearing the fug from his mind, he narrowed it down to two reasons. The first was that he was fifteen years too late: the second wave of Mods was nowhere near as stylish as the first. How could it be? Through Claud and Vaughan, he had been exceptionally lucky, but for other would-be Mods the clothes and scooters, which were so essential, simply weren't available.

To Andy, the whole Mod movement was far better as a vivid black and white fantasy than a tawdry pale colour revival that bore little resemblance to the original. And then there was the music. How could the rough, amateurish sounds of The Chords and the Purple Hearts compare to the sweet, sublime soul of the sixties? It was like comparing antique furniture with cheap reproduction. And for Andy, the final straw came when people proclaimed The Jam a Mod band and Paul Weller 'The Modfather'. It just showed how little they knew.

More importantly, Andy had no wish to be part of a crowd. The people at those gigs reminded him of the congregation at St Andrew Bobola's, all desperate to conform to some kind of creed, all looking for something to worship.

So would he move on and transmogrify into a Ted, a punk, a skinhead or a soulboy? Absolutely not. Why should he? He was there first and he genuinely loved the old music, the clothes and the scooter. His cousin Alison was now looking at him with a huge glint of admiration in her eye. And, as he filed into assembly with the rest of the sixth form, he decided it was worth it just for that.

35

It was the last full assembly that St Bede's would ever be able to hold, the last one where the sea of green blazers at the front could still be complemented by a small pool of black ones at the back. From September, there would only be green, the sixth form hived off to St Saviour's for ever. The next logical step, thought McLafferty, as he took to the stage, would be for Pete Roberts to suggest dispensing with the green blazers too. Scrap the uniform and, hey, let the kids express themselves. It was an emotional moment for McLafferty, more poignant than even he had realised it would be. Everyone in the hall could sense it too. For once, there wasn't the usual scuffling hubbub, which he would need to extinguish with a hard, steely glare. Six hundred silent faces stared up at him as he spoke.

'This is a very significant day for me,' he began. 'It marks the end of St Bede's as we have always known it, a school where boys could stay until they had completed their A levels and were ready to go out into the world, either to university or to take their chances in the great university of life. At which point I would shake their hands and say goodbye, knowing that I and every member of staff here had done our best to prepare each boy academically, socially and spiritually for what lay ahead. We would know that we'd done all we could and that the rest was up to him.'

He paused, then adopted a candid, almost self-deprecating tone that no one in the hall had ever heard before. 'I'm well aware,' he continued, 'of the criticisms levelled at this school. Too strict, too harsh – the word "brutal" occasionally crops up – but I can assure you that the end has always justified the means. When you come across an ex-pupil of St Bede's you will usually find a fine, intelligent, compassionate man with a strong sense of decency and fair play. Most have gone on to do very well in their careers and I, personally, am very proud of that. It's the reason that parents from all over London have wanted their sons to come here. Every year we could fill our places ten times over. And the boys, including all of you, whether you admit it or not, have been proud to wear the green blazer and even prouder to wear the black one, because you know that you had to earn the right to wear it. Sadly, from September, that will no longer be the case.'

Every word he had spoken so far had been the truth, as he saw it. Now, however, he began to lie. 'The fact that St Bede's will be turning comprehensive and admitting a wider cross-section of pupils, regardless of their ability, will do nothing to diminish its reputation. The fact that we will no longer have a sixth form is a shame, but St Saviour's will be a centre of excellence and I'm sure that anyone who goes there will be given every opportunity to do well.'

Then he reverted to the truth and said something that, even two minutes earlier, he'd had no intention of saying. 'I've been at this school for thirty-two years – more than half my life – and I feel that perhaps now would be a good time to move on and retire from teaching.'

This came as a palpable shock – particularly to the staff, who'd had no idea of McLafferty's plans. Father O'Shea was especially aghast: as deputy head, he would be expected to take over.

McLafferty continued, 'I've been offered the chance to return to pastoral duties, running a small parish not far from Loch Lomond, and at this stage of my life I think it's too good an opportunity to turn down.'

His voice remained calm and even. 'I'd like to thank all of the staff for their unstinting support in making St Bede's what it is and always has been.' He paused once more. 'But most of all, I want to thank you boys, your elder brothers, and anyone else who has attended this school over the last thirty-two years. I'm proud of each and every one of you, and will always be grateful to you for making my life's work so rewarding.'

He had held his tone right up to the last word but there was an audible crack on 'rewarding', which suggested that this hard, emotionless figure was uncharacteristically close to tears.

The younger boys, though surprised and moved, felt a sense of relief and good riddance to the old bastard. The older ones, however, Dave and Andy included, had known their headmaster a long time. Of course, they loathed him, but that loathing was undeniably flecked with grudging respect. They were starting to feel proud of who they were and what they now felt they could achieve, and they knew it was due, in no small part, to Johnny Mac. They knew him well enough to read between the lines. He would rather have died than relinquish his post. Why was he really retiring? What did he know that they didn't?

It wouldn't take them long to find out.

36

Dave, however, had something else on his mind: the fact that he'd never slept with anyone. He'd had sex loads of times but, on each occasion, had been wide-awake throughout. He had never actually spent the night with a girl, so the thought of this coming Friday and spending the night with Rachel was making him ill. Anyone who had seen him that day would have assumed that he was in the advanced stages of Sydenham's chorea. He literally couldn't sit still. He was fidgeting, pacing up and down, convinced that he had somehow swallowed Olga Korbut because someone inside his stomach was performing somersaults and flick-flacks.

Rachel's parents and her younger sister had gone to their house in Marbella the previous morning but, since Suzy's eighteenth birthday party was on the Saturday night and Rachel didn't want to miss it, she had been allowed to fly out by herself on Sunday morning

She remembered a piece of advice from a magazine – if you like him, sleep with him, but if you really like him, wait. Rachel did really like him, and she had waited long enough.

*   *   *

Dave, despite desperately wanting to, had never suggested they test out the Cortina's reclining seats and sports suspension. He was dying for this. Having shown Rachel a level of patience and chivalry he had never shown anyone else, he felt he had earned it.

It was the first date Dave had ever had that had started with a prayer. It was something along the lines of 'For what we are about to receive, may the Lord make us truly thankful' but since it was in Hebrew, he had no idea what he was saying.

'*Kiddush*,' Rachel explained. 'Like grace before meals.' Then she handed him a piece of chollah and a glass of red wine.

It was the traditional Jewish Friday-night ritual, and it was supposed to be comforting but fairly dull, and weighed down with religious significance. With Rachel's smooth, sallow complexion and velvet brown eyes subtly illuminated by candlelight, Dave had never found prayers so sexy. He had always been fascinated by this Friday-night meal and had frequently quizzed Rachel about it, so she had decided to indulge him with his own personal shabbat. He found the whole ritual so gentle and stylish, especially when he compared it with the equivalent in his own house: fish and chips out of the newspaper in front of the telly while guffawing at *Love Thy Neighbour*.

Sinatra's *Songs For Swinging Lovers* – recommended and supplied for the occasion by Johnny Birdsall – crooned softly from the music centre in the corner. 'He's a baritone with a two-octave range,' Johnny had explained to Dave's uncomprehending expression before sighing. 'In other words, he's a fucking good singer. Never mind all that smoochy soul stuff – too obvious. What's that you've got in your hand? Rose Royce, *Love Don't Live Here Anymore*. Love won't live anywhere if you take that along.' He handed him the Sinatra LP. 'This is what you want. Trust me.'

He was right, Sinatra's mellifluous swagger and Nelson Riddle's impeccable arrangements provided a backdrop of cool sophistication that was perfect for the occasion. If you wanted to caress and carouse like a grown-up, you could hardly look to punk, glam or disco for inspiration, but *Songs For Swinging Lovers* offered some idea of what it meant to be an adult. Rachel, hugely impressed, brought in the second course – chopped liver. Dave had had an aversion to liver ever since he worked at the Irish Meat Market. In fact, if working-class vegetarians had existed in the late seventies, he would have become one immediately. But this was different – coarsely chopped and sort of de-livered by the addition of onions and herbs. It was delicious. Next up was chicken soup. Again, this was not what he had been expecting. It bore no resemblance to the tinned creamy slime he was used to. It was a gorgeous clear broth, which tasted, amazingly enough, of chicken. By the time he'd worked his way through more chicken, this time served with tiny roast potatoes and fresh vegetables, a scrumptious confection known as lokshen pudding and a couple more glasses of red wine, he realised he had made a terrible mistake. His enthusiastic embracing of the Jewish Sabbath and his orgiastic immersion in its attendant cuisine had rather defeated the object. He had rendered himself unable to move, unable to breathe – full up to the throat. He had left just one sultana from the lokshen pudding untouched on his spoon. He knew that if he'd eaten it, he would have exploded. Sexual intercourse, even with the most desirable girl in the world, was the last thing he wanted.

Nonetheless, he was led by the hand, wheezing with indigestion and heartburn, up to Rachel's huge mauve bedroom with its own double bed. Wow – his own bedroom in Kilravock Street would have slid comfortably into her walk-in wardrobe. Every night, he slept on a narrower-than-normal single bed because anything bigger would not have fitted into his room. He collapsed on to the bed and began to laugh. He hadn't had much wine and there had also been a colossal amount of food to soak it up but he had no tolerance at all. This was a boy who could get drunk on a packet of wine gums. 'Oh, God, I'm sorry,' he spluttered. 'That food was so good. I can't even breathe.'

Rachel looked down at him and grinned. The mobile pub, his initial reluctance to kiss her, the Frank Sinatra LP and now this. Once again, he had confounded her expectations. She had been so nervous but he had unwittingly put her at ease. Nestling her head on his chest and almost causing him to vomit, she fell asleep in his arms.

* * *

At about three in the morning, Dave awoke to find that his stomach had flattened nicely while the bit beneath it had gratifyingly grown. In that gorgeous state of not quite awakeness, he and Rachel made love. It didn't last very long. At seventeen, it seldom does, but at least at that age a boy can swiftly offer a repeat performance, needing only a few minutes to reload the gun.

On the second attempt, he was as he had been for his driving test, much improved. He didn't make love *to* her: he made love *with* her. Making love *to* a girl always implied that she was just a passive recipient, taking no active role in the process. Rachel took a very active role and, in the throes of her passion made Dave feel as though they were re-enacting that famous scene from *Don't Look Now* where Donald Sutherland and Julie Christie made urgent, heartfelt love. The scene was not about the sexual act but about the two people involved in it. She was impressed by how long Dave was managing to keep going, having no idea of the mental exercises he was desperately employing to achieve this. Silently reciting his nine times table was always a good one, though on the previous attempt he'd only made it as far as 27. This time he sailed passed 108 and moved on to the 1966 England World Cup team: Banks, Cohen, Wilson, Stiles ... When he got to Nobby Stiles, he realised that just the mental image of that balding, toothless little man was enough to discourage any sort of climax ... Charlton, Hurst, Peters.

Back to the tables – the tens, the elevens, finally on to the twelves. He narrowly failed to reach 144 but was delighted to discover that it was Rachel's failure to hold back that had made him let go.

As he eased himself back and prepared to drift off into his first-ever post-coital sleep he thought that at that moment, full of love, lust and lokshen pudding, he had never, ever been happier.

37

As Rachel, too, drifted down into that sensual satisfying slumber, it hadn't yet occurred to her that falling in love, particularly for the first time with someone you hadn't planned on falling in love with, turns your life upside down, inside out and, while it's in the mood, back to front as well. Good becomes bad, bad becomes good; things that were fun are suddenly facile and meaningless, and the most mundane activities can become the most pleasurable sensations you've ever known.

The first thing Dave did was ruin Suzy's eighteenth birthday party. It wasn't his fault, he wasn't even there – not invited, working anyway. For months, Rachel had looked forward to this extravagant bash at the King David Suite near Marble Arch. What's more, she had fancied Michael Kaplan since she was thirteen and now, having split up with Sharon Charkham, he and his brand new Fiat X1/9 were just gagging for Rachel. She slow-danced with him to 'Wishing On A Star' – rude not to – but as he tentatively tilted his head to the right, she would quickly tilt hers to the left, until, after three and a half minutes he got the message. All she wanted was Dave, who then went on to ruin her twelve days in Marbella. This was something she always looked forward to – Edgware in the sun. A lot of her friends would be out there too, as would some of their hunky, beach-bronzed elder brothers. This time, however, even lying by the pool in glorious sunshine, her heart was in a grey and distant land, aimlessly cruising its scruffy streets in a second-hand Ford Cortina.

Without Rachel, Dave, back in Kilravock Street, felt bereft. It was as though he had been lifted to a lovelorn level he had never experienced before and someone had kicked away the ladder. He found himself counting the hours, as he had done on those wretched family holidays in Ireland, until a state of happiness could be restored. For her part, Rachel had also ruined a party in Notting Hill that Dave had been looking forward to. He'd gone there after the cinema had closed, and although he could see that it was crammed with booze, beautiful women and an earth-shattering sound system, his heart wasn't in it. He felt more like a spectator than a guest. He wasn't drinking, he was missing the love of his life, so after a couple of hours he made his excuses and left.

He walked out to his car with reggae still ringing in his ears. The thud of the giant bass bins had hammered its way inside his ribcage and given him an extra heart with an irregular beat. He'd had to leave the party early because he could no longer work out whether he was alive or dead. For the short journey home, there was no need to switch on the radio. He just wound down the windows and could still hear the booming, disjointed rhythms of Dennis Brown, Big Youth and King Stitt filling the cool night air.

It was ten past one when he put the key in the door so he was surprised to see the kitchen light on.

Oh, shit, the game was up. Joe and Eileen had always assumed he got home around eleven. They were always tucked up in bed and oblivious to the fact that it was often four or five hours later than that.

Dave's late arrival was the least of his mother's worries. In fact, as she sat sobbing at the kitchen table, she hadn't even noticed him come in. Tears were seldom seen at 76 Kilravock Street. It was a happy, but stoic household. Eileen was one of life's troupers, the sort of woman who gave birth in the morning and did three loads of washing in the afternoon. Dave was shocked and worried by what he saw. 'Mum?' he said gently, and although he was frightened of what the answer might be, he had to ask, 'What's the matter?'

The answer was tear-soaked and unintelligible but he did manage to make out the name 'Bill.'

'Who's Bill?'

'Bill,' she wept. 'The electricity bill. Your bloody Uncle Patsy. I knew I should never have got involved with his little scam. He's been getting me into trouble ever since we were kids.'

Uncle Patsy? Scam? Then Dave remembered the needle in the electricity meter.

'Bloody needle fell out, didn't it?' she explained.

'When?'

'Judging by the size of this bill, about five minutes after he put it in.'

'Oh dear,' said Dave, with a sigh

'Right through the winter I've had fan-heaters blasting in every room. It's been lovely, hasn't it?, not waking up to sheet ice on the inside of the windows, and we've been able to heat up that freezing cold bathroom. I switched the cooker over from gas to electric, and I've been using the washing-machine and spin-dryer without a second thought. And now this . . .' She handed him the crumpled electricity bill and said, 'It's usually about twenty-eight quid.'

Dave uncrumpled the bill. Ninety-three pounds fifty-six.

'What did Dad say?' was Dave's first question, and suddenly realised that the tears had been brought on by a lot more than an electricity bill.

'I haven't told him.' She sniffed.

'Yeah,' said Dave. 'Probably best not to. He'd go berserk.' It then occurred to him that his father wouldn't go berserk at all. It would be far, far worse than that. He would be 'disappointed'. His open happy face would fold into a sad, bewildered frown when he thought about his wife trying to con both him and the Electricity Board.

'He's upstairs, sound asleep. He doesn't know anything about it. Doesn't know anything about anything.' She sighed heavily. 'You've no idea what it's like being married to him.'

'You're not unhappy, are you?' said Dave, shocked at

the very idea that they might be. Divorce among Catholics was unheard-of. Catholic marriages were happy even if they weren't. Maureen Breslin, for example, was still happily married to a man she hadn't seen for twenty-odd years.

Eileen pulled herself together and attempted a wan, watery smile, 'No, of course I'm not unhappy. He's the nicest man in the world, God love him. He doesn't smoke, hardly drinks, wants nothing for himself and hands over all his money for me to run the house. He never complains. And he's not like some of those hypocrites up at the church – all smiles at mass and right bastards in their own homes.'

'So what's the problem?'

'Well, when we first came over, we had nothing. That was fine but . . . oh, I know this sounds awful, but by now I thought we might have a little bit more.'

Dave knew exactly what she meant. It was the same feeling that had made him so desperate for cash, clothes and Cortinas.

'I love him every bit as much as when I first met him. He's a man in a million. Every Sunday I'm told how lucky I am. All those old biddies up at the church who say, "Ah, you're married to a saint." It never occurs to them that I might be the saint for being married to him. He'll work at the gasworks till he retires, no interest in bettering himself. Can you imagine how hard it's been to stretch his meagre pay packet just to provide the basics for you and the girls?'

Dave looked down.

'Oh, don't worry. It's not your concern,' Eileen said, drying her eyes on a tea-towel, 'but . . . well . . . his bloody religion has robbed him of any ambition.'

Dave knew this was true. He, too, had been frustrated by his father's humility for as long as he could remember. Yet he also knew that there was another side to the coin. 'Yeah, but it's his religion that makes him such a good, unselfish man.'

'I know. And, to be honest, I wouldn't have him any other way. I knew it when I made my vows. For better for worse. For richer, for bloody poorer.'

And she began to cry again. 'How the hell am I going to pay this bill?' she wept, 'We'll get red letters, final demands, threats from the courts. And bloody Derek the postman will tell everyone. You know what he's like – he can't stop himself. Oh, the shame.' She buried her face in her hands once more and began to sob.

Dave had no choice. Saturday was always the most lucrative day. A double shift meant he had been fiddling since one o'clock in the afternoon. He took the proceeds from his pocket and placed them – four twenty-pound notes, one ten and one five – on the kitchen table.

His mother looked up as though she had just witnessed a miracle.

'Take it,' said Dave quietly, with more pride at doing this than he had ever felt about doing anything before.

'Oh, God,' she gasped, 'where did you—' Then she

decided she didn't want to know. 'Look, you can't be expected to – I'll pay you back.'

Dave shook his head. 'No,' he said. 'I think it's about time I started paying *you* back.'

38

'Well, I've seen Number One, and I've seen Number Two,' she'd sigh. 'Oh, well, I suppose I'd better see Number Three.' She was in her sixties, well-dressed, beautifully spoken, and she said the same thing every Saturday afternoon. She had never seen anything showing in Screens One or Two. She only ever came to Screen Three but, in her half-disguised embarrassment, she felt compelled to deliver this sad and unconvincing little prologue.

The other regulars didn't bother. Some would shuffle in and mumble, 'Numfree, please,' while others would say nothing: the mere raise of a shy, shifty eyebrow would be deemed sufficient to indicate which film they wanted to see.

The films, like those who came to see them, were fairly harmless. They weren't hard-core Dutch porn, just silly, almost innocent British sex comedies – a natural extension of What the Butler Saw machines, Donald McGill postcards and Carry On films. *Housewives on the Job* or *Confessions of a Window Cleaner* were about the limit of their depravity. The audience weren't perverts fumbling under grubby raincoats, they were just ordinary members of the public whose sex lives were either over or never likely to begin, there to see their humdrum fantasies brought to life.

Dave's fantasy was to see one of his teachers slide furtively into the queue for a ticket – McLafferty without his dog collar, perhaps, or maybe Father Quigley the parish priest without his. Best of all, though, would be Paddy Keane, the world's most sanctimonious man. Not content with receiving Holy Communion every Sunday, Paddy now stood alongside the priest giving it out too. Every Sunday, he would read from the letters of St Paul to the Corinthians, the Thessalonians or some other unfortunate group of people who had had no desire to hear from him. Paddy then took the collection plate round and gave a slightly reproving glance at any contribution which he thought was a bit on the light side. After mass, he would hold court outside in the car park, flanked by his ghastly wife and five ugly children. Even as a small child, Dave had found himself curiously repelled by the very sight of the Keane family, and particularly by the unctuous, smiling patriarch. There were plenty of good Catholics in the parish, his own father being a perfect example, who were neither conceited nor ostentatious about their faith. Why was Paddy so keen to be seen as holy? What was he trying to hide? Probably nothing, but the thought of being able to tell the world that he had torn Paddy Keane's ticket for *Come Play With Me* was something about which Dave fantasised every Saturday.

Deep down, he knew that this particular dream would never come true. If Paddy ever found himself seized by the urge to see Mary Millington naked, he'd make sure he yielded to temptation a long way from Kensal Rise. Dave had always been disappointed that among the Screen Three Saturday-afternoon stalwarts, he had never seen a face he recognised. However, on Wednesday afternoons, it proved to be different.

'Dave?' said a shocked and horrified voice. 'What are you doing here?'

'Well,' replied an equally shocked but slightly amused voice, 'I . . . er . . . I work here.'

'Well, yes, I knew that,' stuttered the first voice, 'but I thought that was only evenings and weekends.'

'And the occasional afternoon.'

'You won't tell anyone, will you?' the voice pleaded.

'Of course not,' said Dave. Then, for a few seconds, he and Derek the postman stood staring at each other.

Dave tried to make a joke of it. 'Pretty rich coming from you, Derek,' he grinned. 'You're the biggest gossip I've ever met. It's quicker to tell you something than put an ad in the *Kilburn Times*.'

Derek was in no mood for persiflage. He seemed terribly ashamed, but at the same time strangely liberated. 'Well,' he said, 'I know you all think I'm queer—'

'No, we don't,' said Dave, too quickly.

'Oh, come on,' said Derek, 'everyone does. They always have.'

'Wouldn't matter if you were,' said Dave, truthfully.

'Yeah, well, I'm not,' said Derek sadly. 'I've always

fancied women, they've just never fancied me.' Looking at the unkempt, overweight postman with a physique like a damp loaf of bread, Dave had to admit that it wasn't hard to see why.

'I've just never been particularly masculine. I was the boy at school who always played with the girls and, as I got older, the other boys just assumed I was a poof.'

'Did they bully you?' asked Dave.

'No, it was worse than that,' said Derek. 'They didn't bother. I wasn't even considered interesting enough to be bullied.'

Dave knew that Derek loved a chat but usually about other people's business. It must have been a refreshing change for him to talk about his own, although Dave was rather taken aback by his poignant candour. Derek was now in full flow. 'You know, Davey, you and I have a lot in common.'

Oh, Christ, please tell me we haven't.

'Just like you, I've got two sisters, only mine were much older. One eight years older, the other ten. I was obviously a mistake. Soon as they were old enough, they were off. One was a GI bride, went out to live in South Dakota, and the other one went off to Stevenage when they first built it, just after the war. I was going to be off too, but then Dad died and I just couldn't leave Mum. Not immediately, anyway. I was desperate to get off the estate. I must have been the only kid in Kilburn who was looking forward to National Service. When I got called up, I joined the Navy because I reckoned that was my best chance of getting away.'

'And did you?'

'Did I heck! I spent most of those two years behind a desk at the Admiralty. I was home every night for my tea. When I came out I went straight back to the Post Office and I've been there ever since. But you can get out, Dave, you must. You don't want to end up like me.'

Dave wanted to tell him how popular he was, how his tuneless whistling and cheery salutations brought happiness to almost everyone on the estate. But he knew that this wasn't what Derek needed to hear. This was not what he had wanted from his life. Pointing it out, even in the complimentary way it was intended, would only remind him of what might have been, what should have been but what plainly hadn't been.

Derek paused, gathered his thoughts and continued. 'Just remember one thing,' he said. 'Please, if you remember nothing else in your life, remember this. When you're a kid, life is weighted very much in favour of the rough kids. All that matters is how tough and streetwise you are, whether you can handle yourself in a row. The posh kids can't so they're the ones at the bottom of the heap.'

Dave wasn't sure where this was going. 'Yeah,' he said curiously. 'And?'

'Well, that state of affairs doesn't last. Gradually, the balance starts to shift – it's like a seesaw. Being tough becomes less and less important until it ceases to matter at all. It's the posh people, better-educated, more confident, who start to come out on top. And that seesaw never swings back. This carries on right through into old age. Posh people usually end up loaded, all their money nicely invested, plenty to leave in their will. Now the ones who were once tough kids finish up without a pot to piss in, worried about how they're going to pay their rent. Trellick Tower's full of them. All these years as a postman mean I've delivered to every sort of household – believe me, I know. So, just remember these two words – get posh.'

'Get posh?'

'I don't mean going all lah-di-dah and putting on airs and graces. Just get yourself qualified, develop a taste for nice things and move on. You've got your O levels. Now get your A levels, get to university and get out of Kilravock Street. I know it's not a bad place to be, but once you start thinking like that you're finished. You'll be there till they carry you down the road to Kensal Green cemetery.'

Suddenly Derek's onslaught of heartfelt advice was over and they both remembered why he was there. The wise and wordly man became timid and sheepish again. 'You won't tell Mum, will you?'

'Of course I won't.'

''Cause this is about the nearest I'll ever get to any sort of female companionship.'

Again, Dave felt almost obliged to say something along the lines of 'Hey, you never know.' But they both did, so he kept quiet.

As he wandered off towards Screen Three, Derek was forgetting that he hadn't done anything wrong. He'd finished work for the day, and was perfectly entitled to spend his afternoons however he saw fit. Dave, on the other hand, was breaking the law on two counts; by playing truant and by sitting watching a smutty film that he still wasn't old enough to see.

39

Rachel had become the person Dave talked to in his head, the one with whom he wanted to share whatever had happened to him that day. He was dying to tell her about Derek. It would do no harm, she didn't even know him. He had kept his word and not told anyone on the estate, but Rachel's knowing couldn't affect the poor postman. Dave was counting the hours until he could see her and tell her, and on Sunday at 1600 hours, he could finally stop counting. Rachel was back behind the kiosk, her caramel tan making her sexier than ever. Both felt the primal urge to rip off the other's unappealing man-made fibres and make immediate love on the foyer floor, but they had to wait six hours for even a peck on the cheek. They'd kept their relationship a secret from everyone but Andy. No reason, they just felt more comfortable that way.

The following Sunday, however, Rachel seemed different. Dave couldn't quite put his finger on what it was but things just didn't seem the same. She was as keen as ever, if anything even more so, but she seemed a bit serious. Perhaps this was what people meant by 'getting serious'. Oh, God, he hoped not. Their relationship was 'serious' specifically because it wasn't.

Perhaps she had met someone else in Spain. He remembered how he had once two-timed Bernadette Ward. He had been slightly distant, over-compensating now and again with a sudden guilty burst of affection. This possibility saddened him but he was neither jealous nor possessive. He had never suffered from are-you-looking-at-my-bird? syndrome. What was the point? He'd been quick to work out that all you could ever do in a relationship was your best. You couldn't be perfect – nobody could. All you could do was treat a girl well enough to ensure that she didn't want to go off with anyone else. If she still did, well, there was nothing you could have done anyway. By the end of an unusually quiet shift, he had to ask, 'Everything all right?'

She looked ashamed and guilty. Oh, no: Dave's instincts had been right.

'I'm late,' she said quietly.

Dave still didn't get it. 'Late for what?'

'My period,' she explained, as though she were talking to a five-year-old, which she might as well have been.

Dave hadn't done Human Biology for O level but knew enough to grasp that this was not good news. 'But I – I – thought you were on the pill,' he said, in bewilderment.

'Well, you thought wrong. I got my dates mixed up. I thought we'd be all right.'

Dates mixed up? Dave's mind had to zoom back to the horribly embarrassing sex-education lessons with

Father Ryan, which at St Bede's were, rather tellingly, part of RE. He vaguely remembered something about the 'rhythm method' and it having nothing to do with dancing.

On the night, he had considered bringing a packet of condoms but since he'd never got the hang of using them, he'd fallen back on two reasons for their absence: one was that contraception was strictly forbidden by the Catholic Church, and the other was that he hadn't wanted to look presumptuous. Now, like so many teenage boys before him, he'd have given anything to turn back the clock and look presumptuous.

'Still,' he said, scrabbling around in the dark for some sort of bright side, 'it's not definite.' He thought of Rizzo, the old slapper from *Grease* squealing with delight at Kenickie, her boyfriend, 'I'm not pregnant!'

On the way home, however, he gazed up at Trellick Tower and wondered whether, despite all his intentions, that was where he was going to end up. Having to 'stand by' his girlfriend, who had been disowned by her family, marrying her in a shabby, joyless registry office and living in claustrophobic poverty on the twenty-eighth floor.

He'd thought it best not to ask her whether or not she was going to keep the baby until he knew whether or not there was even a baby to keep.

The next couple of weeks brought the return of Olga Korbut to his stomach. This time the constant flick-flacks made him feel cold, depressed and ill. Rachel, naturally, was even more troubled by her stomach but prayed that there was nothing more than butterflies inside it. Her prayers were in vain and, when she told Dave the news he obviously didn't want to hear, she was reassured by his calmness. Years of awaiting various forms of barbarism at St Bede's had taught him that the anticipation was usually worse than the punishment. He was fine. At least he now knew that Trellick Tower was a distinct possibility.

'I'll support you,' he told her gently, 'whatever you decide to do.' Dave had omitted to mention the great big caveat which accompanied that statement and read 'as long as you don't decide to keep the baby'. As a Catholic, he had been brought up to believe that human life began at conception and that abortion was murder. Indeed, in a rare show of political militancy, his parents had both taken part in a mass rally – in this case a mass followed by a rally – and marched from Kilburn to Downing Street to protest against David Steel's 1967 bill through which abortion had been legalised. Yet that sacred tenet, everything he was supposed to stand for, was abandoned in a nanosecond when he gave himself the stark choice between spending his life in Trellick Tower or 'murdering an innocent child'. He was ashamed to say that it was no contest but, fortunately, he didn't have to make that decision.

'So, what are you going to do?' he asked.

'I'm having it out on Thursday,' she replied, as though it were a troublesome tooth. 'I know it sounds callous but, realistically, what choice have I got?'

At that moment, Olga Korbut stopped flick-flacking

and Dave's first selfish thought was, thank God for that, although he knew that this was probably not the sort of thing for which God would want to be thanked.

He drew her gently towards him in an embrace full of concern, relief and guilt. 'Do you want me to come?' he offered, trying not to sound as though he was hurrying her along.

'No, it's fine,' she said. 'Suzy's going to come. It's more of a girl thing.'

'Well, do you want me to pay for it?' he said, now trying to assuage the guilt he felt for not being the one who'd have to experience it.

'No,' she said, with a watery smile. 'I've nicked almost as much money as you have. Mind you, this wasn't quite how I intended to spend it.'

That was when the rush of Catholic guilt tidal-waved over him. What goes around comes around. He'd had it too good for too long. This was his punishment for all the cash he'd stolen. Except that it wasn't. He was getting away scot-free. Rachel was the one being punished. Perhaps Jewish guilt and come-uppance were even more severe than the Catholic variety.

Rachel was lying. Suzy wasn't going with her. She might have been her best friend but even she couldn't be trusted with this one. Rachel couldn't risk having half of north London gossiping about her. Even if Suzy kept quiet, there would still be a certain 'I told you so' about her kindness and support. That's what happens when you go out with a *yok*.

No, this was something she would have to go through alone. There was a very good clinic in Finchley, well known for terminating Jewish (or, more often, half-Jewish) pregnancies, but it was too close to home. Instead, she drove out to a discreet place in Twickenham where a friendly doctor who introduced herself as Sally told her what she told all patients. 'Just remember,' she said, 'that terminations are a lot more common than you think. I can almost guarantee that a lot of girls you know, perhaps some of your closest friends, have been through this but obviously they're not going to tell you about it any more than you're going to tell them.'

This, although undoubtedly true, did nothing to allay the fear and loneliness she felt as the anaesthetist put her to sleep.

The following morning, as she drove back across London, she felt numbed and empty, more guilty and less relieved than she had anticipated. For the first time in her life, she knew the real meaning of being too upset to cry.

She also knew that she never wanted to see Dave again. This wasn't strictly true. She was desperate to see him again, but knew that she couldn't. His presence in her life would always remind her of this harrowing experience so she'd have to cut him out completely. On the one hand, she blamed him for making her pregnant in the first place, and on the other, she felt guilty for having let him assume that she had taken precautions and for the enormous distress she must have caused him. She was moving out to Edgware and leaving the cinema anyway. Her A levels were looming, and perhaps if she threw herself into her work, then Dave Kelly and his mobile pub would soon be forgotten forever.

Dave, brooding alone in Kilravock Street, felt the same way. He was desperate to see her, too, but had neither the maturity nor the experience to get over this. He felt guilty that he hadn't taken precautions but also resentment that she hadn't either. Best not to see her again. Her sudden departure from his life and the great gaping wound that she had left made him realise that, emotionally at least, he hadn't got off scot-free at all. For the first time ever, he felt that plunging himself into his studies would be the best way to forget.

However, since he was being forced to swap St Bede's for St Saviour's, this was not going to be as easy as he thought.

40

It was a disaster from day one. Dave, Andy and every other ex-member of the Lower Sixth at St Bede's were subjected to the most alarming culture shock. They were expected to complete their studies with unfamiliar teachers in an extremely unfamiliar environment.

Gone for ever was the brutal McLafferty. In his place was the nice, idealistic and utterly useless Mr James Langfield. Langfield wasn't the headmaster – no, no, he was the 'principal'. St Saviour's, as he liked to point out, wasn't a school: it was a 'college'. Those in his charge were not 'pupils', they were 'students'. It was Langfieldesque language that, in later years, would transform 'passengers' into 'customers' and the Police 'Force' into the Police 'Service'. Futile semantic exercises, which were carried out to disguise the fact that real, useful work was not. Langfield was the sort of person who had splinters in his backside from all the fences he'd sat on. Amiable, open-minded, always willing to see both sides of the argument, he was possibly the only man in Britain who neither loved nor hated Marmite. He thought it was okay. He thought most things were okay and, with no clear views or direction of his own, was exactly the sort of person you don't want as a headmaster or even a 'principal'.

The swottier pupils welcomed this new approach, having been cowed and terrified by the old one. Oh, they thought it was great. They were 'students' now and they had girls in their class. How amazing was that? And, hey, no school uniform – a chance to wear cagoules, brushed denim flares and Marks & Spencer's trainers. This was going to be fun, wasn't it? Not like strict, boring old St Bede's. They liked the fact that their new young teachers, barely out of college themselves, were relaxed enough to say, 'I'm Mr Chandler but you can call me Tim.'

However, those who felt this way were a small minority – boys who so far had had little experience of pubs, clubs and parties, those whose mothers and sisters were the only girls they knew. Boys who would acquire confidence later in life, then over-compensate desperately by playing zany, wacky drinking games in the student-union bar.

The vast majority were not quite so enamoured. Their response was rather different.

'I don't want to call you "Tim", I want to call you "sir". I don't want you to be my mate, I've got plenty of those, thanks, I just want you to be my teacher. I need to know where I stand, where the boundaries are. I want to feel that if I step outside them, I'll be punished. It's your job to help keep me on the straight and narrow. In case you hadn't noticed, "Tim", I've got some A levels to take at the end of this year and you're supposed to help me get them. Help me, Tim, help me.'

It's hard to imagine how any of the boys could miss the violent clerics of St Bede's but within a couple of weeks, most of them were missing their old mentors and tormentors dreadfully. These boys' parents had no concept of further education or careerism, so could offer no practical guidance. The boys needed the input and coercion of their teachers to get them through and, in this respect, they were failed miserably. It gradually dawned on them that, far from having had it hard at St Bede's, they'd had it easy. It's far easier to concentrate and learn when there's the constant threat of a thrashing if you don't. Once the boys' attention was secured, the teachers' passion for their subjects, their compendious knowledge and their great desire to impart it, started to come through. The boys, whether they liked it or not, found themselves propelled towards academic success.

At St Saviour's, 'Tim' and his ilk took the easy option. They put in very little effort under the guise of treating their students like adults. 'Hey, you're working for yourselves now. If you don't want to come to lessons, then that's up to you.'

How many teenagers would respond positively to that? Naturally, 'college' was rarely attended by Dave, Andy or a significant number of their classmates. Even when they did turn up, it wasn't a particularly edifying experience. Their teachers had neither the charm nor the experience to moisten their traditionally dry subjects. Tim, the head of English, singularly failed to convey the importance of W.H. Auden and his unique feel for human suffering. For many pupils, it took John Hannah, fifteen years later, in *Four Weddings and a Funeral* to bring that quality to life.

Still, Tim was encouraged by the fact that Dave, Andy and the rest of his English 'group' were not disruptive. In fact, they were extremely well behaved. When you're half-asleep, you generally are.

It didn't take Dave long to figure out that any time spent at St Saviour's would be about as much use as a glass eye at a keyhole. Under the tutelage of the various Tims, he had virtually no chance of getting the grades he'd need for university.

Andy's dreams of becoming the Petrocelli of Shepherds Bush now looked increasingly unlikely, as did any chance of following his father into dentistry. Although he had always scorned the idea, it had never occurred to him that he wouldn't gain the requisite qualifications, and that the nearest he'd get to being a dentist would be helping Mrs Wizbek with the filing.

The boys' futures, which had once looked so bright, despite the misery and oppression of St Bede's, now seemed, in the sunny, liberal environment of St Saviour's, exceedingly bleak.

Their one consolation was the cinema. The cash and worldly experience that each had acquired from working there had made them the very consuls of cool. Almost every girl at St Saviour's wanted a lift home either in Dave's Cortina or on the back of Andy's

Vespa. They had replaced Cronin and Harte as the twin strikers and top scorers of their year.

They had very little competition. Harte, no doubt inspired by Warren Beatty in *Shampoo*, had embarked on a career as London's most libidinous hairdresser. Cronin, meanwhile, like so many mature teenage heart-throbs, was way ahead of his time. He was the first one into the pub, up the aisle, into the delivery room and on to the council-house waiting-list. And twenty years on, at the School reunion, he would be the fat, bald, old-looking bloke with little to say for himself. And, rather sadly, still ahead of his time: the only one with a grandchild.

This was the position Dave had always wanted to hold, that of most-fancied bloke in his year but, like Andy, he had found himself in love with a girl he could never have – or, at least, in his case, never have again. Rachel could convey more sex appeal in the raise of one eyebrow than the rest of the girls at 'college' could muster collectively with their whole bodies. He missed her wit, style, elegance and beauty. He missed the easy companionship of having a girlfriend, and even though there were plenty of girls whose heads had been turned by his cool confidence and even cooler Cortina, he couldn't have cared less about any of them.

Some of the more earnest students had already begun to pair off. One couple, Mark Halsey and Jane Murphy, seemed inextricably entwined. They walked around the 'campus' as though they were taking part in a three-legged race and were particularly proud of their new

T-shirts. Jane's said, 'Hands off – I'm Mark's', while Mark's proclaimed, 'Hands off – I'm Jane's'. Since Jane's nickname was 'Pusbucket' on account of her acne and Mark's was 'Frankie', short for Frankenstein, on account of his comedically large forehead, it was unlikely that anyone anywhere would want to put their hands *on* either of these two. In his mind, Dave tried to be charitable. Wasn't it sweet that two such unappealing creatures had found each other and were so in love? In a word, no. It was quite revolting, and he found himself gripped by the urge to vomit profusely over their smug, deluded and horrible T-shirts. In his opinion, these two nauseating specimens typified St Saviour's and, before long, its utter futility had convinced him that the most sensible thing he could do was spend his afternoons working at the cinema, amassing as much money as possible. He'd need it to supplement the miserable life on the dole that seemed to be awaiting him.

It wasn't long before Andy came to the same conclusion. They were more grateful than ever for their employment at the cinema: it saved them from noticing how cruelly and randomly their education and futures were being snatched away from them. It saved them from submitting to evil thoughts of sneaking back into 'college' one night with matches, rags and petrol.

Thank God they still had the cinema.

Though not, it would seem, for very much longer.

41

The car was going too slowly – dead giveaway. The first thing any driver who knows he is over the limit will do is drive very, very carefully. He might as well put a sign on top of the car alerting the local constabulary: 'I'm pissed. Please pull me over.'

So, to Sergeant Alan Keal's weary, seen-it-all-before eye, the sight of a car crawling along a deserted Ladbroke Grove at three in the morning at twenty-six miles per hour was cause for suspicion.

Tony Harris was driving and, as usual, when he knew he was two sheets to the wind, was wearing a chauffeur's cap. This did not look out of place at the wheel of a Jaguar and always ensured that he was spared the attentions of the Old Bill. Generally chauffeurs don't drink and drive, and are rarely stopped. On this occasion, however, Keal and his rookie assistant, PC Prentice, gently overtook the car and motioned for Tony to pull over, having noticed he was wearing his cap back to front.

This was not good news. Neither Keal nor Prentice were regulars at the Bramley Arms. In fact Prentice, fresh from cadet school, would have had trouble getting served. No more than twenty, he looked like a child at a fancy-dress party. Surely that was a toy truncheon and they were plastic handcuffs. The old maxim was certainly true about knowing you're getting old when the police start looking younger. Mind you, you weren't really getting old until popes started looking younger. Keal looked distinctly irascible as he began the standard procedure.

'Would you get out of the car, please, sir?' Only the police can make the word 'sir' translate into 'you piece of shit'.

'Unusual way of wearing a cap, sir.'

Tony thought it best to remain silent.

'Been drinking, have we, sir?'

'Er . . . well, you know, just a glass of wine.'

'Pint glass, was it, sir?'

Oh, Christ, a comedian as well. Tony smiled along with Keal's little crack. Pass the attitude test, he thought. That's the thing with the Old Bill. They're quite willing to play ball as long as you remember whose ball it is. If they can see you're harmless, they'll usually let you go.

Not when you've been drinking and driving, they won't.

'I'm afraid I'm going to have to ask you to take a breath test.' The boy Prentice silently passed the breathalyser to Keal. 'If you could just blow into the bag, please.'

'And what if I don't?' asked Tony, just wondering.

'Then,' said Keal impatiently, 'you'll have to accompany us to the station for either a blood or a urine test'.

Tony weighed up the odds. He'd been gambling round at Totobags in Blenheim Crescent. He'd hit a lucky streak and was wondering if it was still with him. He decided to have one more throw of the dice. 'Okay,' he said. 'I'll come down to the station.'

'Very well, sir,' said Keal, with a weary sigh. 'If you insist.'

Tony climbed into the back of the panda car and Prentice, watching in solemn silence, couldn't understand why Tony was wasting everyone's time like this. Ladbroke Grove police station was two minutes away: he was hardly going to sober up by then. And, anyway, he was so far gone that they could have breathalysed the inside of the car and the crystals would have turned bright green.

When they arrived at the station, Keal marched Tony into an interview room. 'It's all right, Prentice,' he snapped. 'I'll deal with this.'

'Righto, sir,' replied the child in the funny hat.

Blimey, thought Tony, it speaks. He was also struck by much more sobering thoughts. How could he have been such a fool, putting that fucking cap on back to front? It was only a matter of time before he got his collar felt. Oh, he'd played right into Patterson's hands now. Drink-driving was grounds for dismissal and Patterson would have no qualms about wielding the P45 that would introduce bingo to Westbourne Grove. By his own stupidity, he was about to bring down the huge red velvet curtain for the very last time.

Sergeant Keal, who clearly had better things to be

doing, was not happy. 'I'll be back in a minute,' he said, and went out. On his return, he dropped the sarcasm and descended into plain, straightforward anger.

'For fuck's sake, Tony,' he growled, 'what the hell do you think you're playing at?'

Tony buried his face in his hands. 'I know, Alan, I know. What can I say?'

'How about, "I'm a stupid fucking idiot and I could have killed someone"?'

Tony nodded remorsefully and Keal continued, 'If I'd been with anyone but Prentice, I could have just taken your car keys, bunged you in a taxi, end of story. But he'd never buy that.'

'Who? Dixon of Camberwick Green?'

'Oh, don't underestimate him. He may look like he's just left kindergarten but he's keen, very keen. Does everything by the book. Bullied at school, I reckon, and now he's going to take it out on everyone else. Should have been a traffic warden, but for the time being I'm lumbered with him.'

Tony shook his head. His lucky streak really had run out now. Even he couldn't talk, bribe or beg his way out of this one. They sat staring for a moment at the sample bottle on the table in front of them. 'I'll lose my job,' said Tony, more to himself than to Keal.

'I'd lose mine, Tony, for a lot less than this.'

'The cinema will close down.'

'And whose fault will that be?'

Tony's gaze returned to the sample bottle. Any minute now, he would have to fill it and, in so doing, consign himself and the cinema to history. However, the dice he'd thrown by refusing the breathalyser were still rolling. Then they stopped.

'I've been drinking myself tonight,' said Keal.

Tony was puzzled by this sudden confession.

'Only water, mind. And do you know something, Tony?'

'What?'

'I'm dying for a piss.'

Tony looked at the dice: double six.

Keal unzipped his fly and filled the bottle. Tony wanted to weep with gratitude: such was his popularity around Notting Hill that a seasoned police officer was willing to risk his own career to save Tony's.

'Okay, Mr Harris,' he said, all official again, 'we'll send this sample off to the lab. You're free to go.'

Tony fell into the nearest taxi. When he emerged fifteen minutes later outside his terraced house in Acton, birds were twittering and milkmen whistling. He was almost sober now and genuinely shaken by his ordeal. He vowed that it would never happen again, and he meant it.

Like he did last time. And the time before that.

42

Tony awoke a few hours later to the sound of a jumbo jet landing by the side of his bed. Ungluing one weary eye, he realised that it was Linda, his wife, and her purgative use of the vacuum cleaner. Before he had a chance to pitch face first into the traditional post-binge bad mood, which only another drink, a stodgy fry-up or both could alleviate; he realised that he wasn't in a bad mood at all. He was Scrooge on Christmas morning, delighted to be alive, delighted to have been given a second chance, and still be the proud owner of a job, a wife and a driving licence.

He unglued the other eye, tried to get out of bed, failed, lay back on the pillow for a moment and thought about stunt doubles. In the thousands of films he had seen, the stars' dangerous stunts were invariably performed by doubles. Christ, wasn't it time he got a stunt double to do his drinking for him?

Once she was satisfied that the vacuum cleaner had awoken him from his drunken slumber, Linda would hit him with the deafening roar of silence. Far more effective than nagging. The nagger gives the naggee the right of reply, the chance to present a different point of view. The naggee can then launch a counter-attack, perhaps blaming the nagger for whatever has happened. The naggee's own grievances can then be aired, and item one is invariably a hatred of being nagged.

Tony Harris, once again the recipient of the passively aggressive silence, was denied these options and he couldn't bear it. He was a great apologiser. He'd had plenty of practice, and once he'd shown his contrition, he expected instant forgiveness and *carte blanche* to do it all over again. This morning, however, he thought it best to say nothing, not least because every cell of his anatomy was severely hung-over, including his tongue, which no longer seemed to fit, and he wondered whether he'd ever form a coherent sentence again.

Staggering up and managing to remain vertical at the fourth attempt, he tried, in his self-imposed silence, to focus his thoughts. Why did he do it? Why did he never spend his evenings with the wife he adored, who had borne him those three lovely children? Well, it was work, wasn't it? Nature of the business, unsocial hours. Millions of men have to do the same in theatres, restaurants, nightclubs and factories up and down the country. So why didn't he come home? Why the after-hours drinking? Why was he on first-name terms with Bayswater prostitutes, like Pat from Moscow Road? Why would a happily married man be out flirting and carousing almost every night of the week? Why?

Part of it was because it made no difference. Linda usually went to bed at eleven, so on the rare occasions that he had rushed home to see her, he was usually five minutes late, so he might as well have stayed out until four in the morning. His life was like that Marty Feldman sketch where the timid suburban husband would say to his wife, 'Just off to put the cat out, dear,' and then embark on all sorts of fantastic, swashbuckling adventures. Except that Tony's adventures were real. Why did he feel the need to have them?

It was simply because one part of his life sustained the other. He needed the heedless drinking and gambling to make him appreciate the happiness and stability of the life he had at home. Likewise, he needed the boredom and drudgery of his home life to heighten the buzz of drinking contraband rum and playing three-card brag. Despite appearances, he was never unfaithful, although he had nightly opportunities. Like many people, he just liked to know that he could be if he wanted to. It wasn't the going to the party that was important, it was the fact that he had been invited.

Still, even with a hangover that had left him barely able to see, speak or walk he was feeling lucky this morning. He'd just have to feel the pain and gamely stagger through it.

He called out to Linda. He wanted to tell her how much he loved and appreciated her but knew it was pointless. No matter what he said, there would be no reply. Not for a couple of days at least. With a momentous effort, he managed to make a brief phone call before he hauled himself round the corner to Len's Café: having witnessed this sight many times before, Len would take one look at him and administer the full English breakfast with a huge mug of strong black coffee.

As he left the house, Linda heard the clumsy slam of the front door. Shortly afterwards, she heard the doorbell. Silly sod's forgotten his keys. Well, he can just wait a minute. The bell rang again and, on seeing the outline of a figure in a crash helmet outside, she realised it wasn't her beloved spouse.

'Telegram for you.'

'Oh,' she said in bewilderment. 'Er . . . thanks.'

She opened it and read it:

SORRY, I LOVE YOU. BACK IN 20 MINUTES. I HAD
A GOOD NIGHT. LET ME TAKE YOU TO HARVEY
NICHOLS TO SPEND MY WINNINGS.

43

Tony had got away with it again, but even he was forced to concede that he had no more tricks up his sleeve. Next time, her silence might be permanent, her only communication through solicitors' letters. It was a sobering thought. Literally.

His relief that the telegram had worked was what carried him through the day, but when the shopping trip was over, his marriage remortgaged for a taxi full of Harvey Nichols bags, the evil hangover returned with a vengeance. 'Got to get to work a bit early,' he said, using his last milligram of energy on a sunny, apologetic smile. '*Quadrophenia*, you know. It's really busy.'

Thank Christ, he thought, for those two boys. Andy and Dave they were a real find. Tonight – in fact, any night – he could leave them to run the place. He stumbled into the foyer three hours early with a face so white and eyes so black he looked like a cross between Chi Chi the giant panda and Dusty Springfield. He managed to locate the office door, fall through it and collapse with a groan on to the sofa. Maureen, sitting at her desk, didn't even glance up from her paperwork. She knew he wouldn't stir for hours but she, too was reassured that those two boys would take care of everything. It would be busy – *Quadrophenia* was proving enormously popular because, in 1979, Sting was cool.

He was worshipped by women and admired by men for both his physical pulchritude and his musical genius. Stars didn't come much bigger than Gordon Sumner, so when he rode along the seafront in Brighton, blond hair cut short and immaculate, Italian suit and long leather coat, astride a beautiful scooter in *Quadrophenia*, thousands of girls almost passed out with excitement.

And so did one boy. Sitting on the usher's seat at the back of Screen One, finally watching the film he had been so desperate to see, Andy Zymanczyk felt his knees go weak. He understood now how teenage girls had let out involuntary screams at the sight of the Beatles, the Osmonds or the Bay City Rollers. He, too, let out an involuntary emission. 'Fucking hell!' he cried, at the sight of Sting's magnificent Vespa. 'That's my scooter.'

They'd added an extra rack at the front to accommodate a ludicrous amount of lights and mirrors but it was unmistakably his Vespa GS160, and now he knew why Claud had borrowed it.

'I couldn't tell you,' Claud explained, with a laugh. 'God knows why but their lawyers made me sign a bit of paper saying I would not divulge any secrets about the production. I supplied every one of those scooters – most of them were shit-heaps, took a hell of a lot of work to get them going, especially the old Lambrettas.

I'd been looking everywhere for a good original GS. I couldn't believe it when you turned up with one. God, I'd have paid money to see your face when that Sting rode up on it. What did you think?'

There were two answers to this. The first would have been the truth.

'Well, I don't know, really, Claud, I've got mixed feelings. I'm naturally shy, you see, and I know it's unusual in a Mod but my obsession with my scooter, my clothes and my music has nothing to do with narcissism. It's my own private escape. The fun, flamboyance and danger of the Vespa, the rarity and elegance of my apparel, the hedonistic influences of American music, English tailoring and Italian scooters were my way of coping with the regimes of Polish austerity at home and Irish Catholicism at school. Don't get me wrong. I adore that scooter and I can't thank you enough for restoring it but I love it for what it is, not for the fact that Sting rides it in *Quadrophenia*. I adore the sense of fun and freedom it has given me. You should see me on it. The new engine has made it so fucking quick and I've become really skilled at weaving in and out of the traffic. It's the best fun I've ever had. Now everyone at school has seen the film and more girls than ever are queuing up to ride pillion. Thing is, I never bring a spare helmet. I just tell them it's too dangerous, which, of course, just ramps up their desire for a lift home. The truth is something I can never admit. I may be riding the coolest scooter in the world but my parents have no idea that I ride it. They'd go mental if they ever found out. I'd have to sell it and they'd never let me work in the cinema again. Funny, really, I've passed my mum on it quite a few times. She crossed the road right in front of me on Shepherds Bush Green. I thought she might recognise the parka but she didn't. Anyway, only one person has ever been on the back of that scooter and, as far as I'm concerned only one person ever will.'

However, in reply to Claud's question, he thought it best to give the second answer, also true. 'Yeah, it was amazing. I couldn't believe it.'

44

Guy Patterson was delighted with the figures. He smiled with relief and satisfaction. Despite the enormous success of *Quadrophenia*, the numbers had finally dropped below what was commercially viable. The Westbourne Grove Gaumont was making a loss. Not even Tony Harris could defend it now. The game was up. Or rather, as he liked to look at it, another game was about to begin. Eyes down for a full house.

However, Patterson was not one to gloat. Ambitious, yes; spiteful, no. He'd decided to be magnanimous in victory. 'Well, Tony,' he smiled, after their perfunctory handshake, 'I've got to hand it to you.'

Tony rolled his eyes and looked at his watch. 'And what exactly have you got to hand to me?'

'Well, I underestimated you. I never thought you could keep it going for so long.'

Tony was in no mood to be patronised. 'Oh, spare me the crap, Patterson. We both know why you've got me down here. You're closing the cinema. Please don't insult me with one of your "with the greatest regret but at the end of the day it's the bottom line" speeches. You've been wanting to turn the place over to bingo for years and now your bosses are finally letting you do it. Well, I hope you're pleased with yourself.'

Until that moment Guy *had* been pleased with himself. He really was trying to break the news amicably and compassionately, but Tony clearly hadn't read the script.

'Of course I'm not pleased,' he said.

'Prove it.'

'What do you mean, prove it?

'Prove it by fighting the decision.'

'Tony, believe me, I'd love to, but at the end of the day it's a commercial decision and—'

Tony cut him short. 'You know, I actually *over*-estimated you. I thought you were a man of vision. I thought you were Don Quixote.'

Patterson was confused now. Don Quixote? Wasn't he in *The Godfather*?

'Tony, I am a man of vision. And, much as you may not like it, bingo is the future. We've had this discussion so many times. Cinema is dead and buried. These new video-recorders—'

Tony cut him short again. 'That's what I'm talking about. These new video-recorders are going to revive everyone's interest in film. It's already starting to happen in the States. You can borrow films like library books and watch them on your video machine. If you were a man of vision, you'd be playing the long game. Instead of tearing cinemas down, you'd be investing in them – better seats, Dolby Surround Sound – so that when people come flocking back to the cinema, which they will, you'll be ready for them.'

'And if they don't?'

'Their appetites for film will have been whetted by all those videos, so I think they will.'

'But you don't know.'

'Oh, come on, nobody knows anything for certain.'

'Well, that's the difference between you and me, Tony,' said Patterson, condescendingly. 'You like to gamble with your money. You're in the bookies, you're playing poker, always hoping for that big win, which never seems to come. Now, me, I prefer my money in a high-interest savings account. Not so glamorous, maybe, not so exciting, but offering a far better chance of a return.'

He was pleased with his little analogy, but Tony found it rather unfortunate. 'I think that's a rather cruel irony, don't you?' he said quietly. 'All those mug punters playing bingo, always hoping for the big win that never seems to come. What they're doing is putting their money into this company's high-interest savings account.'

Patterson tried to bring an insincere trace of sadness to his smile. 'That's just the way it is,' he said, 'but they love it. If they didn't, they wouldn't come.'

Tony couldn't argue with this. 'But do we really need a bingo hall in Westbourne Grove? There are great big ones already in Kilburn and Shepherds Bush.'

'Too far away,' said Patterson, dismissively. 'They need to be within walking distance. People who go to bingo can't afford cars. Why do you think they're playing bingo in the first place?'

'Why can't you just give it time?' said Tony. 'Videos will lead to the rebirth of cinema.'

'When? Two years? Three? What if they don't catch on? We need to be making money now. And bingo is doing just that for us in every site we've converted.'

'So, when are you planning to convert this particular *site*?' Tony almost spat the last word, unable to think of his beloved cinema as a mere plot of land.

'Well, obviously not for three months,' said Patterson, 'that being the lead time on the films you've already booked. But we simply cannot let the place run at a loss for any longer.'

'Three months, eh?' Tony muttered morosely,

'Three months,' confirmed Patterson. 'If you can turn it round in three months, it can stay open.'

This was his clumsy, ill-judged attempt at levity. They both knew it was impossible, like trying to turn round an oil tanker the size of the *Amoco Cadiz*. Tony thought of his patient, adoring wife and three children and faced up to the fact that he'd better spend those three months looking for another job.

45

Linda Harris was just about to go to bed when she heard a sound she didn't often hear: her husband's key in the door. And even when she had heard it, it was usually followed by a lot of staggering, stumbling and bumping into things. But not tonight. He walked into the sitting room, raised a resigned eyebrow and simply said, 'It's all over.'

Linda knew exactly what he meant and was overcome with relief. At last, after all those years of lonely evenings, she and the children would finally see more of him. He could work regular hours, they could be like a normal family. However, she took one look at him and stopped herself saying so. He looked like a loud, colourful and exuberant jukebox that had just been unplugged. His expression was not unlike Jack Nicholson's at the end of *One Flew Over the Cuckoo's Nest*, just after his frontal lobotomy. She knew in an instant that the man she had been unable to resist since the moment she met him was the man he was because of the Gaumont cinema. It was his love of that place and his pivotal role there that had put the wind in his sails and the spring in his step. Without it, would he still be the man she had always adored? She kept her response fairly minimal. 'How long?'

'Three months.'

'Well, you know, there are other cinemas.'

'I know.' He sighed. 'I know.'

Tony wasn't given to self-pity. He'd always felt that it was a rather repellent emotion, which people had no right to express. If someone else felt sorry for you, fine, but it wasn't your place to decide that you were entitled to sympathy. He smiled warmly but there was no power behind the smile. 'Something will turn up,' he said. 'It always does.' But he knew that nothing quite like the Westbourne Grove Gaumont was ever likely to turn up again.

Tony found himself going to bed at the same time as his wife, which was something of a novelty, and at the same time as most people in London, instead of several hours later.

The Zymanczyks were also going to bed, but Andy found it hard to sleep with the thought of the Gaumont cinema's imminent closure fuelling his insomnia.

A couple of hours later, however, he had dropped off and was having one of those dreams. We've all had them: the ones where you're not completely asleep, retaining sufficient consciousness to realise that it is a dream but not enough to have any control over it. Although you have half an idea of what's going to happen, you're still surprised when it does.

Andy's semi-dream involved a beautiful woman but

he was not enjoying it. The dream was not exactly erotic since the woman in question was Our Lady of Czestochowa and she wasn't very pleased with him. She'd escaped somehow from the gilt-framed picture downstairs and was now standing at the end of his bed. She folded her arms across her chest, and looked down at him sternly. 'All right,' she said flatly. 'Enough is enough.'

Andy knew what was coming

'Just because I haven't said anything,' she continued, 'doesn't mean I don't know what you've been up to. Contravention of the eighth commandment – "Thou shalt not steal".'

The dream then went a bit weird as dreams always do, and she briefly became Jack Regan from *The Sweeney*, slamming her fags on the table and shoving him up against a wall. 'You've been a very naughty boy.'

Andy discovered that it was also one of those dreams in which you open your mouth to speak but nothing comes out.

Regan morphed back into the Virgin Mary and she continued, 'I didn't say anything because I felt sorry for you. I've been hanging on that wall since 1962. I've watched you grow up and, grateful as I am for your parents' goodness and their devotion to me, it was always you I felt sorry for. You needed to have some fun, a life of your own and I was pleased to see that the cinema provided that for you. It's finally allowed you to be who you want to be.'

Andy nodded.

'Look at you,' she gestured to him with her hand, 'beautifully dressed with that fantastic scooter and all those records. I love them, especially "Heatwave" by Martha and the Vandellas – that's my favourite. I can hear you playing them from downstairs, and I know that just listening to them has put you in touch with your emotions, taught you about love and joy, about pain and heartbreak. They've taught you more about life than I ever could, but I'm afraid the party's over. The Gaumont is about to close down for ever. Tony will be down at the job centre and he's got a wife and three children. And how will Maureen cope?'

Andy's voice returned: 'But what can I do?'

'I'll leave you to work that one out. You're a clever boy. It shouldn't take you too long.'

And with that she was gone, leaving the dream to take one more surreal turn. Andy's last glimpse was of Our Lady of Czestochowa, umbrella aloft, dressed as Mary Poppins and disappearing over the rooftops of Shepherds Bush. It was an image that would remain with him for ever.

46

'A reading from St Paul to the Kellys.' There was a
pause. 'All right, just the one Kelly, David Michael
Kelly of 76 Kilravock Street, London W10.'

Dave's Catholic guilt had also come to haunt him
in a dream, but a very different dream, one with no
visual content just a disembodied voice. 'Who's that?'
he shouted.

'Well, who do you think it is?' said the voice. 'Weird,
isn't it? This is what it was like for me on the road
to Damascus. Got knocked off my horse, and I saw
the error of my ways – best thing that ever happened
to me.'

'What do you want?'

'Oh, I think you know the answer to that. When
I said to the Corinthians, "Through your union with
Christ Jesus you will become rich in all things," I wasn't
talking about clothes, records and cars. What you're
doing is wrong. It's theft. Fortunately you had the
sense not to steal from the Variety Club collection box,
although I know you were tempted. Now look what
you've done – that cinema's about to close down.'

'It would have closed anyway.'

'That's not the point. Your dishonesty certainly

hasn't helped. I've turned a blind eye to what you've been doing for too long. I mean, stealing from the sweet kiosk hardly compares with stoning Christians to death so I was in no position to criticise. But I found redemption and so must you, but it's almost too late.'

'What do you mean *almost*?'

But the voice didn't answer, leaving Dave to work it out for himself.

The following morning, as he parked the car in St Saviour's car park, Andy pulled up next to him on his scooter. Though neither gave details of the ways in which their consciences had manifested themselves in the night, they had both come to the same conclusion.

47

They had both decided that there were two ways of looking at it. One perfectly logical way would be to think that the cinema was closing anyway so they had three months to bleed it dry. Now was the time to steal like they'd never stolen before. Alternatively, they could yield to the force of long-overdue guilt. They could think of other people – Tony and Maureen, for example, who'd always been so good to them. They could consider old George, Lily, Doris and Ida, whose work at the cinema kept them from going senile (or, in George's case, even more senile). They could think of Les and Gary, the projectionists, both with young children and for whom no work could be found in a bingo hall. They could thank God, St Paul, Our Lady of Czestochowa and anyone else for all the money they'd had and decide to take no more. They could make sure that, from now on, every penny went where it was supposed to go, and if the fortunes of the Gaumont were reversed, who knows? It might even be reprieved. Got to be worth a try.

Despite common sense and natural greed pulling them towards the first option, innate Catholicism pulled them harder towards the second. And, as the old maxim goes, once a Catholic . . .

Behind the kiosk, however, Dave was still fiddling furiously. Patrons were being overcharged more than ever, but he didn't take a single penny from the huge surplus accrued by the end of each shift. Instead, he would spend it over at the box office in an effort to boost the takings. He was beginning to regret being so derisive about people with Post Office savings accounts. He had a car to run, a lifestyle to maintain, people to impress, and was now in dire need of a little slush fund to keep these things going. Still, it was only a temporary glitch. If they managed to keep the Gaumont open, they could return to business as usual. Catholic guilt only stretched so far.

His and Andy's efforts bore fruit immediately. Maureen was stunned as she went through the figures, especially those relating to sales of Coke and Fanta, which seemed to have quadrupled overnight on account of not one empty cup being washed up and resold. Box-office takings had increased dramatically too. This was due to all tickets being torn and none resold, but also because all the old arrangements had been cancelled. Film fans from all the local shops who had been paying for entry with clothes, cakes and hamburgers were now being asked to pay with hard cash.

Maureen couldn't understand how the cinema's fortunes had been so suddenly turned round. She had a feeling, however, that it would be too little too late. The place was still going to close and she'd still have to earn a living. Bingo wouldn't be the same, even if Patterson did make her the manageress. He wouldn't, of course. She wasn't taken in for a moment by his tawdry blandishments. She didn't want to be in charge anyway – that was what Tony was so good at, and she worried most of all about him. He'd never know how his faith in her ability all those years ago, had restored her confidence and optimism.

And that confidence and optimism told her that Tony was right. After years of steady decline, the fortunes of the cinema industry were about to rise. She'd say nothing, keep her fingers crossed, keep up the steady flow of prayers to St Philomena and perhaps the faceless mandarins at Head Office, who pulled Guy Patterson's strings, could be persuaded to change their minds. She'd sent the latest figures through to them and was expecting a call. She knew that these figures would flummox them. She knew that, upon receipt of this unexpected bonus, Head Office would be straight on the phone.

Presently the phone rang, and after a lengthy conversation, even she was surprised at the outcome. On replacing the receiver, she knew that at last her worries were over.

48

Contrary to what Eileen Kelly had always believed, Maureen Breslin was not still 'holding a candle' for the husband she hadn't seen for twenty-three years. They had married in the mid-fifties because she'd thought she was pregnant. It was a false alarm, followed by several more – for which Jim Breslin never forgave her. He had been keen to have children for all the wrong reasons: he was a handsome and deceptively charming man, whose immense arrogance had made him want to fill the world with miniature versions of himself. He didn't care who provided them. However when his young wife failed every month to do so, he would beat her up so viciously that she was too terrified to call the police in case the next attack was even worse.

Yet she remained with him. She went through all the usual emotions, chronicled a million times in women's magazines and on daytime TV shows. First the naïve vanity – the vain belief that the bastard had a kind side that would be brought out and nurtured by 'wonderful me'. Then the 'challenge' – the harder and harder that fabled kind side is to locate, the more determined the poor deluded wretch is to find it. Then the fatal mistake, the one that causes more misery than any other notion: the idea that the love of a bastard is somehow more valuable because it isn't so easily given. Maureen was too callow to realise that a bastard isn't a bastard to everyone, only to those who let him get away with it. For every Frank Sinatra, there's an Ava Gardner, and the mistake so many women make is to believe that they are all Ava Gardners when their willingness to put up with systematically vile treatment has already proved that they're not.

More than any of this, however, it was Maureen's belief in the sanctity of marriage as a holy sacrament and her refusal to recognise divorce that bound her to Jim. He would drunkenly accuse her of trapping him into wedlock then beat her up again. After a particularly savage assault, he disappeared, surfacing a few days later to say he wasn't coming back. Ever. Maureen was heartbroken. For days, she wouldn't emerge from the house. She was too ashamed and, as innocent victims often do, she turned the blame on herself. If she could only have borne him a child, he'd still be there. They'd have been a happy little family. As time wore on, however, she woke up to the fact that that wouldn't have been the case: a violent, abusive alcoholic like Jim Breslin could never have been part of a happy family. He liked to think of himself as a free spirit, the Wild Rover. Child or no child, he would still have left her and, after a while, she was thankful that she hadn't been left to bring up one, or maybe several children on her own.

She began to count her blessings and rebuild her life.

Fortunately she had a roof over her head in Kilravock Street but she needed a better paid job to keep up with the rent. She decided to leave B.B. Evans, the Kilburn department store where she'd worked with Dave's mother, and start afresh where nobody knew her. She could work as an usherette at the Westbourne Grove Gaumont in the afternoons and evenings seven days a week, until eleven every night. Why not? She had nothing else to do and she needed the money. She was promoted to the box office and, years later, Tony Harris made her assistant manageress.

Throughout all this, she remained married to Jim. She still felt forbidden by her faith to divorce him, though even if she had, her confidence and self-esteem were so damaged that she would have been unable to make a success of another relationship. She sought comfort in that traditional repository for lost and unhappy souls: the Catholic Church.

Jim never contacted her again. She didn't even know where he was. She neither knew nor cared whether he was alive or dead. Finally she found out. That phone call hadn't come from Head Office but from a Mr Clark, a solicitor in Manchester. Jim had been killed in a car crash on the M62. There had apparently been several subsequent girlfriends but no children. Legally, she was still his wife and therefore his next of kin. Mr Clark just wanted to know where he should send the cheque for half a million pounds.

49

Suddenly Maureen was like one of those pools winners who vow that their gargantuan windfall will not change their lives. In her case, it didn't. She went without the brand new Mercedes and the huge detached house in Totteridge. Instead, she bought the most unusual things: popcorn, boxes and boxes of popcorn, Mars bars, Maltesers and chocolate raisins. She bought hundreds of empty Coca-Cola cups at a price that was supposed to include Coca-Cola. She didn't want the Coke, just the cups. She didn't even want those, she just took them home and destroyed them. But more than anything else, she bought tickets – hundreds and hundreds of tickets for films she had no intention of seeing.

It would seem like madness, but there was a cool method in it. She had access to the figures and knew that even the spectacular recent improvements would not be enough to save the cinema. She'd thought about donating one lump sum at the end of the three months, whatever was needed to change Head Office's mind, but knew that that would arouse suspicion. So, when no one else was around, sometimes early in the morning, sometimes in the middle of the night, she would let herself in and dramatically augment the takings to show the sharp but steady increase that would keep the Gaumont open.

It was a huge risk. What if they decided to close it anyway? She'd spent twelve thousand pounds already. And even if they kept it open, she'd never see that money again – and how long would it be before the forces of bingo regrouped again outside the main doors? She couldn't keep pouring money in. As it was, she felt guilty enough about subsidising a huge profit-making organisation when she thought of what Oxfam, CAFOD or the Red Cross could have done with twelve grand. But she trusted Tony. She envied the way he seldom thought too hard about anything, just followed his instinct. He rarely made a mistake when booking the films, sniffing out the most unlikely hits like a pig snuffling for truffles. While everybody else was saying that these new videos would kill off cinemas for ever, he was saying the opposite.

He also believed that a bingo hall in this area would, as he put it, 'go down like a shit sandwich', and nobody knew Notting Hill better than he did. He was sensitive to the slightest nuance in its atmosphere, the smallest vagary in its vibe. And he thought he could feel something changing. Bohemian people had always lived there but more affluent ones were trickling in from Kensington and Holland Park. It would probably be years before it became apparent but he was sure it would. And these people, he contended, would prefer Bergman to bingo.

Yet she kept quiet. She'd kept quiet about Jim's violence, she'd kept quiet about the way he'd abandoned her, she'd kept quiet about the fortune he'd unwittingly left her and, most of all, about how she was now using it. So she kept quiet about the figures and the hopes she had of turning the tide. She didn't discuss them with Tony. She never did. He wasn't interested. He could see by the number of hands he pumped and backs he slapped in the foyer whether or not the Gaumont was doing well. He'd accepted that his time in Notting Hill would soon be over, and had plunged himself into all the blues joints, shebeens and gambling clubs as never before, enjoying them until he was either made redundant or banished to a distant suburban cinema where the only pleasures on offer would be washing the car, trimming the hedge and attending the wife-swapping parties at number thirty-seven.

Every evening, Andy gazed up at the portrait of Our Lady of Czestochowa, looking for her approval. It was very odd: he was now enjoying honesty almost as much as he'd enjoyed dishonesty. It showed just how far his moral standards had plunged that he felt virtuous and almost saintly simply by not embezzling the company he worked for. He couldn't help thinking, though, that it was all going to be in vain.

50

Andy's pessimism was misplaced. Before the three months were up, Guy Patterson had received a call from his boss, Jack Pulman. Jack was an old-fashioned cinema man, who had secretly shared Tony's distaste for bingo. Even though he was running a business, not a charity, and felt a duty to his shareholders, Jack had shown great clemency to Tony Harris and the Westbourne Grove Gaumont. Despite Patterson's constant protestations that it would be far more profitable as a bingo hall, Jack was always willing to give it just one more chance. Finally, though, even he had run out of benevolence. Guy was right: the plug would have to be pulled. However, on receipt of the astonishing figures Maureen had sent through, he was forced into a sudden rethink.

'Have you seen these figures, Guy?' he said, waving the sheet of paper at his area manager.

Patterson had to think about his reaction: ever ambitious, and assiduous in keeping on the right side of his boss, he was also reluctant to lose face by admitting that his judgement might have been wrong. 'Yes,' he said. 'Very interesting.'

But Jack wasn't prepared to let him off the hook. 'So, what do you think?'

'I have to think about what's best for the company,' was Guy's bland, convictionless reply.

'Yes, you do. And in my view, Guy, we may be acting a little too hastily. Bingo has been good for us and will continue to perform well. However, perhaps we shouldn't put all our eggs in one basket. Spread your risks, Guy, that's the secret of success. It might be wise to keep this site as a cinema, just in case these video-recorders do create an upturn in demand. We've got plenty of bingo halls to bring in the money. And, anyway, Westbourne Grove seems to have got its head above water.'

In his heart, Patterson couldn't have cared less whether Westbourne Grove was a cinema or a bingo hall. His only concern was what was best for Guy Patterson. At the moment, it seemed to be an embarrassing climbdown. Although, of course, it needn't be presented as such. He decided to break the good news in person, and arrived at the cinema just before seven when he knew both Tony and Maureen would be there.

'You've no idea how hard I've had to lobby for this, Tony,' he said, 'how long I've battled to convince Jack. But I thought about what you said and, well, knowing how hard you've worked to keep this place going, at the end of the day, I just couldn't let them close it.'

Bollocks, thought Tony. He knew the change of heart had come from Jack Pulman and not from Patterson. The secret of telling lies convincingly is to keep as close to the truth as possible but Patterson had never quite mastered this. By claiming that Tony worked hard, he'd veered too far from veracity, so Tony rightly assumed that everything else he had said was a lie too.

Maureen, sitting next to him, didn't need to assume: she knew that it had been her twelve grand, not Patterson's 'lobbying', that had tipped the balance. Tony, however, was in celebratory mood. If Patterson wanted to claim credit, let him. He wasn't fooling anyone – least of all Dave and Andy, who had been invited in to share in the glad tidings. They didn't believe Patterson either because they thought that their own dishonest take on honesty, fuelled by Catholic guilt, had been wholly rather than fractionally responsible for the cinema's reprieve. Only Maureen knew the real truth and as she watched Patterson taking the credit that was rightfully hers she found herself shamed by a delicious desire to shut his hand in a car door.

Naturally, there was a huge party in the foyer to which Patterson had not been invited. Tony had always planned to go out with a bang and invite all the regulars to the best bash they had ever attended. Just because the place was no longer closing down, he saw no reason to cancel it. In fact, there was more reason than ever to hold it.

The whole of Notting Hill seemed to be at the party but Andy eschewed the huge quantities of food, drink and dope that were there for the taking, concentrating instead on the sounds provided by Duke the DJ's sound system in the corner. These records were fantastic;

he'd never heard them before and had to make a note of them – 'King Of Kings' by Jimmy Cliff on Stateside, 'Night Train To Jamaica' by Danny Davis and Byron Lee on yellow MGM; and two on black Atlantic, 'Smokey Joe's La La' by the Googie Rene Combo and 'Jamaican Ska' by the Ska Kings. He'd be down at Johnny B's first thing in the morning to see how many, if any, of these rare gems he had in stock.

Johnny had them all. They cost Andy a small fortune, but what the hell? Normal service could now be resumed: he'd fiddle back that money in no time.

Or would he?

51

Jack Pulman had come down in person. He was much older and his Jag was much newer but, otherwise, he and Tony Harris were remarkably similar. Both had that easy charisma, and as they shook hands in the foyer, they displayed a genuine warmth for each other that neither would ever feel for Guy Patterson.

'Jack, come and meet the boys,' said Tony. 'Dave, Andy, this is Jack Pulman, top man at Gaumont Cinemas, took me on as an usher at the Willesden Empire in nineteen . . . well, long before either of you was born.'

'Good to meet you both,' said Jack, in his rich, biscuity voice. 'Tony tells me that you, Andy, run the box office and you, Dave, run the kiosk. Is that right?'

Both boys nodded.

'Well,' said Jack, 'what I'm about to tell you is almost too good to be true.'

For Dave and Andy, however, it was too true to be good. The cinema, its future now secure, was going to have a much-needed refurbishment, starting with the box office, as Jack proudly explained. 'Your job,' he told Andy, 'is going to be a piece of cake. You'll be getting these flash new ticket machines, all computerised.

They log exactly what you've sold. No more tearing tickets and having to balance the books every night. The computer will do all that for you.'

It got worse.

'And as for you, Dave, over on the kiosk,' he beamed, 'you're even luckier. At long last you'll have a proper till. Not just that but one of those new ones that you see in some pubs – I think McDonald's have got them too. You just press a button for, say, a packet of popcorn or a large Coke and the price comes up automatically. It logs exactly what you've sold, all on computer, no more nightly stock-take.'

Tony then took Jack triumphantly into his office for Scotch and cigars, leaving Dave and Andy to stare at each other in horror. They'd each managed a weak smile for the sake of their bosses but this was a catastrophe. The huge cut in real earnings that they'd only intended to be temporary was now going to be permanent. All their fiddles, which had brought them more money than they'd known what to do with, were to be wiped out at a stroke by new technology. Yes, they could re-establish their old reciprocal arrangements with people like the Harlequin Hippies and Mustapha from the Wimpy Bar, but those little perks were a mere bagatelle compared with the rich rewards to be garnered from the judicious use of untorn tickets and washed-up Coke cups.

'What are we going to do?' Dave almost wailed. He was at yet another crossroads in his life. He had taken rather well to dishonesty. Since the collapse of any academic ambitions he might have had, a life of villainy had seemed his best chance of escape from Kilravock Street. Except that this was more like toy villainy, and he knew that he had neither the physical nor the emotional hardness to embark upon the real thing. He and Andy were in crisis now. They sat outside the Gaumont for over an hour after their shift had finished, discussing their rather Pyrrhic victory.

'There's not a lot we *can* do,' said Andy, revealing that, despite superficial similarities created by so many shared experiences, they still had very different characters. Unlike Dave, Andy was curiously relieved to find his days of dishonesty curtailed. He could look Our Lady of Czestochowa in the eye again. He had more clothes than he would ever find time to wear, more records than he would ever find time to play, and the thirst of his Vespa could be slaked with minuscule amounts of four-star. He really didn't need the excess cash. Yet, without it, his life seemed horribly empty. It wasn't the money but the wicked thrill of iniquity that he knew he was going to miss. The Mod revival had meant that his beautifully crafted new image was now far from unique and the glorious feeling of rebellion that had set his soul on fire had been dampened and almost extinguished.

The following morning, he decided against going to St Saviour's, opting instead for a ride in the sunshine to Richmond. He rode through the park to the top of Richmond Hill, removed his helmet outside a pub called the Roebuck, and took in a truly majestic view of the Thames. Its splendour, however, could not lift his spirits, which were being dragged down by the feeling that it was all too easy. He could saunter back for double history in the afternoon and none of the staff would know or care where he'd spent the morning. He longed to feel the fear of McLafferty catching him, and running the risk of suspension or possible expulsion. It made him feel young, alive and rebellious. If there's nothing left against which to rebel, life can become rather dull. He found himself loathing Langfield's liberal laxity more for this than for the fact that it was slowly robbing him of his A levels.

52

It was an unusual way for Ewa Zymanczyk to find out about her son's habitual truancy. Until Tuesday 14 May she had no idea that most of his history lessons were spent in second-hand-record shops, most of his English lessons in second-hand-clothes shops, and most of his economics lessons on the usher's seat at the cinema. On this particular afternoon, it was 'Economics', so when she phoned the school she was alarmed to discover that he was not where he was supposed to be.

Dave Kelly, for once, was exactly where he was supposed to be and found himself summoned to Mr Langfield's office where the principal came straight to the point. 'Do you know where Andy Zymanczyk is?'

'No, sir, I don't. Why? What's happened?'

What had happened was that Jerzy Zymanczyk had been performing root-canal work on his old friend Henry Kobus. They were chatting (well, Jerzy was chatting and Henry was gurgling) about the Pope's forthcoming trip to London, a big mass at Wembley Stadium. Oh, what a wonderful day it would be. A day both men had waited years to see. Suddenly their conversation had been brought to an alarming halt. Mrs Wizbek, Jerzy's assistant, had come rushing in when she heard the crash of the toppled table and the metallic clatter of the neatly arranged dental implements as they skittered across the floor.

Henry Kobus was in a difficult position. What do you do if your jaws have been clamped apart with dental scaffolding, your mouth is full of gauze, your tooth has been removed, its nerves painfully exposed and your dentist suffers a heart-attack? Compared with the poor dentist, who's going to feel sorry for you?

Jerzy was rushed to Hammersmith hospital but was dead on arrival. It had been immediate. He had suffered no pain. Which is more than could be said for his patient.

Dave had lied to Mr Langfield. He knew exactly where Andy was, and as soon as he left the principal's office, he headed straight for Westbourne Grove. It was an uncomfortable journey. What should he tell his friend? The truth? That his father had suffered a heart-attack and had been rushed to hospital. Or the whole truth? That the heart-attack had been fatal. Shit, which was worse? As he pulled up outside the cinema, he decided to tell him the whole truth. Andy would work out that Langfield had told Dave and would wonder why Dave had not told him.

He went straight into Maureen's office. 'Is Andy here?'

'Yeah, Screen Two.' She looked at him. 'Is everything all right?'

'Um . . . No, not really. I've got some very bad news.'

'What's happened?'

'His dad's just died. They were looking for him at school.' Maureen hadn't realised she'd been harbouring a truant. Dave asked her if he could use the phone.

'Yes, of course,' she replied.

Dave dialled the number. 'Mr Langfield? It's Dave Kelly. I've found Andy and we're on our way to the hospital now.'

Langfield couldn't help but admire Dave. Zymanczyk had obviously been skiving but his friend had not told on him and had also shown courage and consideration in making this call. Yes, technically both were in breach of college regulations but now was not the time for punishment.

'Okay, Dave, thank you for letting me know.'

That had been the easy bit. Oh, Christ, Dave was not looking forward to the next thirty seconds.

'I'll just go and get him,' said Maureen tactfully. She went in and brought Andy out to the foyer. As soon as he saw Dave's face, he realised something was very wrong.

'What is it?' he asked.

'Maybe it's best,' said his friend gravely, 'if I tell you outside.'

In the event, Dave didn't have to tell him anything.

'It's my dad, isn't it?' said Andy, as they walked out on to the pavement.

Dave bit his lip and nodded.

Andy turned very pale. 'He's dead, isn't he?'

Dave bit his lip even harder, looked his friend briefly in the eye, looked back at the ground and nodded again. He looked up. 'I'm so sorry,' he said. Instinctively he opened his arms and hugged his friend's face into his shoulder and, to his surprise, he found that tears were streaming down his own cheeks too. They had arrived for several reasons: obviously out of sympathy for Andy, and also because the burden of having to tell him had been lifted from his shoulders. They were tears of guilt too, that it hadn't happened to him, and then the realisation that some day it would. He was overcome with a depth of love for his own father that he hadn't known was there, and a terrible dread of the day when he, too, would be in this position.

Andy was sobbing. He'd tried for a few seconds to keep his finger in the dyke – after all, no eighteen-year-old boy wants one of his mates to see him crying. However, Dave had already witnessed the trickle, so he might as well witness the flood. Andy's shoulders were heaving and from deep within him came a primal, unintelligible moan. Yet reaction to bereavement can be very odd. Through all this he couldn't help thinking, oh good, perhaps now we can get a telly.

As Dave drove to Hammersmith hospital, the silence was only broken by Andy's occasional sniffs. 'You don't me mind crying, do you?' he said, his voice snuffly but not quite so quivery.

'I'd have thought it very strange if you hadn't,' replied Dave, sniffing in solidarity.

'I mean, I shouldn't be surprised,' said Andy, staring into the middle distance. 'He's had this heart condition ever since I can remember – always in and out of hospital – but I suppose it was bit like a James Bond film. No matter what happens to the hero, you know he'll be all right in the end. You know he'll always get up. And this time he hasn't. I don't know why but it's sort of made me even less prepared.'

'Well, at least he didn't suffer,' said Dave, trying his best to be reassuring as they drew up outside the hospital gates. 'Do you want me to come in with you?'

'No, thanks, I'll be fine,' said Andy, drying his eyes. He took a deep breath and headed for the cardiac unit on the third floor. When he arrived, the sight of his mother and assorted Polish relatives made him burst into tears again.

'We've been so worried about you,' said his mother, hugging him tightly and crying into the side of his neck. 'Where have you been?' Andy didn't need to reply. He was wearing a red Crimplene jacket and a bow-tie, and he still had a torch in his hand.

53

The gates to the cemetery in Zakopane bear the motto 'A nation is its people and its graves.' Another cemetery, the Powazki in Warsaw, is a national monument. Then, of course, there is the famous Polish War Memorial on the A40, just near RAF Northolt. All of which would indicate that the Poles have a great reverence for the Grim Reaper. That evening, having returned home from the hospital, Andy and his mother found themselves enveloped in a warm duvet of Polish sympathy. Father Lizewski was first to arrive, followed over the next few hours by the Markiewiczs, the Januszeskas, the Pskadlos, the Mruks, the Kluczniks, the Sztukowskis, the Wizbeks and, of course, poor old Henry Kobus, who could only mumble his condolences through the side of his numb and swollen mouth.

Toasts were solemnly drunk, memories shared and tears shed until gradually they all drifted off home and Andy began to dread being alone with his mother. I was something he had seldom experienced. His parent had always come as a matching pair – buy one, get one free. Jerzy really had been Ewa's 'other half' and Andy wondered how on earth she would manag without him.

She had married at nineteen and now she was fifty-eight. Her whole life had been devoted to *Pan Dentysta*. She had never worked, only as his receptionist; she had always been there for him, cooking his meals, washing his clothes and attending to his every need. He had been equally devoted to her, in a more patrician way, and their marriage had worked very well, even though, in the process, she had become enfeebled by his tyranny. Ewa and Jerzy had been as happy as could be expected for two ultra-devout Catholics who wouldn't have known how to allow themselves any form of fun. What would she do now? She had nothing else in her life. She was frozen in time, mentally and emotionally embalmed as an innocent teenage girl but, in reality, just eighteen months away from drawing her pension.

She'd had a few glasses of vodka and although she was not drunk, the alcohol combined with the raw pain of bereavement to make her a little less inhibited in what she was saying. She was gazing straight ahead, watching an old film that no one else could see. It was a private screening in her own head, starring herself and Jerzy in a story of love and devotion. As she watched it, her cheeks became wet with a mixture of salt water and running mascara. Andy couldn't help noticing that his mother was looking more and more like Alice Cooper.

'For years we lived there,' she said, to no one in particular. 'Sixty-four Colville Square in Notting Hill, just around the corner from that cinema of yours. It was a very rough neighbourhood, dangerous, even. Most of the houses were owned by this man called Peter Rachman. Polish man. Very bad man. Slum landlord. The houses were in a terrible state, full of rats and cockroaches – horrible. He didn't care as long as he got his rent. And if he didn't, he'd send round a gang of thugs to throw the people and all their belongings out on to the street.'

Andy stifled a yawn. He couldn't count the times he'd heard these terrible tales about Rachman but, given the circumstances, he knew he would have to listen politely. Or perhaps if he joined in and at least turned her monologue into dialogue, he'd stand a better chance of staying awake. 'So why did you live there?' he wondered aloud.

'Well, you know your father,' she said. 'He always wanted to give help to those who needed it most. He was doing good work in a very poor community. Secretly, I wanted him to get a practice in somewhere nice, like Kensington or Ealing, but I had to stand by him. As his wife, it was my duty.'

'So Rachman didn't bother you?' he asked.

'Not really,' she said. 'You see, your father had known him back in Poland. Rachman's father was a dentist and your father had trained under him, so Rachman was always very nice to us.'

'You liked him?'

His mother was outraged. 'No, we did not.'

Andy smiled inwardly at the 'we'. His parents had always been united in every opinion and belief.

'No,' she exclaimed, with all the power of offended

dignity. 'We detested his greed, his ruthlessness and the violent thugs who did his dirty work, but he never did us any harm. Your father needed a surgery and Rachman sold us this huge house very cheaply. The surgery was in the basement, we lived on the ground floor and the rooms upstairs were let to all sorts of people.'

Oh, no, thought Andy. Here we go. She's going into her Notting Hill League of Nations routine.

His mother continued, 'They came from everywhere, Ireland, the West Indies, Portugal, Spain, Morocco. I lost count of the people who lived in that house.' She paused again, 'But there was one girl I'll always remember, a little Irish girl, Teresa, I felt so sorry for her.'

'Why her?' asked Andy. 'I'd have felt sorry for anyone who had to live in a place like that.'

'Well, she was so innocent, so vulnerable. She was only seventeen and she'd come over from this little village in Ireland. She hadn't wanted to come.'

'So why did she?'

'Her family had disowned her. She was ... you know ... having a baby, and she wasn't married so they threw her out. She came to London because no one would know her, she could have the baby, then go back to Ireland. It used to happen quite a lot. She was so scared. We used to hear her every night, sobbing herself to sleep.'

'Did she have the baby?'

'Yes. We were at home that night and she suddenly

started screaming. She'd gone into labour, poor girl, she didn't even know what was happening to her. There wasn't time to get her to hospital and the baby was born in our front room.'

'Oh, and what happened to it?' said Andy, on automatic pilot. He was indulging his mother: he wasn't really listening, he didn't really care. His mother had gone very quiet. He looked at her. She looked at him. Suddenly he thought he was going to be sick.

Ewa had always wanted to tell him. She felt that if he had known from day one, it wouldn't have been a problem. She could explain, as adoptive parents always do, that he was special, he was loved, that they had adopted him because they really, really wanted him, but Jerzy had forbidden her ever to mention it. 'Over my dead body,' he had thundered. And now she was taking him at his word.

But how could she do this to Andy? His father had died that very day and now she was telling him that he wasn't his father at all. Oh, and by the way, she wasn't his mother. How could she heap shock upon grief like this?

It was no snap decision. She had spent years turning it over in her mind. While her husband snored softly beside her, she had spent countless nights lying wide awake wondering when would be the best time to tell him or whether she should tell him at all. She'd finally decided that there would never be a good time, but assuming he was eighteen and had a legal right to know, just after Jerzy's death would probably be the least awful time to break the news.

She remembered the war, the Jewish friends she'd had in Poland who had been dragged off to concentration camps. As one shock or tragedy was piled on top of another, the effect of each was slightly diminished. When your heartbreak is continuous, you cannot help but become toughened to it. She reasoned that Andy would be heartbroken at the death of his father. Far better to give him this terrible shock while he was already in shock than to let him recover only to hurt him again.

Andy was hot, cold and dizzy all at the same time but speechless. Absolutely speechless. Finally, he found some words. 'So then you moved over here?'

'Well, even your father had to admit that Notting Hill was not the best place to bring up a child, and once the church round the corner became a Polish church, he couldn't wait to move.'

Another disturbing thought suddenly crossed Andy's mind. 'So everybody knows?' he mumbled. 'Auntie Ania, Uncle Krzys – all of them?'

'No, they don't. Nobody does.' This second revelation was even more astounding than the first.

'How can they not know?' Andy wailed. 'You're such a close family.'

'Your father and I were desperate for children,' she explained. 'Oh, we tried and tried but our prayers were never answered. After twenty years, we knew they never would be. We tried to adopt, but it was hopeless. I mean, we were good, prosperous people, but to the English authorities, we were still just Polish immigrants. We hardly spoke the language and they preferred English babies to go to English homes. And by this time, anyway, we were too old. I was forty and your father was forty-seven. There was no chance. When Teresa came along and said she would have to put you up for adoption, we knew it was the last opportunity we would ever get. That maybe our prayers had been answered. Teresa was just relieved that you were going to people she knew would love and care for you.'

Andy's mind turned to Teresa, the hopelessly naïve little girl who had given birth to him. 'Why didn't she want me?' he asked,

'Oh, she wanted you. She wanted you so much that she couldn't even bear to look at you. Couldn't hold you because she said that if she did she would never be able to let you go. But she knew she couldn't keep you. She was no more than a child herself. She didn't have a penny. She wasn't ready . . .'

'So, who's my father?'

'She never said. All she'd say was "someone back home". I don't think he was her boyfriend and he never knew about you. Probably still doesn't.'

'Where is she now – my . . .' Andy found himself struggling with an everyday word that he had said a million times before, the meaning of which he thought he knew but now realised he didn't. 'My . . . my . . . mother.'

'Well, she always kept in touch. Whenever she moved, she'd send her new address. She went to America about ten years ago. And, as far as I know, she's in Boston.'

Andy remembered his original question. 'But how come nobody knows? How could you keep it a secret?'

'Well, your father was so desperate for a child, he would leave nothing to chance. So I had to pretend I was pregnant.'

Andy just looked at her with a silent, slack-jawed stare. He tried to speak. 'H – w – I mean, did – but how . . .'

'Well, it was 1961 – a very cold winter. Had it been summer, we could never have got away with it, but at the time everyone was wrapped up in coats and hats and scarves, so no one could tell. I would pad myself every morning with cushions . . .'

Andy found himself wanting to laugh. This was like an episode of a really bad sitcom, but he had to admit that it would have been an easy trick to pull off. No one was likely to say, 'Excuse me, that bump, is it a baby or a cushion?'

'I only had to do it for the last three months. We told the family that we hadn't said anything before because it was my first child and I was forty and we were terrified something would go wrong. They all knew how much we had always wanted children so they understood.'

Andy was appalled but somehow impressed by the nature and scale of the deceit carried out by the two most honest, upright, God-fearing people he had ever known. 'But how about when I was born?'

'There was a midwife who lived across the square – a big Jamaican woman called Pam. She delivered you.'

'But surely my birth certificate—'

'It says your parents are Ewa and Jerzy Zymanczyk. No one knows any different.'

'And are you ever going to tell anyone?'

'Well, that's up to you, Andrzej. Whatever you wish. I don't mind.'

To her surprise, Ewa found herself wanting to tell everyone. This terrible secret had been a thorn in her side for eighteen years. She was a very honest woman – this had been her one aberration. She had never been comfortable with it. But it couldn't have been any other way. No one would have allowed two ageing childless Polish immigrants to adopt a newborn baby. Had Teresa's name been on the birth certificate, there would always have been a chance that she might try to take the baby back. They couldn't risk it.

Jerzy had never given it another thought but, then, it was much easier for him, because he would never have had to experience pregnancy and childbirth anyway. Once the baby was presented to him, that was it – he was convinced that the child was his. In the same way that he was convinced that the Pope was infallible and that Jesus had walked on water.

Ewa had always felt a bit of a fraud. She adored Andy more than anything else in the world. She had loved every moment of bringing him up. She was proud of the way he had turned out, but perhaps it was time to come clean. All Catholics have an inbuilt desire to confess. No one could take him away now. Anyway, he was eighteen – he could take himself away if he wanted to.

Andy couldn't bear the strain of living with this secret. Now that he knew, he could never unknow, so he made his decision at once: 'Tell them.'

54

It was only ten minutes on the scooter, twenty on a pushbike and forty on foot, but time meant nothing to Andy that night. Nothing meant anything to Andy that night. He didn't know who he was or even what his real name was supposed to have been. The one thing that became clear to him that night was the concept of sleepwalking. He now understood that it was possible to walk for forty minutes, from Askew Crescent to Westbourne Grove, without remembering a single moment of the journey.

Ewa had been right. The revelation about his adoption had lessened the pain of his bereavement. After all, most people at some time in their lives will have to deal with the death of a parent. Far fewer had to contend with discovering that their fine upstanding parents were, in fact, a pair of law-breaking impostors.

He arrived at the cinema and walked into the foyer, where Dave was putting the shutters on the kiosk. It all seemed much harder work without that cushion of cash at the end of each shift. Andy looked across at him. 'Just come to get my scooter. And my coat. Thanks for today. You're a real mate.'

Dave nodded and smiled. 'You'd have done the same.

Look, hang on, I'll only be five minutes.'

As they walked outside, Andy pointed to Dave's Cortina. 'Can we sit in the car for a minute?' he said.

Andy looked very pale and still, and Dave didn't quite know what to say, especially when Andy finally spoke. 'My dad's not really dead, you know.'

Oh God, he's gone mad, poor fucker, thought Dave. I knew it would hit him hard but . . .

'No, he's still alive. At least, I assume he is. He might be dead, though.'

Dave wasn't ready for this. He was only eighteen: he had no experience of bereavement counselling.

'I mean, Jerzy Zymanczyk is dead but he wasn't my dad.'

What the fuck was he talking about? 'What do you mean?' asked Dave gently.

'I mean that the man who died this afternoon was not my father. I was adopted.'

Dave felt his mouth fall agape, then go up and down like a goldfish's as he groped in vain for words that wouldn't come. When, after what seemed like an eternity, they finally did, they formed themselves into the standard response: 'Well, it's sort of good, isn't it?' he croaked. 'That means your parents really wanted you, which is more than some people can say about their real parents.'

Andy thought for a moment about telling Dave everything – cushions being stuffed up jumpers, the whole lot – but decided against it. No one would believe that. His friend would think he was overwrought with grief and had completely lost his marbles. Anyway, that wasn't the issue – it wasn't the reason for the dry tears of resentment pricking at the backs of his eyes. His voice was cold and bitter as he began to list the litany of crimes that he felt had been perpetrated against him. 'Polish school,' he began, 'Polish Cubs and Scouts, Polish books and newspapers, the *Dziennik Polski*, the Polish Social and Cultural Centre, the Polish church and youth club, the Polish folk-dancing troupe, St Andrew fucking Bobola.' His voice rose. 'The Katyn Memorial, the grave of General Komorowski, the Sikorski Museum, having to speak Polish at home, only eating Polish food – *bigos*, *golabki*, pickles, and beetroot soup. My whole life has been wasted on Poland and all things Polish.' He reached his climax and sobbed, 'And it turns out I'm not even fucking Polish!'

Dave didn't know what to say. Best to let Andy's stream of cathartic consciousness continue.

'Have you any idea how much I envied you, Cronin, Clancy, Harte, even Fishy Wilkins, because no one, not even the other Polish kids in our school, had a home life like mine? I must have been the only one who looked forward to Monday mornings and dreaded the weekends.'

'But they weren't bad parents, were they?' said Dave. 'I always liked your old man.'

'I know,' sighed Andy, calming down a bit. 'Everyone did. Christ, I can't believe I had to go through all that for nothing.'

'But it wasn't for nothing, was it?' said Dave, rather feebly. 'I mean, it's always good to have a second language.'

Oddly enough, this made Andy smile.

'And another thing,' Dave reminded him, 'you have got very good teeth.'

55

At the funeral, Andy felt strangely detached, maybe because he wasn't related to the deceased. Ever the film fan, he had begun, since Ewa's startling revelations, to view his life as a movie and he felt as though he was watching this particular scene from the usher's seat at the back of Screen Two.

It was an impressive turnout even though, this being a Polish funeral, the numbers had almost certainly been swelled by a slew of professional mourners, there to pay heartfelt respects to a fellow Pole whom they had never met. Andy looked at himself, sharper than ever in his best black mohair suit and skinny silk tie, leading his 'mother' to the front pew. He had been worried about her ability to cope but was surprised to see an underlying calmness and serenity in her expression that seemed to support her obvious grief. It was as though she, too, had been gently released and would now perhaps form her own opinions, articulate her own views and live her own life, without constant deference to her kind but domineering husband.

Andy let his imaginary camera pan round the church. As he looked at all the solemn, tear-stained faces, some half buried and snuffling into handkerchiefs, he was overcome by a sudden rush of love for all things Polish. Now that his Polishness was no longer compulsory, he could see its many benefits. The Poles were fine, brave, noble people, who had a goodness and spirit that neither Fascism nor Communism could crush. They were quirky, stylish, warm-hearted and generous. They were fiercely proud and protective of their nationality, but always willing to welcome outsiders into the fold. This, again, made Andy feel happy.

He was happy that so many people had gathered to say goodbye to the man he'd always thought was his father. So many people thought that Jerzy Zymanczyk's was a life worth celebrating and that he was a man worth saluting. An empty 'Eleanor Rigby' style funeral had to be the saddest epitaph to anyone's life.

He was happy not to experience the guilt felt by so many at the funerals of their parents. He hadn't fallen out with Jerzy, and had done everything he could to be a model Polish and Catholic son, even though it had often made him miserable. There had been no quarrel that could never be patched up. *Pan Dentysta* would be lowered into the ground immensely proud of his boy because, although he'd never know it, he had got out just in time.

Had that heart-attack not been fatal, there would have been terrible trouble between father and son. Jerzy would have been apoplectic with rage at the lousy A-level grades that Andy would soon be receiving. His dreams of his son matriculating at 'The Cambridge University' before training as a dentist would have crashed and burned. As Andy, legally an adult, struggled to assert his independence and make his own decisions, there would have been more rows. And rows can turn into irreparable rifts, so Andy was happy that he was spared the anguish of having them.

He was happy that his mother was selling the house. It had always seemed to be a dental surgery first, a shrine to Marian Catholicism second, and a family home a rather poor third. She was buying a much smaller house round the corner from his Auntie Ania and Uncle Krzys in Ealing, where she and Andy could start afresh.

He was also happy that Ewa had had the courage to tell him the truth about his parentage. Although the news had thrown him into turmoil and he was in the midst of an identity crisis, he found it all curiously cleansing. He was a new person, free to dance to his own tune and be whoever he wanted to be.

However, one thing made him happiest of all. A couple of scenes after the funeral service, he was back at home with about a hundred merry mourners, floating along on a sea of vodka. He watched himself seek out one mourner, a beautiful girl whose black two-piece suit accentuated her white-blonde hair. He watched himself approach her with new-found confidence. 'Well,' he said, with the raise of an eyebrow, 'out of bad things come good and, well, since it seems we're not cousins any more, will you go out with me?'

56

The passage ended with the words 'Anna Victrix'. In order to answer the question, Dave needed to know what happened next? He hadn't a clue. He'd never read the book. 'Tim' had pulled off the rare feat of making *The Rainbow* by D.H. Lawrence more boring than it was in the first place and Dave, along with the rest of St Saviour's A-level English class, had switched off a long time ago. He could only recall that Lawrence seemed to see phallic symbols in everything and the only legacy of this book would be Dave's inability to look at rhubarb in the same way again.

He sat in his A-level English exam, wondering how the hell he was going to while away the next two hours and fifty-four minutes. The second section of the paper concerned the *Four Quartets* by T.S. Eliot. All Dave could remember about Eliot was that his name was an anagram of 'Toilets', but thought that this was unlikely to impress the examiners.

In time-honoured fashion, he hoped that this was a particularly unpleasant dream from which he would soon wake up. It was, however, all too depressingly real. He looked at the other blank, uncomprehending faces and realised that St Saviour's had failed them all. Only Catherine Philpot, tongue protruding approximately a quarter of an inch from the side of her mouth, concentrating heavily and scribbling furiously, looked like she had the remotest chance of passing. Dave, like many a natural optimist, was doomed to disappointment. He'd honestly believed that A levels wouldn't be too taxing. Why else would the St Saviour's regime have been so lax? Surely they wouldn't send them into battle so ignorant and ill-prepared. He'd be able to blag his way through, he'd thought, just as he had with his O levels. But when he looked down at the questions in front of him the cold realisation struck him that it was critical analysis, not blagging, that was required.

Andy was having similar thoughts. Except that he was surprisingly unconcerned. Recent events had diluted the significance of his A levels to pure H_2O. In a funny sort of way, Jerzy's death had done him a favour. When his results arrived, everyone would cite the sudden death of his father and the discovery of his adoption as the reasons for them being so pitifully short of what had been expected. No one would know that, even if Jerzy had lived, Andy would have failed them anyway. He couldn't have cared less about his results. He now felt almost duty-bound to follow a different path from the precisely paved Polish one that Jerzy had laid out for him. And, naturally, the first step involved failing his A levels.

Dave wasn't quite so sanguine. Like almost everyone else in the hall, his whole future was at stake.

He remembered the confidence imbued in them by McLafferty on their first day as green-blazered first-formers. The world is your oyster, they were told, you can be anything you want – prime minister, anything. Dave Kelly's stewardship of 10 Downing Street was now looking very unlikely.

He'd let everyone down: his parents, who'd been so proud of him for getting into St Bede's, all those neighbours who had waved him off on his first day, the teachers who'd got him through his O levels and had left him primed to pass three A levels. Even Derek the postman. Especially Derek the postman, whose impassioned advice had affected him far more deeply than anyone else's. Kilravock Street had been the desert island from which he'd promised Derek he'd escape, and St Bede's was supposed to be his life-raft. Now he had fallen off, and could only watch in impotent despair as it slipped further away from him, further and further away.

He looked down at the exam paper again. Part III concerned Virginia Woolf's To the Lighthouse. There was no longer a lighthouse in sight. No future. A recession was looming, jobs were scarce – particularly for unqualified school-leavers too clumsy for manual work.

He didn't know who Pete Roberts was but, as chair of the local education authority, Pete had been aware that there would be, as he put it, 'adjustment casualties' as the borough changed over to a wholly comprehensive education system. Privately, he had admitted, 'One year will have to be messed up,' and, sadly, it was Dave's.

The living embodiment of an adjustment casualty stared sadly at the blank sheets of paper, which were waiting in vain to be written on. His situation was hopeless. Trellick Tower was beckoning. What the hell was he going to do?

Twenty Years Later

'One of London's best-loved cinemas is to close tonight after more than sixty years. The curtain will come down on the Westbourne Grove Gaumont in Notting Hill for the last time at around ten thirty and the final film, appropriately enough, will be *Notting Hill*. Speaking on BBC London this afternoon, Guy Patterson, chief executive of Gaumont Leisure PLC, blamed the closure on the recent opening of two twelve-screen multiplex cinema complexes within a three-mile radius of the Gaumont. "It's a terrible shame," he explained, "but ironically the Gaumont has fallen victim to the massive resurgence in the popularity in cinema over the last fifteen years." Cinema fans around West London, however, aren't entirely convinced by Mr Patterson's explanation, citing the huge increase in property values in the Notting Hill area, especially since the site occupied by the cinema is a prime one and will almost certainly be re-developed for residential use. This is Sheena Craig for BBC London in Westbourne Grove.'

Dave Kelly had caught the news bulletin as he pulled in to the driveway of his large detached house in Bushey. He glanced at his watch – eight fifteen. As he walked through the front door, his wife was tiptoeing down the stairs, one finger raised to her lips and a pleading look in her eye.

'I've only just got them off,' she whispered. Dave smiled and nodded. He would have liked to have seen his two small children. He'd wanted to get them out of the bath and swaddle them in towels before reading them each a bedtime story, watching with amusement as their little eyelids drooped while they fought and lost their battles with fatigue. Tonight, however, the traffic had been particularly bad and he'd had to be content with saying goodnight to them on his mobile phone from a tailback approaching Staples Corner.

He slumped down on the sofa next to his wife, spent the next twelve seconds fidgeting distractedly and suddenly stood up again.

'I've . . . er . . . got to go out,' he announced.

'What?' she replied. 'You've only just come in.'

'I know but . . .'

'Where are you going?'

Dave paused. He hoped she would understand. 'It's the old Westbourne Grove Gaumont,' he explained, 'I've just heard on the news, it's closing down tonight. I wanted to have one last look.'

'Oh God,' she groaned with a weary smile, 'you are a sad old git. Off you go then. You'll regret it tomorrow if you don't.'

He bent down and kissed her, got into the car and drove off. At the end of his road, he watched an imaginary barrier lift and usher him into a time tunnel.

As the years began to peel back, his brand new BMW became his old gold Cortina and, even after all this time, his most potent memory was of Rachel. He'd met a lot of girls since meeting her and had slept with quite a few of them, yet none had ever come close to exuding the allure that she had. No one else had ever activated his sensual sensors in quite the same way, making them crackle and fizz with love and lust with little more than a smile. In the years that followed their break-up, he'd almost convinced himself that it wasn't the girl he'd been in love with, but the time. It was just his own teenage years that he remembered so fondly and Rachel was a mere symbol of this.

But no, that theory was blown apart about ten years after she'd checked into that clinic and out of his life. He'd been with a group of mates on a hot summer's evening sitting outside a pub in Hampstead when he saw her. She too had been with a group of friends, sitting just a few tables away. It was definitely her because only she had the password for the sensors that had immediately sprung into action and for the klaxons that had also gone off in his head. He'd turned very pale and had totally lost the power of speech. His mate Terry noticed it first. Pointing at the half drunk pint of shandy, he'd laughed, 'God, look at the state of you, Kelly, one sniff of the barmaid's apron.'

With a momentous effort, Dave had snapped himself out of it, even managing a weak smile but he kept looking over, heart pounding, pulses racing in his wrists, in his ears, in the sides of his neck, in places he hadn't realised pulses could race. Now's your chance, he'd told himself, if you don't do it now, you'll never get another opportunity, Go on, go on, but he found himself powerless, unable to cope with the force of his feelings. Instead of pulling him magnetically towards the great lost love of his life, those feelings were so strong, so heavy that they rendered him unable to move from his seat.

And now, even though he was happily married with two adorable children, just the thought of the Gaumont and Rachel Harvey had him revisiting the pain of that night outside the old Bull & Bush. He knew now that the attraction he felt for her all those years ago happens maybe once in a lifetime and for many people, not even that. He hadn't known how rare that 'chemistry' would turn out to be but boy, did he know it now.

Still hurting, he made his way along Westbourne Grove and pulled up outside the Gaumont. He looked at the posters of Julia Roberts and Hugh Grant outside but still felt no desire to see *Notting Hill*. Like many people with fond memories of a rough, cosmopolitan, ungentrified neighbourhood, Dave couldn't bear to go and see the celluloid celebration of what it had now become.

It was just after nine o'clock when he stepped once more through the old swing doors. All the films had started and the foyer was deserted apart from a sullen youth with a pierced eyebrow who was securing the shutters on the kiosk.

God, thought Dave, a computerised till and a CCTV

camera pointing straight at him. No wonder he's miserable.

He looked at Dave and raised his forehead. To ask 'Can I help you?' would evidently be too much like hard work.

'Hiya,' said Dave with a grin, 'I used to work here. About twenty years ago; on the kiosk, same as you.'

Common ground established, the youth's expression softened slightly and he managed a syllable, 'Yeah?'

'Yeah,' Dave continued, 'and when I heard that the place was closing, I just wanted to have one last nose around.'

The youth seemed to have no feelings either way, so Dave pressed on. 'Who's the manager now?' he asked, convinced it would still be Tony Harris.

'Mr Clay,' he replied

'Not Mr Harris?'

The youth shook his head, 'Never heard of him.' Then he seemed to brighten up a bit. 'Tell you what,' he suggested, 'why don't you come back at about half ten? They're going to have one last organ recital then you can have a quick look round after that.'

'Okay,' said Dave. 'That'd be great. See you later then.'

He spent the next fifteen minutes taking a slow tour of the surrounding streets, astonished at how much they had changed. The boarded up shops along Ledbury Road were now chic boutiques. Scary pubs were now gastropubs and coffee shops, restaurants, gyms and juice bars had proliferated over the face of The Grove like spots on the face of a teenage boy. He was aware that at this speed in a BMW, he might be mistaken for a drug dealer, then he wondered if the area still had any left. He parked the car and decided to explore on foot. Looking around, he decided that there were probably more drug dealers than ever; they were just a lot more subtle and well-heeled. As he walked, he marvelled at the way the crumbling old houses had been renovated and colonised by the only people who could now afford them. There were still pockets of squalor, and Dave had the impression that you could only live in Notting Hill if you were either very rich or very poor. He wondered whether any 'normal' people still lived there but then looking back, he wondered whether any 'normal' people ever had. He then felt ashamed of his inverted snobbery: if he objected to the middle classes moving in, wasn't he just as bigoted as those who had objected to the influx of West Indians in the 1950s?

He returned to the cinema where his new pal with the pierced eyebrow was now removing the big red letters which spelt NOTTING HILL from the canopy above the entrance. To Dave, the dismantling of those words seemed to symbolise the dismantling of the very soul of London W11. Looking up as the letters came down he recalled how, on Saturday nights, it had been his task to arrange them into the names of the following week's films. He remembered the puerile delight that he and Andy had taken in arranging them so that, just for a few minutes, the main feature would be called FUCK OFF. He was still grinning at the thought of this when a coach disgorged a group of people on to the pavement next to him, a group he'd seen many times before: organ enthusiasts. It was late, so on this occasion they would have eaten first and had therefore come without their usual flasks and sandwiches. Some were older than the Wurlitzer they had travelled one last time to worship and Dave was amazed to see so many of them still alive.

He followed the elderly throng into the foyer and up the grand staircase then took his seat in Screen One. For sentimental reasons, he sat on the usher's seat at the back and looked down fondly at the monogrammed carpet from which he had scrubbed vomit on his very first day.

He was delighted to see Ted Hogarth, now in his seventies, his goatee snow white, sitting at the keyboard. He was probably the only person still alive who knew how to play it and, as he launched into his familiar repertoire of old favourites, it was clear that time had not tarnished his touch. Ted finished with a stirring rendition of the national anthem and Dave, along with everyone else, got to his feet. He wondered how many others in the audience also had lumps in their throats and tears in their eyes.

After a couple of sniffs, he left the auditorium. Ted was greeting his ancient groupies in the foyer, so Dave didn't like to intrude. However, before he drove home, he decided to have that last look around he'd promised himself. He wasn't really supposed to, but what was the worst they could do? Throw him out? And anyway, he'd already cleared it with Pierced Eyebrow. He slid secretly out of the foyer, along the passage by the side of Screen Two and right down to the back of the stage to take one final mental snapshot of the old dressing rooms. In the damp, empty silence, he discovered that well-worn cliché to be true. When you say goodbye to a place that holds so many personal memories, you really do hear the voices of the people who shared those times with you. He heard old George, Lily, Doris, Tony, Maureen, Andy and, of course, Rachel.

'You won't find any Coke cups down here,' a voice was saying. Dave, adrift in his own sentimental reverie, was unable to distinguish between reality and aural illusion. After a couple of seconds, it struck him so hard that he almost keeled over. That voice had been real.

Looking in an old make-up mirror, he saw a face that had barely changed in the twenty years since he had last seen it. It was tanned and broke out into a wide, friendly grin revealing a dazzling set of perfectly capped teeth.

Dave thought he was hallucinating. 'Zymanczyk,' he said, 'what the hell are you doing here?'

'Same as you, I guess,' replied Andy. 'I heard the old place was closing and just wanted to pay my respects.'

Dave stared incredulously at his old friend. He may have looked the same physically, give or take the odd decade, but his accent was totally different. This was a boy who had started primary school, unable to speak English and even when he did, it was a long time before his Polish accent was entirely eradicated. It had gone completely now, as had the native London that had replaced it. Vocally, Andy Zymanczyk was American.

'How are you, man,' he said, shaking Dave's hand firmly with one hand and embracing him warmly with the other.

'I'm fine,' said Dave. 'You?'

'Yeah, I'm good.'

'So, well, I mean, well, look at you,' said Dave, stepping back. 'Either you've spent the last twenty years in the States or you're part of a Beach Boys tribute band.'

Andy laughed, 'Is it that obvious? Yeah, I've been living in LA since 1980. You?'

'Bushey,' said Dave with a light smile, 'Didn't even get as far as Watford.'

'Why would you want to?'

'True.'

They stared at each other again in bemused, delighted silence for a few moments before Dave, always the more voluble, continued, 'Christ, I wonder what happened to everyone. How about Tony? I honestly thought he'd still be here.'

'Oh, I saw him on TV,' said Andy. 'On CNN of all things – must have been about five years ago.'

'CNN? What was he doing?'

'Shaking hands with Tom Cruise and Nicole Kidman; welcoming them to some big premiere in Leicester Square. Bit fatter, bit greyer but it was definitely him. What about Maureen?'

'Oh, she retired,' said Dave. 'Went back to Ireland a few years ago. My mum told me. Apparently, she bought this unbelievable farmhouse set in about four acres. Nobody could work out where she got that kind of money.'

'Same place we got ours,' said Andy with a laugh. 'Mind you, I can't see it somehow.'

Again, a strange, almost reverential silence fell upon them and again Dave was the one to break it. 'Glad I made the effort, aren't you? This chance would never come again.'

'It wouldn't,' said Andy looking at Dave again. 'Sure is good to see you.'

Dave looked at his watch. 'Look, we'd better get out of here or we'll get locked in and turned into a block of luxury flats.'

'Okay,' said Andy. 'Well, let's get a drink.'

Dave laughed. 'The place may have changed but licensing laws haven't and I doubt if any of those old blues joints are still going.'

'Well luckily,' said Andy, 'I'm staying round the corner at The Portobello. Very rock'n'roll. The residents' bar is open twenty-four hours.'

They strolled out of the Gaumont for the very last time, each genuflecting at the kiosk and the box office in a gesture of thanks for all the cash that each outlet had provided and walked round to the Portobello Hotel and its funky subterranean bar. They sat down and ordered two cranberry juices; Dave because he was driving, Andy because he was from California.

'Right,' said Dave, 'twenty years in twenty minutes. You first, Mr Zymanczyk, your time starts . . . now.'

'Oh, man,' said Andy taking a gulp of his drink, 'where do you want me to start?'

'Well,' said Dave, 'how about when I last saw you: 1980, Terminal One at Heathrow, Boston bound, looking for your real mum.'

'Oh yeah,' said Andy, 'well, I found her.'

'Christ, how was it?'

'All a bit embarrassing really. She was married with three young kids. Hadn't told her husband about me.'

'Whoops,' said Dave.

'I was expecting to be welcomed with open arms but it was awful. I almost felt sorry for her. She was in a terrible state. We went to this coffee shop two blocks away and I had to pretend that I was some sort of distant cousin. She just didn't know what to say to me. I can see now that it was her way of coping; to pretend to herself that I didn't exist. She was sobbing, kept apologising and making me promise not to contact her again.'

'So what did you do?'

'Well, it was the first night I'd ever spent away from home. I had nowhere to go, so I booked into this cheap, depressing motel. It was probably the worst night of my life. I had intended to go straight home the following day; that would have been the easy option but I just couldn't. Not to all that Polishness, back to everything I had only just escaped from. The thought of going back to St Saviour's to retake my A levels forced me into a life-changing decision.'

Andy paused for a moment. 'I know this sounds really American,' he continued, 'but I had to find myself. I didn't know who I was. I couldn't go back to who I used to be. That's why I lost touch with everyone. That night in the motel room, it was like I had to give birth to myself all over again.'

Dave couldn't help grinning.

'If you'll forgive the California-speak,' Andy continued. 'By the morning, I'd decided to go the other way – West Coast rather than West London, thought I'd try my luck in LA. I'd read *The Moon's A Balloon* on the plane and thought if it worked for David Niven, it might work for me.'

'And did it?'

'I suppose it did. I bummed around for a while, living off the cash I still had from working at the cinema. Then I got a job at Paramount Studios, you know, just sweeping up, doing whatever I was told to do. I mean, with my upbringing, that was like second nature. They were real good to me, loved the fact that I was English but sort of Polish and that I'd worked in a movie theatre while I was at "high school" and my obsession with films certainly didn't do me any harm. I was very lucky, they made me assistant to a guy called Rob Lambert.'

'Who's he?'

'Probably the greatest cameraman in the world and he kind of took me under his wing, taught me everything I know.'

'So that's what you are now, a cameraman?'

'Yep. I love it. I go all over the world. Last shoot, believe it or not, was in Warsaw.'

'How was that?'

'Interesting. Suddenly a lot of things made a lot of sense. Only trouble is, I'm always away on location and that does take me away from the family. Here . . .'

Andy took his wallet from his pocket and pulled out a photo and pointed out the subjects with his little finger. 'That's my wife, Kim and that's Michael, Matthew and Megan; eleven, eight and six. Taken about a month ago. Kim reminds me a lot of my first love – the girl I'd always thought was my cousin.'

'You kept that quiet.'

'Well, wouldn't you?'

'Anyway,' said Dave with a chuckle, pointing at the vintage Vespa on which all three kids were sitting, 'surely that's not the same one?'

'It is,' said Andy, 'first thing I did when I got settled over there was to have it shipped out.'

'Bet they love all that in Hollywood,' said Dave, 'bit of British eccentricity.'

'I suppose so and it's perfect for LA. I go everywhere on it.'

Dave, remembering the shy and desperately conformist boy from St Bede's, was fascinated. 'And now?'

Andy smiled with genuine modesty. 'I'm doing just fine. Good cameraman trained by Rob Lambert, I can pretty much write my own cheques. Mind you, I had to spend a dollar or two in therapy so LA was ideal. They're not embarrassed by that sort of thing. The way they look at it, you hurt your leg, you get it seen to. You hurt your mind; you do exactly the same thing. Well, you can imagine, they had a field day with me.'

'Did it help?'

'Are you kidding? Two hours a week just talking about yourself. You wanna try it, it's great. Anyway, enough about me. What about you?' Always one to appreciate good tailoring, Andy leaned over and took the cuff of Dave's Richard James suit between his thumb and forefinger. 'You seem to have done pretty well for yourself.'

'Well, I was lucky too. I got into the City just at the right time, early eighties, just as it was all taking off. Couldn't really fail. I work in the money markets.' He took another sip of his drink. 'The box office and the kiosk turned out to be the perfect training for what I do.'

'Married?' asked Andy. 'Kids?'

'Yeah. Boy and a girl. Five and three.'

Andy looked at his old friend. 'It's so good to see you.'

'Yeah, you too.'

'No, I mean it,' said Andy. 'You'll never know how much you helped me.'

Oh God, thought Dave, he's developed that Californian lack of emotional inhibition.

'You know what my home life was like,' said Andy. 'If I hadn't worked at the cinema with you, I'd never have had the confidence to do what I did.'

With a nod and a smile, Dave accepted the compliment. He could see that Andy meant it. 'So, do you get over here much?' he asked.

'Yeah, all the time. London's become quite a hip location. Especially round here.'

'And yet you've never got in touch?'

This seemed to embarrass Andy. 'Well, I guess I was too busy "finding myself" but on the last few visits, I tried very hard to find you.'

'Yeah?'

'Yeah,' said Andy, 'I started with that Friends Reunited thing but you're not on it.'

'You mean People Who Never Had Any Friends Reunited. Too right I'm not on it,' said Dave with a laugh.

'Then I tried to get hold of your mum and dad,' said Andy, 'but they've moved, haven't they?'

'Gone back to Ireland.'

'Yeah, because a couple of years ago, I got a cab from my hotel over to Kilravock Street. It's gone a bit upmarket now. The girl who bought your old house was gorgeous. Something big in publishing, apparently.'

'Unlike my old man,' said Dave with affection, 'who was something small at the gasworks.'

'But when I found out that the Gaumont was closing,' said Andy with an earnest glint in his eye, 'I came straight over. I had a hunch you might turn up there, it was my only chance, I was right out of ideas.'

Dave couldn't quite take this in. 'Hang on,' he said,

'are you saying you flew in from LA just to find me?'

'Absolutely.'

'Eh? What? Why?' said Dave, not sure whether to be flattered or alarmed by this.

'Well, I was at a big post-production party a couple of years back and I got talking to a guy called Marty Kaufman, very famous screenwriter and as we chatted about our lives, Marty decides that my English/Polish/Catholic/Mod/Adopted/Real-mother-didn't-want-to-know-me sort of life would make a great movie.'

'Well, now you come to mention it . . .' said Dave.

'Well Marty keeps bugging me about it. Believe me, this is an honour. Marty Kaufman doesn't need to bug anyone. He wants to centre the whole story around the cinema – a movie about a "*movie theater*" – and I keep saying to him, this project cannot go ahead until I find Dave Kelly. He was with me through all that, through the most pivotal part of my life.'

Dave was astonished. He liked Andy and had very fond memories of the time they'd spent working together but could never have appreciated the esteem in which Andy still held their friendship.

'Believe me, if Marty Kaufman writes something, the green light is a mere formality. This movie will get made.'

Dave's head was swirling. He was convinced that his cranberry juice was spiked. He closed his eyes, counted to three and opened them again. Andy was still there

'If you want to do it, I really need your help. The fact that you showed up at the cinema tonight tells me how important it was to you. Your memories of the place and of St Bede's, St Saviour's and all that will be crystal clear and anyway two heads are better than one. The whole of Hollywood is waiting for you.'

Dave, who didn't know what to say, said, 'I don't know what to say.'

'Well, Marty's desperate to meet you. He called me just as I got to the airport and said if I find you and you'll do it, he'll be on the next plane. He's written a full synopsis. Don't go away, I'll just pop up to my room and get it. Just wait till you see who wants to play you.'

Andy disappeared upstairs and Dave, heart and pulses racing again, reached for his mobile and scrolled down to 'Home'.

'Hello?' said a familiar semi-sleepy voice.

'Hi, it's me,' said Dave, now almost hyper-ventilating. 'Listen, don't wait up, I'm going to be very late but you'll never guess who turned up at the cinema: Andy Zymanczyk. It's a long story but he's been in Hollywood for the last twenty years. They want to make a film of his life, based around the cinema.'

'Based around the cinema?' said Rachel, suddenly as excited as her husband. 'In that case, who's going to play me?'

Don't miss Paul Burke's previous novel,
FATHER FRANK, also available from Flame

FATHER FRANK

Father Frank Dempsey is a Roman Catholic priest who harbours an almighty secret: he doesn't believe in God.

Despite this, or maybe because of it, he is brilliant and hugely successful as a priest. His unconventional methods, which include driving a taxi to raise funds, bring his flock together and transform what was once a drab North London parish.

It's all going beautifully until Sarah Marshall hops into his taxi and into his life, slowly putting his vows under incredible strain.

'A dazzling first novel – funny, thoughtful and original'
STEPHEN FRY

'Fast-moving, witty and highly digestible' TIM LOTT

'Refreshing' ADELE PARKS

Read on for an extract . . .

First published in Great Britain in 2001 by Hodder and Stoughton
A division of Hodder Headline

1

The church was packed. Of course it was. This was
Kilburn, 1970, home to the largest Irish community
in Britain, and the Catholic church in Quex Road was
its epicentre. It was a huge church, bigger than many
cathedrals – high Gothic arches, acres of stained glass.
Such was the concentration of Catholics in Kilburn that
Quex Road needed eight full-time priests to cope. Every
Sunday more than ten thousand people attended mass
there, requiring services on the hour in the church and
on the half-hour in the church hall to accommodate
them. A total of fourteen Sunday masses in all, standing
room only in each.

This was the eleven o'clock mass – particularly popular as it finished rather conveniently at ten to twelve,
which left just enough time for a fag and a cough in
the car park before the pubs opened at noon.

Inside, the smell of incense was floating down from
the altar, along the aisles and into the furthest recesses
at the back. Right down into the corners it wafted,
so that the slackers who stood there rather guiltily,
the ones who had shuffled in just before the Gospel
and would shuffle out just after Communion, were
aware that they were attending Sunday mass. Aware

that mortal sin had been avoided and their weekly obligation fulfilled.

Most of the congregation were just going through the motions – mindlessly mumbling the words of prayers they'd mumbled a million times before. Prayers they knew so well that they didn't know them at all. There was, however, one parishioner, seated six rows from the front, who was considering the broader picture, asking himself the bigger question: why are we here? Not 'Why are we here?' in the deep, philosophical sense: why were we put on Earth? What is our ultimate purpose? What is the meaning of life? No, nothing like that. When eleven-year-old Francis Dempsey asked himself, 'Why are we here?' he meant why are we here in the Church of the Sacred Heart, Quex Road, Kilburn, spouting what sounded to him like rubbish?

Francis, you see, was breaking the habit of a lifetime. He was paying attention. His father Eamonn, having seen the boy gazing vacantly into space yet again during the Gospel, had nudged him sharply and told him to listen to what the priest was saying. Francis had always used his weekly trip to mass as an opportunity to catch up on his daydreaming – would England win the World Cup again in Mexico this year? His collection of Esso World Cup coins was almost complete. Only Brian Labone and Ian Storey-Moore to go. Which member of Pan's People was he most in love with? Cherry, Dee Dee or Babs? This morning, though, he was listening to the liturgy, the absurdity of which he found rather disturbing.

'We believe in one God, the Father, the Almighty, creator of Heaven and Earth, of all things visible and invisible . . .'

'Lord, I am not worthy to receive thee under my roof but only say the word and my soul will be healed . . .'

'Lamb of God, you take away the sins of the world . . .'

Lamb of God? What on earth were these people talking about? What is the Lamb of God anyway? And since when could a lamb take away the sins of the world?

A few of the flock, particularly those nearest the front, looked worried – very worried. There was a lot of bead-jiggling and breast-beating going on. *Mea culpa, mea culpa, mea maxima culpa.* Old Mrs Dunne looked terrified. What dreadful sins had she committed as a girl in Ireland? What could have made her so desperate for forgiveness? She was praying now, eyes closed, beads clutched, with the speed and delivery of an auctioneer: '. . . hallowedbethynamethykingdomcomethywillbedoneonearthasitisinheaven . . .'

As Francis joined the queue to receive Holy Communion, the opening bars from a familiar hymn struck up with a mighty resonance from the organ loft at the back: 'Praise my Soul, the King of Heaven' which, according to the hymnbook, had been written by somebody called H. F. Lyte. 'Praise Him, Praise Him' was the chorus and general gist of it. It was the general gist of most hymns, and Francis found the sentiments expressed by H. F. and his ilk rather disquieting.

If God is up there now, His beady eye trained on Kilburn, what must He think of the grovelling musical tributes ringing out of Quex Road? Doesn't He find them horribly embarrassing? Having 'Happy Birthday' sung to you was bad enough so how excruciating was this? Surely He's not enjoying this cringing sycophancy. If He is then He's very conceited. If He's conceited, He's not perfect. If He's not perfect, He's not God.

Francis felt the familiar hot pang of Catholic guilt for entertaining such thoughts. How could he even consider such evil, blasphemous ideas about Our Lord? But wait a minute – he wasn't thinking anything bad about God. On the contrary. He was assuming that God was a nice man, a modest man, a man who had no desire to be fawned upon in this way. Having pulled off this neat feat of self-exculpation, Francis reboarded this train of thought, which was now calling at all stations to Eternal Damnation.

What about all the other things he and his fellow parishioners were asked to do in the name of the Lord?

It all began with baptism. At Quex Road, they were very proud of the fact that they had the highest rate of baptisms, the busiest conveyor belt of freshly minted Catholics, in the country. More than six hundred babies a year, apparently, most of them no more than a couple of weeks old. Baptisms were arranged in great haste to secure the infant's place in Heaven. Any child tragically returned to The Manufacturer before making it to the font would, regrettably, not be eligible for a place at His side, condemned instead to float for ever between Heaven and Hell in the land of Limbo – where innocent babies go if death tightens its icy grip before the Catholic Church does.

And Francis Dempsey, along with every other Roman Catholic, was seriously expected to believe this.

His mind then turned to Holy Communion. Now, that was a good one. How could that tiny round wafer actually be a part of Christ's body? If you stuck enough of them together would you be able to make a long-haired bearded man in his thirties? And even if those little wafers really were tiny pieces of a man's body, why on earth would you want to eat them? And how could that old bottle of Mosaic Cyprus Sherry possibly be Christ's blood? And again, even if it were, why would you want to drink it?

How about confession? What, in the name of God, was that all about? Kneeling inside a wardrobe and telling a strange man your innermost secrets. Francis tried to remember the justification for this most peculiar of sacraments. Oh, yes, inside our bodies, we have a heart and soul. Funny that the latter had never once figured in human-biology lessons. And, as far as Francis was aware, no doctor had ever been called out to treat a suspected soul-attack. Yet, apparently, there it was, pure white but picking up little black marks every time its owner committed a sin. So confession was a bit like a trip to the launderette with a packet of metaphysical Persil. Those emerging from the wardrobe with their sins absolved, their souls cleansed, were supposed to feel as though they were wearing clean white shirts inside their bodies as well as outside.

Francis looked up at Jesus, depicted high above the altar, nailed to a cross. Who said he looked like that anyway? A bit like George Harrison on the cover of *Abbey Road*. Not Matthew, Mark, Luke or John. He'd caught that little snippet on a religious-affairs programme. Not one of the Gospels contains any reference to what Jesus actually looked like. All we know for certain was that he was Jewish. Well, Gus Harvey, who used to live next door, was Jewish, so that was how Francis always imagined the Son of God. It was Gus Harvey healing lepers, Gus Harvey turning water into wine. So two days after Gus died, Francis half expected him to rise from the dead.

This remarkable trick, allegedly performed by Jesus, was celebrated every Easter and Easter was just two weeks away. So today, the priest was clad in rather fetching purple vestments: purple for Lent and Advent, white for weddings and christenings, black for funerals and the standard green for any other time.

Francis felt a sense of dread as he anticipated Friday week – Good Friday, a misnomer if ever there was one, it being the most miserable day in the Catholic calendar, the day Our Lord was supposedly crucified. Any display of happiness or cheer on Good Friday was strictly forbidden. The Dempsey household, like hundreds of others in Kilburn, was subject to a blanket ban on all forms of pleasure. Watching TV, playing records in the front room or football in the park –

forget it. Good Friday was a day devoted to solemnity – or, rather, mock-solemnity. Wasn't it all a bit of a charade, rather like an old Hollywood movie that was shown every year? Yes, there is a weepy bit where the hero gets nailed to a cross but we all know he's not dead really and gets up to live happily ever after.

Easter Saturday was a bit odd too. If people are going to pretend to be miserable on the Friday because Christ is dead then surely they should still be grief-stricken on the Saturday. He's still dead, isn't he? And yet every year on Easter Saturday smiles return to Catholic faces as they pile into Woolworth's on Kilburn High Road to buy each other Easter eggs.

All very strange. And yet here he was at mass, surrounded by grown-up, intelligent people all buying into this nonsense – Jim O'Hagan, Mr and Mrs Quinn, the Mackens, the Hennesseys, the McKennas. Surely these thoughts had occurred to them too. Did any of them truly believe the stuff they espoused every Sunday?

Francis only really believed in the things he had seen, which was why he no longer believed in monsters, ghosts or Father Christmas. There was, of course, one ghost in whom he was still supposed to believe: the Holy Ghost, recently rebranded as the Holy Spirit, as if making him sound less like a ghoul and more like a bottle of whiskey would give him more credibility. Francis believed John Shanahan was the toughest boy in the class because he had seen him beat up Richard Fisher in the playground. He believed that the E-type

Jaguar was the most beautiful car in the world because he had seen one parked on Brondesbury Road and had gazed at it for ten minutes. But God? These people believed in Him not because they had seen Him but, paradoxically, because they hadn't.

Most baffling of all was that missing mass on a Sunday was considered a mortal sin on a par with murder or armed robbery. Why? Almost on cue, Joe Brennan handed him the most likely explanation.

Joe was a friend of his father's – a good man, parish hero, a Knight of St Columba. Big and burly, Joe was dressed in his Sunday best: blue suit, brown shoes, tiny crucifix half buried in the cloth of his lapel. As he leaned towards Francis, he emitted the faint whiff of last night's Jameson's and this morning's Old Spice. He was passing Francis the collection plate. Ah, so that was it. Receiving no money from the State, the Catholic Church was wholly dependent on the contents of that plate. Without these enforced attendances every Sunday, the health and wealth of the Church might be terminally affected. So why not just admit it? Why threaten everyone with the roaring fires of Hell if they didn't turn up? It was clear that Francis Dempsey and his fellow parishioners were not, as the old cliché goes, singing from the same hymn sheet.

It got worse. After mass, Francis noticed the titles of some of the Catholic Truth Society's pamphlets on sale in the repository. One was called *Wrestling With Christ*. What was that all about? Did it feature pictures of Jesus grappling with Mick McManus or Jackie Pallo?

Did Jesus form a tag team with the Holy Spirit? That would be some tag team – one invincible, the other invisible. Well, Jesus might have had the rest of the congregation in a half-nelson but Francis was refusing to submit.

He wandered behind his mother, father and two sisters into O'Brien's newsagents for the traditional after-mass treat. While picking up the *News of the World*, the *Sunday Press* and forty Majors, his father would bestow a shilling upon each child to spend on confectionery. They would always eke it out – Francis in particular. He'd fill the little paper bag with Black Jacks, Fruit Salads, little chewy Frother bars, spreading that shilling over at least a dozen items. This Sunday he was in a different state of mind. Hang the expense: he was living dangerously now. He was going to blow the whole lot on something really decadent like a Tiffin, an Aztec or an Amazin' Raisin bar. He was breaking old habits, and by the time they'd all walked back to their terraced house in Esmond Road, he'd decided to break the biggest habit of all. He'd made an important decision. A decision for life. Francis Dempsey did not believe in God.

Odd, then, that years later he would return to Quex Road and, witnessed by hundreds of people, would appear to proclaim the opposite.

2

There are generally two routes to choose between when emigrating from Ireland to London. It's either Dun Laoghaire to Holyhead or Rosslare to Fishguard. The Holyhead train comes into Euston, the Fishguard train into Paddington. Those arriving at Euston tended to settle a couple of miles north in Camden or Holloway. Those arriving in Paddington would often head a few miles west to Shepherd's Bush or Hammersmith. Kilburn, however, lying between the two termini and equally convenient for either, attracted far more Irish settlers than any other area in Britain.

Eamonn Dempsey was one of thousands who arrived at Euston in the mid-fifties to help rebuild a nation still recovering from the Second World War. He headed up to Camden, the weight of his battered old suitcase blistering his fingers. Up and down he trudged, street after street, before eventually he found a house that wasn't displaying the almost standard 'No dogs, no blacks, no Irish' sign in its window. It was a huge, once grand Victorian villa in Gloucester Crescent, now in the depths of decay and carved up into a dozen damp and dismal 'bedsits'. Each contained an old, cripplingly uncomfortable bed and one dangerous-looking gas ring. Basic sanitation was shared with several other homesick, lonely immigrants in a freezing cold privy at the end of a corridor. With only this to return to, was it any wonder that Eamonn preferred the warmth and conviviality of North London's many pubs?

The house was a short walk from Camden Town tube where Eamonn and scores of others would gather at six thirty every morning when the building-site foremen or 'gangers' would come looking for casual labour. It was like the feeling they'd all experienced at school while waiting to be picked for the football team, but this was rather more important. If you didn't get picked, you didn't get paid, which meant that you couldn't afford to eat. Or, more importantly, you couldn't afford to drink.

That was the other route to gainful employment. You soon discovered which gangers drank where, and or quite a few, it was Kilburn High Road. The Cock, he Old Bell and the Cooper's Arms were particularly ruitful. Fortunately for Eamonn, aged twenty-two and lready built like the brick walls he would soon be recting, he was never short of work, never left standing t Camden Town station and never needing to give oo much of his green and folding to the publicans of ondon, NW6.

Mary Heneghan had also arrived in London courtesy f the Holyhead train. She, too, hauled her suitcase p to Camden Town and was given a tiny room Arlington Road by her sister Eileen whose hus- nd John was a leading hand (whatever that was) at the Black Cat cigarette factory in Mornington Crescent. She found work as an auxiliary nurse at the Whittington Hospital in Archway, and it was at a dance at the nearby Gresham Ballroom that she was swept off her feet by Eamonn Dempsey. Well, swung off them, really. They were dancing the Siege of Ennis, a complex Irish reel, involving dozens of participants, which had long served as an informal mating ritual. Eamonn had grabbed hold of Mary and had never, ever let go.

In those days Catholic courtships were fairly brief and to the point. If there was a solid attraction between you, it was usually deemed good enough for Holy Matrimony. A physical attraction could never be more than visual attraction since sex before marriage was strictly taboo. The proposal, when it came, was low-key. Eamonn did not fall to one knee (only Our Lord was worthy of genuflection). He did not produce a big diamond ring and beseech Mary to marry him or his heart would surely break and his life become worthless. 'Mary,' he'd said, over a quiet drink in the Archway Tavern, 'will we get married?'

And in response, Mary did not scream, 'Yes, yes, yes,' and burst into tears of orgasmic delight. She just nodded, and within a matter of weeks they were in their first home together – a small flat in Kilburn. If that is, the lower half of an unconverted house could be described as a flat. Mr and Mrs Dempsey lived at the bottom of the stairs, Mr and Mrs Ward at the top. Agnes Ward was from Leitrim, and every Sunday morning she would clip-clop around the bare floorboards of the upstairs 'flat' so that Eamonn and Mary, sleeping peacefully below, would be startled from their slumbers in time for the eight o'clock mass.

They'd lived there for just over a year when Mr Thompson, the landlord, gave them notice to leave. He was selling this and the various other dilapidated houses he owned around Kilburn and Kensal Rise and was retiring to the south coast. This was a pity. Despite Agnes Ward's stiletto-heeled reveille, Eamonn and Mary were happy there. They didn't want to move and seemed no nearer the summit of the London Borough of Willesden's council-house waiting list. They asked Mr Thompson how much the house would cost to buy.

'Two thousand pounds,' he replied, almost embarrassed by the certain knowledge that this was far more than the charming young couple could afford. And he was right, but Eamonn and Mary asked him to give them a month before he placed their home in the hands of the estate agents on Salusbury Road. He agreed, and over the next four weeks they hardly ate, didn't go out drinking or dancing and shelved their hitherto immediate plans to start a family. They scraped together every pound, shilling and penny they could find, plus many more borrowed from various members of their family to piece together the two hundred pounds required by the Allied Irish Bank as a deposit. They only ever managed a hundred and ninety, which meant that, ultimately, they would be hundred pounds short of Mr Thompson's asking price.

When the month was up, he came to see them. 'Will you accept nineteen hundred?' said Eamonn.

Mr Thompson pushed some Old Holborn into the bowl of his pipe, lit it, took a couple of puffs, gazed quietly into the middle distance and considered the offer. Or, at least, he pretended to. They were good tenants; they'd never damaged his property or been late with their rent. Such was his regard for them that he'd probably have let them have it for even less. 'Okay,' he said, after what seemed like an eternity, 'on one condition – that you can raise the money within, say, three weeks. I've got my eye on a nice little bungalow in Bournemouth, and if I'm not quick, I'm going to miss it.'

'Three weeks. That'll be fine,' said Eamonn. He'd get the money, even if it meant robbing the Allied Irish Bank to do so. He held out his hand for Mr Thompson to shake, but in his excitement he'd alarmed his soon-to-be-ex-landlord by spitting on it first.

3

On a fine August morning in 1977 Francis, now eighteen – tall, dark and almost handsome – was sitting in the box room of that very house in Esmond Road. You could call it a box room for two reasons: first, because it was a little square bedroom, the smallest in the house; and second because it was filled with boxes – long wooden ones that had once contained little bottles of Britvic orange juice but now housed Frank's huge and ever-increasing collection of seven-inch singles. He'd stopped answering to 'Francis' years ago. It was too reminiscent of St Francis of Assisi, open-toed sandals and sackcloth robes.

Old singles were his passion and his collection was now approaching four figures. He'd long ago made the sweeping generalisation that, with the noble exception of the Beatles, most tracks on most albums were crap. He couldn't bear the overblown pomposity of even the most revered examples – tracks like 'Supper's Ready' by Genesis or Led Zeppelin's 'Stairway To Heaven'. How could this pretentious drivel ever compare to Levi Stubbs pouring raw emotion into every line of 'Baby I Need Your Loving'?

For Frank, the three-minute single best encapsulated

what pop music was all about. He'd picked up most of his older ones for next to nothing in junk shops and jumble sales. For a few of the choicer items, he'd paid a little more at specialist outlets like Spinning Disc in Chiswick or Rocks Off just behind Tottenham Court Road. They resided alongside the shiny new punk stuff, often on brightly coloured vinyl with picture sleeves.

Recently, Frank had been putting his collection to good use. Since passing his driving test a few months earlier, he'd been allowed occasionally to borrow his dad's old Corsair to embark upon a part-time career as a mobile DJ. He'd saved his Saturday-job money from Riordan's butchers in Kilburn High Road and invested in a rudimentary disco unit, a pair of bass bins and a set of flashing lights. He'd been playing records at parties for years. At each one, he'd gravitate towards the music centre in the corner and have a quick flick through the host's (or the host's parents') record collection. Then, almost like a good chef supplied with even the most unpromising ingredients, he could concoct a selection of tunes that would turn a bad party into a good one. He seemed to have the knack of finding the right track at the right time.

Today, he was looking for the appropriate track to clatter on to one of his twin BSR turntables. It was one of his oldest singles, released in 1957 on the purple HMV label, the label on which you'd also find the very early Elvis singles. Frank had them all – 'All Shook Up', 'Paralysed', even the rarer than rare 'Mystery Train', all on purple HMV with the gold lettering. Now, in August

1977, with the King having recently joined the queue at the Great Hamburger Joint in the Sky, the value of these waxings had increased a hundredfold.

He found it – 'The Banana Boat Song' by Harry Belafonte. He wanted to hear that famous chorus 'Day-o, day-o, daylight come and she wanna go home'. The record had surely been made for this occasion. Frank had just received his A-level results – a D, an E and an O. 'DEO, DEO, daylight come and she wanna go home.' Well, Frank thought it was funny. Though in reality, these grades were no laughing matter. Oh, they weren't disastrous – nothing to be ashamed of, and considering how little effort had gone into them, they were remarkably good. They just weren't going to be much use.

Harry Belafonte was faded out and replaced by a spinning blue Phillips label – Dusty Springfield singing the painfully apposite 'I Just Don't Know What To Do With Myself'. As he listened to Dusty's peerless vocals, soaked in hopeless self-pity, Frank couldn't help feeling the same emotions seeping through him. It dawned on him then that there was no point in leaving school at eighteen. No point at all. At sixteen, you could get started, as most of his Kilburn contemporaries already had, and begin your apprenticeship as brickie, chippie or spark. Or perhaps put your foot on the bottom rung of any of a number of clerical ladders in the City or the West End. Alternatively, at twenty-one, in your cap and gown, you could take your pick from the world's graduate appointments and set off on a sprint round life's inside track where the chairmanship of ICI awaited you as you breasted the tape.

The primary purpose of A levels is to unlock the doors of universities but the key only turns if your grades are good. Frank had no real desire to go to university. He quite fancied Oxford or Cambridge but only in the same way that he quite fancied Farrah Fawcett-Majors. With his grades, he'd be lucky to loosen the locks of Doncaster Poly, and the thought of spending the next three years sharing grotty digs up north and having to put his name on his yoghurt was wrist-slittingly bad. With a D, an E and an O, he'd fallen between two stools with only a limited number of places to land.

The Metropolitan Police, for instance. Now as much as Frank occasionally fantasised about being in the Sweeney, tearing round London's still derelict docklands before snapping the cuffs on a vicious team of armed robbers, he knew the reality would be rather more mundane: ordering hapless motorists to produce their documents or strip-searching innocent Rastafarians at the Notting Hill Carnival. No, a career in the Old Bill did not appeal. Neither did the thought of working all day on a building site and doing day-release at Kilburn Tech to become a quantity surveyor. Real progress for a lot of boys: one rung up from their bricklaying fathers.

The only career on which Frank had been vaguely keen was journalism, but this budding enthusiasm was strangled at birth by the arrival at his school of a dull old hack from the local paper. He had given a talk explaining how rewarding it had been to spend thirty-six years as part of the local community. 'I've covered their weddings and I've covered their children's weddings' was the phrase that had Frank hanging the noose over the beam. He had imagined a life as a crusading reporter working for one of the broadsheets, but the idea of thirty-six years on the *Kilburn Gazette* covering stories of the 'Man Drops Bag Of Sugar In Supermarket – We Have Pictures' variety had turned him off for ever.

He thought of becoming a full-time DJ, but was forced to concede that this was not a 'proper job'. It was a hobby, and once it became work, the fun would go out of it.

It was with heavy heart and dragging heels that he returned one last time to St Michael's Roman Catholic Grammar School to see Mr Bracewell, who taught English and was head of the upper sixth. Bracewell was the sort of teacher who doesn't exist any more: he had leather patches on the elbows of his tweed jacket, he smoked a pipe, he voted Conservative. He also had access to the understated brand of sarcasm that takes at least thirty years to perfect. Never was it more evident than today at his one-off 'surgery' when he would dispense advice to pupils whose only thought about a career was 'Dunno, sir.'

'Come,' he drawled, in response to Frank's tentative tap on the door. 'Ah, Dempsey,' he said, through an expression that was neither smile nor frown. 'A D, an E and an O.'

Bracewell's expression said it all, and Frank sat down for a perfunctory trawl through all the dull careers for which they both knew he would be completely unsuitable. Having got those out of the way, Bracewell leaned back in his chair and made a ridiculous one-word suggestion: 'Oxford.'

'Oxford Poly?'

'No, Dempsey, Oxford University.'

Frank tried to speak but no words came out. He tried again. Nothing.

Bracewell was either smiling benignly or sneering cruelly, Frank couldn't work out which. The world had turned rather surreal.

'Well, Dempsey, you – lost for words. This is a sight I'd have paid good money to see.'

'But, well, sir . . . er . . . Oxford . . . You know . . . Peter Staunton,' was the best Frank could manage.

Peter Staunton was the class swot. Top every year, he gave the impression of having emerged from his mother's womb already reciting the formula for solving quadratic equations.

'Yes, Dempsey, you're quite right. Staunton has achieved three As and is going up to Balliol to read physics. He is a brilliant scholar who has earned his place on merit.' He paused, almost conspiratorially, and lowered his voice. 'But there are other ways,' he winked, 'of getting in.'

Frank was confused. Only two 'ways of getting in' sprang to mind. First, a sports scholarship but, like most of his mates, Frank had turned his back on any form of competitive sport at the age of fourteen when he had discovered cigarettes, alcohol and the girls from St Angela's Convent across the road. The other way was a music scholarship, but unless you counted being able to play 'Land of Hope And Glory' or 'We Hate Nottingham Forest', as it was better known, on the paper and comb, the doors to the world's most prestigious university seemed Banham-locked and bolted.

Bracewell enlightened him. 'At all colleges, Dempsey, there are certain – how can I put it? – not so popular subjects, which can sometimes be under-subscribed. Those departments are naturally keen to keep themselves going and can therefore be rather more lenient with their entry requirements.'

'But even so, sir, a D, an E and an O?'

Bracewell arched an eyebrow. 'Well, you never know. Though I have to say the only subject unpopular enough to accept you, Dempsey, would be . . . theology.'

That was it. Frank was certain now – Bracewell was having a laugh, wreaking a slow, satisfying revenge for that incident all those years ago with the blackboard duster. Even now, Frank had to suppress a smirk as it flashed into his mind. The way he had removed the tiny red heads of those Swan Vesta matches and inserted them in the folds of the duster. When Bracewell tried to wipe the blackboard, he'd nearly set the school on fire.

But surely Frank had paid his debt to society for that one. Six swift strokes of the cane, delivered with pitiless ferocity across the seat of his pants. So much worse than across the palm of your hand, which was numb after the first three. You could take another twenty without any further pain. What was more, you could run your hand afterwards under the cold tap in the boys' lavatories. Try doing that with your backside.

One question gnawed at the back of Frank's mind: why would Bracewell want to help him into Oxford? This was the man who had written on his report, 'Not content with wasting his own time, he comes to school and wastes everyone else's.' But Frank decided to play along.

'Theology, sir? I don't know the first thing about it.'

'Nobody does, Dempsey. Not even, I suspect, those who teach it. From what I understand, much of it involves eternal questions about life and death. What's it all about? Why are we here? That sort of thing. You can't really get it wrong – just so long as you can assemble a fairly cogent argument to substantiate your theories. Something, if I remember rightly, Dempsey, for which you've displayed quite a talent.'

'Me, sir?'

'Yes, you, sir. Last year when we were studying *Waiting For Godot*, I remember you suggesting that Estragon and Vladimir were Beckett's personification of fish and chips.'

'And I remember you, sir, dismissing that theory as rubbish.'

'Rubbish for a student of English literature, Dempsey, but for a student of theology, quite brilliant.'

Now he really *was* having a laugh.

Bracewell continued, 'Now it just so happens that Professor Gerald Crosby is an old friend of mine. He runs the theology department at Christ Church. If you like, I could give him a call this afternoon and arrange for you to go up and see him.'

Frank began to suspect that 'Professor Crosby' would turn out to be Peter Dulay, long-time host of *Candid Camera*. A secret camera would have been hidden in the 'Professor's' study and their meeting would be filmed. Then, when the whole nation had finished laughing at Frank Dempsey's lame attempt to get into Oxford, Bracewell would appear on screen, wagging his finger in a stern warning to Britain's recalcitrant schoolboys: 'So, think very carefully before you put Swan Vestas into your teacher's blackboard duster.'

Blinking back into reality, Frank realised that Bracewell's expression, accentuated by the half-moon spectacles perched on the bridge of his nose, was deadly serious.

'Er . . . well, um . . . yes, if you . . . er . . . wouldn't mind, sir, that'd be . . . er . . . great, like.'

Bracewell gave a tight smile. 'Good, because I've already spoken to him. He's expecting your call.'

'Did you tell him about my grades, sir?'

'Yes. A D, an E and an O. *Deo*. He thought that was rather amusing.'

Bracewell chuckled and Frank shared the joke. 'Yes, sir. "The Banana Boat Song" – Harry Belafonte.'

Bracewell's chuckle was replaced by a quizzical expression. 'I was thinking of the Latin, Dempsey.'

It was Frank's turn to look puzzled.

'*Deo*,' Bracewell explained. 'With God.'

4

It was a bit of a worry. Frank was making a serious application to Oxford University and he'd never read a book in his life. Ever. His A level in English literature had been acquired without reading any of the titles on the syllabus. He'd simply invested in a copy of *Brodie's Notes* for each, and familiarised himself with the plot and the main characters. Then he had skimmed through *Brodie's Notes* on other books, for example, by Shakespeare or Hardy and compared them. '*Hamlet*,' he'd write, 'unlike *Macbeth*', or '*Tess of the d'Urbervilles*, unlike *Jude the Obscure*', to give the impression that he'd broadened his reading to encompass the author's other great works. But reading – that's what people did at university. Those bearded contestants on *University Challenge* were always *reading* history or *reading* engineering. Perhaps it was time he read something.

As he perused the literature section of the Kilburn Bookshop, one volume in particular caught his eye – *Animal Farm* by George Orwell. It had two things going for it: one, it was a famous piece of English literature; two, it was very thin, little more than a leaflet. Excellent. If he didn't understand it, it wouldn't take him long not to understand it. However, he did understand it. And he enjoyed it. Right, that was the reading cracked, now for the clothes.

In 1977, most London boys between the ages of fifteen and twenty could be roughly divided into three categories: Teds, Punks and Erics. Despite his huge collection of fifties rock 'n' roll and his burning desire to drive a '57 Chevy or a PA Cresta to the Chelsea Bridge Cruise, Frank couldn't be bothered to be a Ted. It was too much like hard work. Having to schlep out to Harrow to have your drape suits made by Jack Geach – and all those hours in front of the mirror with Brylcreem and comb getting the DA and quiff just right. Forget it. Anyway, Brylcreem always seemed to encourage acne and he'd end up looking like his mate Vince Agius, the Teddy-boy son of a Maltese pimp (a devout Catholic pimp, mind you) who had the complexion of a cheese and ham pizza.

Looking vaguely punk was a lot easier. The Oxfam shop seemed to have a limitless line of old narrow-lapelled suits. With a spiky haircut and a smattering of safety-pins you could pass for the bass guitarist of any one of a hundred new-wave bands.

Erics were soulboys. They took their name from Tall Eric, a vicious but sartorially sharp Chelsea hooligan. Eschewing the number-one crop and steel toecaps, he preferred pleated trousers known as pegs, pointed shoes and mohair sweaters.

Frank could have made the journey to Oxford as a punk or as an Eric, but not as an eager, beaming

Christian. What he really needed was to borrow the contents of Peter Staunton's wardrobe. Failing that, he'd have to suffer the indignity of buying some Stauntonesque clothes for himself. But where? Kilburn High Road was out of the question – he was bound to meet someone he knew. Oxford Street? Absolutely not: it was the busiest shopping street in the world and he was more likely to bump into someone there than anywhere else.

The trip to Christ Church was a secret known only to Frank, Mr Bracewell and Professor Crosby, who had, surprisingly, turned out to be a real person. Frank hadn't told his friends or family – he felt he stood less chance of getting into Oxford than he did of getting into Mandy Wheeler-the-most-gorgeous-girl-in-North-West-London. Since the entry requirements for Mandy Wheeler included a brick-thick wad of cash and a set of car keys, Frank's chances were slim, if not anorexic.

What would his mates say? Theology at Oxford? Are you queer, Dempsey, or what? What's wrong with working on the sites, becoming a QS, meeting a nice girl at a St Patrick's Night dance and settling in a semi in Sudbury?

His parents would find it even harder to understand. Their reaction, even if he got in, would probably be a little pinch of pride and a big dollop of dismay. With some justification, they regarded their son as a rather idle student who had 'messed around at school' for long enough. They would now expect him to find a job. And since he had A levels, a job where he wore a suit. At eighteen, it was his filial duty to weigh in with some housekeeping money.

So it was in secret that he boarded the number 36 bus, hopping off at the corner of Westbourne Grove and Queensway. After a quick double-check to make sure nobody was watching, he darted into Whiteley's of Queensway, a gargantuan old-fashioned department store. It was the size of Selfridge's, but without the customers.

It was like stepping into a time-warp, or into a scene from *Are You Being Served?* By the late seventies the store was on its last legs, so he certainly wouldn't meet anyone he knew in there. It would be a miracle if he met anyone at all. As he passed through the perfumery, he cast a furtive glance at the heavily made-up assistants. His mother had once whispered that underneath the four inches of Pan Stik, they were hookers, happy to work there for nothing because of the lucrative contacts they made with wealthy clients.

Frank had always thought this was a ridiculous story, but probably no more ridiculous than Jesus throwing a dinner party for five thousand with just five loaves and three fishes.

He made his way to menswear, which was practically deserted – perfect. The shelves and racks were filled with exactly the apparel he was looking for. He found a white shirt and a vomit-inducing brown knitted tie to be worn beneath a green lambswool V-neck sweater, lovat slacks and a pair of those Clark's Polyveldt shoes, the ones that looked like Cornish pasties. Even thought that open-toed sandals would be taking this ghastly charade a little too far.

As the crusty old assistant, tape measure round his neck, folded the goods and placed them in Whiteley's of Queensway carrier-bags, Frank was wondering, since the interview was a secret, where on earth he was going to hide them. While most of his mates were worrying about where to hide their secret supplies of fags, dope and porno mags, he was panicking about a lambswool sweater and a pair of Crimplene slacks. He had an idea. The train to Oxford went from Paddington station, which was only a few minutes' walk away. 'Um, I was wondering,' he said to the assistant, 'could you keep these for me? I'll pay for them now but I'll come back and pick them up on Wednesday. It's a long story.'

The following Wednesday, Frank returned. Fortunately, the same assistant was on duty. He remembered Frank, possibly because he hadn't had another customer to serve since Frank's last visit. Frank took his purchases, went to the changing room and put them on. He stuffed his Ramones T-shirt, ripped Wranglers and black suede creepers into the Whiteley's bags and went back to the assistant. 'Um . . . sorry to be a nuisance but would you mind keeping these for me? I'm going for an interview and I'll be back later on today. What time do you close?'

'Five thirty, sir.'

'Fine. I'll . . . er . . . see you later, then. Thanks.'

He left the store, and as he strode towards Paddington, had to concede how comfortable the slacks and shoes were. By the time he got there, he was totally in character – he'd even bought a copy of the *Catholic Herald* to read on the train. As he crossed the station concourse, however, he heard something that made his blood run cold.

'Frank?' The upward inflection suggested that the owner of the voice couldn't believe what she was seeing.

Oh, my God, he thought. It's Mandy Wheeler-the-most- gorgeous-girl-in-North-West-London. Never mind, I'll just ignore her and pretend I'm not me and . . .

'Frank?' She was touching his arm now.

He had no choice but to face his tormentor. Mandy Wheeler, the zenith of his desires, the girl with whom he had always tried to cultivate an air of nihilistic chic. Now, at last, she's engaged him in conversation and he's dressed like a paedophile. 'Oh – er – Mandy, hi . . er . . . didn't recognise you there . . .'

'Well, I almost didn't recognise you.' She giggled, pinching the sleeve of the lambswool sweater between her thumb and forefinger. 'What's with the clobber?'

'Er . . . fancy dress party . . . part . . . part . . .' Hang on, something was coming through on the wire. 'I'm auditioning for a part in a West End play. Only a small part . . . er, a Christian youth-club leader.' Very good, well done and, look, Mandy's expression was turning into one of genuine admiration.

'I didn't know you were an actor.'

'Well, I'm not. I just . . . you know . . . thought

was something I might like to try . . . and, well, you've heard of method acting, I thought that wearing these clothes might help so that by the time I get there, I'll be, you know, in character and I'll stand a much better chance.'

She wasn't giggling now, but Frank couldn't be sure whether that expression was one of admiration or pity.

'Anyway, better go,' he spluttered. 'I'm late already.'

'All that time spent preparing, I suppose.'

'Yeah.'

'Well, let me know how you get on.'

Admiration. Definitely admiration. 'What? How?'

'Ring me.'

With a coy but knowing smile, Mandy pulled a pen from her bag and scribbled her number on Frank's newspaper. As she finished, she noticed it was the *Catholic Herald* and she looked at him again. Pity. Definitely pity.